BREAKING BONES

ROBERT WHITE

ENDEAVOURINK

AN ENDEAVOUR INK PAPERBACK

This paperback edition published in 2017
by Endeavour Ink

Endeavour Ink is an imprint of Endeavour Press Ltd
Endeavour Press, 85-87 Borough High Street,
London, SE1 1NH

ISBN 978-1-911445-88-3

Typeset in Garamond 11.75/15.5 pt by
Palimpsest Book Production Ltd, Falkirk, Stirlingshire

Printed and bound in Great Britain by
Clays Ltd, St Ives plc

www.endeavourpress.com

Born in Leeds, England, the illegitimate son of a jazz musician and a factory girl, **Robert White** grew up hating school and was a regular truant. Joining Lancashire Constabulary in 1980 changed his life. He served for fifteen years, his specialism being close protection and tactical firearms. Robert then spent four years in the Middle East where he took up a training role, working alongside retired members of the UK and US military. Robert White's novels regularly appear in Amazon's top ten bestselling Crime and Action and Adventure charts. He captures the brutality of northern British streets in his work, combining believable characters, slick plots and vivid dialogue to immerse the reader in his fast-paced story-lines.

PRAISE FOR ROBERT WHITE:

'Authentic and entertaining. Robert White has written one of the best crime thrillers of the year' – Thomas Waugh, author of the *Kill Shots* series

'Pitch-black and granite-hard, *Breaking Bones* delivers over and over. A breathless, sweeping tale of love, blood, crime and vengeance that grips you by the lapels and forces you along for the ride. Highly recommended.' – Robert Parker, author of *A Wanted Man*

'Reads like a frightening true crime story. An addictive read. Superb.' – Keith McCarthy, author of *A Kiss Before Killing*

'The brooding sense of impending violence keeps you turning the pages. Imagine the eighties with three friends who make the Krays look like pussy cats. You know it won't end well . . .' – Dean Carson, author of *Dead or Alive*

Also by Robert White:

The Fix

The Fire

The Fall

For my wife, Nicola.

Table Of Contents

Author's Note

I have enjoyed writing this work, probably more than any other. Maybe it is because it is set in the town where I worked as a cop for fifteen years. Maybe it is because it falls in the era I consider to be my heyday.

Who knows?

What I will say is this. Contained in these pages are instances of historical fact. The Falklands war and the Maze breakout, being just two. And inserted inside these real events are my fictional characters and their fictional escapades. I have done my best to ensure that the factual information contained in these pages is correct. Any mistakes, however, are my own.

Now, for those legal eagles amongst you, I have to admit to bending some of the rules when it comes to police investigative work, and both military and civilian legality, including coroner's courts' process. They are minor changes, but help to maintain the pace of the tale. I hope it doesn't spoil your enjoyment. Indeed, I hope it increases it.

Robert White.

Preface

Detective Jim Hacker

When I first began to follow the criminal careers of Frankie Verdi, Eddie Williams and Tony Thompson, I had no idea how powerful they would become, or how it was possible for three individuals to nurture such a criminal empire from their meagre beginnings.

During the thousands of working hours spent attempting to bring the three to justice, I cannot say I ever witnessed a single ounce of compassion, remorse or regret from them. I found them to be nothing more than ruthless, violent creatures, incapable of feeling anything.

Not even fear.

*

The three boys were all born within months of each other, lived in the same town and attended a perfectly good school. I would like to be able to explain away their ferocious nature, their calculated coldness, by telling you about their deprived childhood, but I cannot.

All came from average, working-class homes; were neither rich nor poor, and wanted for little. They had summer holidays, birthday and Christmas presents, and parents who loved and cared for them.

I cannot begin to suggest what went wrong, as I am neither doctor nor psychiatrist.

*

Frankie, Eddie and Tony had been inseparable from being small children. They played together in the narrow streets of Preston, Lancashire, and to the casual observer, or neighbour, it would have appeared that they were developing normal friendships and basic social skills.

The fact was, by the time they left Blessed Sacrament Primary, for Preston High School aged eleven, they had formed a relationship so close, so tight and so impenetrable, that neither their parents nor peers could get close to them.

*

It was on 11th June 1976 that the youths gained their now infamous nickname. The boys were in their fourth year of high school and all had celebrated their fifteenth birthdays. During the morning break between lessons, Tony Thompson, who, in these more enlightened times, would be described as a child with "learning difficulties", had been unfortunate enough to run into the school bully whilst enjoying a cigarette behind the science block.

The older, bigger youth had repeatedly punched Tony, bloodied his nose and robbed him of his pack of ten Embassy.

That afternoon, the three friends waited for Tony's attacker to leave the school gates, and in front of dozens of witnesses, including mathematics teacher John Swindles, they fell upon the bully. Armed with compasses stolen from their technical drawing class, they stabbed the youth over a hundred and twenty times.

The one-inch spike on the end of the compass was, of course too short to cause a fatal blow, but the sheer number of puncture wounds inflicted to the boy, including seventeen to his face, ensured he was hospitalised for a week.

John Swindles later told police officers, that even in his days in the parachute regiment, he had never witnessed such a frenzy of brutality and violence.

A *Lancashire Evening Post* crime reporter nicknamed the boys, "Three Dogs", due to the ferocious nature of the assault, and the pack instinct they had used to formulate the attack. That headline, together with mugshots of the dishevelled youths, splashed across the inside of the paper, created instant infamy.

"The Three Dogs" were born, and were never going to look back.

*

One week after the attack, the three were summoned to Preston Juvenile Court. They entered pleas of guilty to wounding and possession of an offensive weapon.

Their parents sat at the back of court in total shock, as Frankie, Eddie and Tony were sentenced to six months in an approved school, the maximum the court could impose.

In the early seventies, the government went to great pains to inform the public that their latest young offenders' institutions, recently renamed "approved schools", were a far cry from the previously badged borstals, first built in the Rochester town of the same name almost a hundred years earlier. These new and improved prisons had moved away from the grim regime of the old institutions and were a shining example of the government's policy to reduce youth offending.

*

Whatever the policy document may have said in 1976, the establishments were still borstals in everything but name.

*

The Three Dogs were detained in Kirklevington Approved School for Boys, Stockton on Tees.

The government's latest arrangements, like most of its money, had failed to reach the North of England, and the establishment had a reputation for taking in naughty boys, and turning out super-fit psychopaths.

The boy's "training" was all six a.m. runs, porridge for breakfast, cleaning, chores, bricklaying, farming in all weathers. And the dreaded birch.

Corporal punishment was supposedly banned in all borstals and training centres back in 1972.

The governor of Kirklevington had no stomach for breaking this ruling, or watching his boys beaten for their misdemeanours. But when his back was turned, his guards were not so squeamish. Indeed, some took great pleasure in dishing out the supposedly banned cane.

The Three Dogs suffered greatly at the hands of one particular prison officer.

P.O. Jeffrey Morris.

He hated the way the boys showed no fear of him, or the harsh regime at the centre. Frankie Eddie and Tony, particularly Tony, were beaten at regular intervals. They each took their physical assaults in silence, just as they endured the removal of any privileges.

Morris ensured that the three each had their detention extended every time they stepped out of line, and it was not until the 8th of July 1977, almost thirteen months after their six-month sentence, that The Three Dogs were released.

*

As the boys had all reached sixteen years old, the Board of Education ruled that they need not return to school.

Tony used some of the knowledge he had gained inside Kirklevington, and took a job as an apprentice bricklayer. Frankie had no choice but to work for his Italian father in the family restaurant, and Eddie found he enjoyed tinkering with cars in a back-street garage just off Plungington Road.

To most onlookers, it would seem that The Three Dogs had been rehabilitated by the harsh prison regime. The boys were all employed, and quietly getting on with their lives.

I, for one, was not so sure.

*

Almost a year to the day of the boy's release, on the 15th of June 1978, Prison Officer Jeffrey Morris was found beaten to death in the front room of his Kirklevington flat. His facial injuries were so severe that the police were forced to use dental records to identify him. The coroner stated that Morris had been systematically beaten, and remarked in his report that the perpetrators had taken hours, rather than minutes, to inflict the horrendous injuries that eventually took his life.

Within days, my suspicion that The Three Dogs had murdered Morris, were to be founded.

Chapter One

18th June 1978

Tony Thompson strolled along Whitmore drive enjoying the warm afternoon sunshine. Three schoolgirls giggled behind their hands as the handsome boy, dressed in the latest fashions, passed them by.

Tony noticed them too, and increased the length of his stride. He didn't like girls his own age. They made fun of him for being "slow". The younger girls, however, liked Tony . . . a lot.

Every few paces he pushed a handful of wayward curls from his forehead. When the girls were out of sight, he stopped, checked that his shoes were as immaculate as they had been when he'd left his parent's house seven doors away, adjusted the waistband of his new flared trousers, and strode into the driveway of Frankie Verdi's home.

He hummed *You're The One That I Want*, the current number one. In fact, watching *Grease* at the Ritz, had almost made him ditch his flash flares for a pair of 1950s style Wranglers with turn-ups; but Tony figured Travolta looked cooler in *Saturday Night Fever*, and stuck with the crisp pressed flared trousers.

He didn't knock on Frankie's door, but simply shoved at it and padded down the carpeted hallway of the Verdi's modest council-owned property.

The parlour door was closed tight and he could hear the hushed voices behind.

He opened it wide enough to push his mass of raven curls inside.

"You two okay for tea?" he asked.

Eddie Williams pointed to a pale green pot, three cups, saucers and spoons, sitting atop a sturdy wooden kitchen table.

"Just brewed," he said.

Tony nodded and gave a broad grin. He loved it when Frankie called a meeting. It made him feel important. "Cool," he said.

Frankie sat holding court at the head of his mother's ancient table, resting his elbows on the heavy chequered cloth.

He was the oldest of The Three Dogs, by four months and had used this to his advantage in the early days. Being physically the strongest ensured he ruled the roost using his size and natural aggression.

As time passed, and the other two could match him, and in the case of Eddie, even out-fight him, nothing had changed. The others seemed simply to accept Frankie as their natural leader. No member had ever said a word about it, and he had never been challenged. It was just the way it was.

"Sit down Tony," he said softly. "Pour the tea and listen. This is important."

The tea tippled and the cups rattled happily on their saucers.

Frankie sipped his briefly before setting it down. "Did you burn all the clothes Eddie?"

Williams gave a withering look. "Done," he said.

"He was just asking Eddie," chipped in Tony.

Frankie held up a hand. "I had to ask, you know me on details. It was the last bit of forensics the coppers could've got us on."

"Well they're ash now," muttered Eddie.

Tony leaned in, he had no idea what forensics were, but it sounded good. "That's cool eh Frankie . . . ash . . . eh? Coppers can't do anythin' with ash mate."

*

The Verdi family had first settled from their Palermo home to Glasgow, but had moved south of the border before Frankie was born; even so the lad's accent was a strange mixture of Lancashire, Italian and Glaswegian. He also bore an uncanny resemblance to Italian Scot, Tom Conti.

He smiled at Tony, reached forward, and ruffled his

wayward mop. It was the action of a loving father or older brother, rather than a mere seventeen-year-old.

"Yes Tony, everything is cool, and ash is just that . . . ash."

Frankie rarely raised his voice. He found the quieter he spoke, the more people listened. He pointed a finger and settled into his rhythm.

"The script is this Tony . . . it was no good topping that bastard Morris, if no one knows it was us what did him in is it?"

Tony looked puzzled.

Frankie spoke slowly, quietly.

"So, we're going to let the cops know it was us what topped him right? . . . that it was us who smashed the bastard's face to a pulp. Obviously, the cops will come down from Kirklevington an' nick us."

"Obviously," mimicked Eddie.

Frankie shot him a look and soldiered on. "But then . . . when they have to let us go 'cos they can't prove anything . . . 'cos were so on top . . . so clever . . . well . . . everyone round here will know it was us what did him eh? Everyone will stand up and notice us . . . The Three Dogs. We'll have the one thing that no one round here has Tony . . . respect . . . total fuckin' respect."

Frankie leaned in. "And with what I've got planned for tonight, the whole town will be talkin' about us."

*

Eddie Williams sipped his tea and set his cup carefully back in its saucer, so as not to stain Mrs Verdi's tablecloth. For a seventeen-year-old, he was a monster. The year in Kirklevington had ensured that Eddie had worked on his body every day.

Unlike the other two teenagers, his almost white-blonde hair was cropped unfashionably short. He visited his barber weekly, spent an average man's weekly wage on his suits, and was a regular dancer at Wigan Casino's "all-nighter". From a tender age, Eddie had been thought of as a lady's man. His clear pale skin, dazzling eyes and natural muscular physique always ensured he had many female admirers.

Secretly, he was anything but.

He was, however, a drug dealer, and it was these activities that made him so popular amongst the Wigan faithful. It was Eddie who provided the dancers with the speed, that kept them spinning all night.

Eddie made a hundred quid a week selling whizz.

This, of course was shared amongst The Three Dogs. It was another of Frankie's rules. Once all dues were paid, everything the three made over and above was either shared equally or saved. Frankie's tips, Tony's foreigners and Eddie's drug money all went into the pot.

This meant that aged seventeen, the boys each had a disposable income of eighty quid a week.

*

The average working man in the north of England earned thirty-five pounds. No wonder the boys were the best dressed on Moor Nook Estate.

Eddie's eyes flashed when he spoke. He was the most unpredictable of the three. This was no mean feat, but his extremely short and violent temper constantly simmered below the surface; waiting to explode at any given moment. His liking for his own amphetamine sulphate did little to calm the ticking bomb.

He looked directly at Tony.

"The plan is to give Fat Les from Marl Hill Crescent the word on the dead screw. He's a fuckin' grass . . . everyone knows that. Once we drop the info to him, he'll be off to the plod like a rocket."

"Les, the ice cream man? He's a grass?" asked Tony.

Frankie stood up and turned to the window. The afternoon sun lit up his face. It gave him an almost cherubic appearance. He had yet to start shaving and his skin was as smooth as it was sallow. His slender frame and boyish good looks belied his uncompromising vicious nature.

"Yeah Tony, Fat Les is a stinking grass. Once we give him the word on Morris, he'll spill his guts to the plod, no danger."

He cricked his neck.

"Anyway, never mind that for now, like I said, there's another job for us to do . . . tonight. And if it all goes according to plan . . . we'll be going into the ice cream

business ourselves . . . and the whole town will be talkin'
about us."

Tony smiled failing to grasp the seriousness of the
conversation, "I like ice cream Frankie."

Verdi placed a hand on Tony's shoulder. "I know you
do Tone, but don't worry, all will be revealed."

Frankie turned businesslike. "Now . . . Eddie . . . you
go tell that grass bastard what we agreed . . . he'll tell that
detective pal of his . . . what's his name? Hacker . . . that's
him . . . Hacker . . . he'll tell the coppers up Stockton . . .
Oh, and Eddie . . . soon as your done with Fat Les . . .
get back here with your motor."

*

Eddie knew better than to ask questions. Frankie would
divulge his plans as and when. He simply pushed his chair
back, lifted his jacket from the back and slipped it over
his massive shoulders.

"I'll go see the cunt now . . . no time like the present
lads."

Frankie turned and pointed a warning finger, "Slip it
in all casual Eddie."

Eddie gave Frankie another look that told him he was
stating the obvious, and stepped from the room, his unusually light footsteps disappearing toward Fat Les' house
three streets away.

*

Frankie returned to his seat at the table and poured more tea for Tony and himself.

He took a sip.

If Eddie Williams' eyes were a sharp, dancing blue, Frankie's were at the other end of the spectrum, a deep chocolate. That said, his irises were unusually small and were overpowered by the jet of his pupils. This gave the impression of a dark, flat void at the very centre of his eye. Despite his diminutive stature, those eyes gave him something the other two would never truly wield.

Frankie Verdi had the power to strike genuine fear into another human being without saying a single word.

Tony took a noisy gulp of his brew, opened a new twenty-pack of Embassy and lit one. He dropped the cigarettes on the table with a nod.

Frankie took one, tapped it on the pack, just as he'd seen Al Pacino do in *The Godfather*, and pushed it into his mouth.

Before Frankie could find a light, Tony had his Zippo open.

Frankie lit up. "Nice," he said, exhaling slowly and eyeing the lighter. "Where'd you get that?"

Tony snapped the gold-plated Zippo shut and gave it to Frankie to admire further.

"That tobacconist shop in town, bottom of Fishergate, near the station, y'know?"

Frankie nodded appreciatively and rubbed his thumb over the cool smooth surface of the item.

"Think I'll nip in tomorrow and get me one. I like the old way, simple, classy, just a wick, flint and petrol. I'm sick of them new disposables."

Tony smiled. It was a broad natural beam that lit up his eyes.

He loved it when Frankie approved of something he did or had. Frankie and Eddie were his world.

Only they understood him; they never took the piss when he got mixed up or made a mistake; never called him thick or retard or spaz.

The two sat smoking in comfortable silence for a while. Some kids began playing in the garden next door, and their giddy laughter filtered through the open window and into the warm smoky room.

Frankie listened to them and tried to remember if he had ever been so innocent.

*

Ever since they were small boys, kicking cans in the street, Frankie knew he'd have a special responsibility for Tony. He knew the lad needed a little extra care and attention. Attention that only he could provide. Frankie knew he must protect Tony from his worst enemy . . . himself.

He pushed the pack of Embassy back across the table.

"Remember, at school when that fat kid punched you in the face and nicked your fags Tony?"

Thompson squirmed in his seat. He didn't like to hear about the school bully; it made him feel weak.

"Course I do."

Frankie allowed himself a kind smile. He loved Tony, and Tony needed to understand the strategy of the group; the reasoning and rationale. Not words he would know, but Frankie would simplify his message. No one would be excluded from any decision he made; especially Tony.

"What we did to that kid . . . the three of us . . . that was because we look after each other, you know what I'm saying mate?"

Tony was wide-eyed.

"Yeah, course Frankie; I know what you're sayin'. You're dead clever mate, I know that."

"Do you Tony? So, do you know why we did that screw in? Messed him up so bad?"

Tony's lip curled. Frankie and Eddie had taught him all he needed to know about vengeance and retribution, even if he could never spell the words.

He shook with anger.

"He . . . he wanted to do bad things with me . . . to me . . . I mean. He beat me Frank. He beat me hard."

Frankie rested a hand on the shoulder of his lifelong friend. "And we could never allow him to get away with that . . . could we?"

Tony grimaced and balled his fists until his knuckles were white, crushing his cigarette between his fingers and dropping ash onto the tablecloth. He looked deep into Frankie's eyes.

There was a tremor in his voice.

"I enjoyed killing that fucker mate. Smashing his face to mush, like a . . . like a lump of mincemeat eh Frankie? He fuckin' screamed Frankie. Just like he wanted me to scream eh? But I wouldn't would I? He beat me . . . and beat me . . . wanted to play with my cock . . . remember? Dirty fucker he was . . . always after feeling up the lads . . . but not me Frankie . . . not me . . . no chance."

Verdi's eyes turned black as coal. He grabbed Tony's fist in his warm hand.

"He's gone now mate. The only thing that matters is us eh? Me, you . . . an' Eddie, The Three Dogs!"

Tony lifted his tea cup and toasted his friend.

"The Three Dogs!"

Chapter Two

Fat Les Thomas was an ice cream man and a cannabis dealer. He kept his business ventures secure, by occasionally grassing up one of his customers. Now you wouldn't think that a man like Les would be allowed to survive on an estate like Moor Nook, but somehow, he managed to keep his balancing act going.

Maybe it was because he chose who to grass up very carefully. Maybe it was because he sold the very best Moroccan resin available; or maybe, it was because his brother was Mickey Thomas, the most feared brawler in town.

To Les, one less dope smoker was a cheap price to pay for the smooth running of his empire.

Today, however, Fat Les had a dilemma.

He'd just had a visit from one of those kids who the papers were calling The Three Dogs, and what a big dog

Eddie Williams had turned out to be. The last time Les had seen him, he was a skinny fuckin' runt playing in the gutter. Now he was built like a brick shithouse and dressed like a millionaire.

The kid bought a quarter of "rocky" from Les and cool as a cucumber let the bombshell slip.

Now Les was perfectly okay dropping a stoner to the cops. But some fuckin' nutter who casually mentions that he and his two mates had battered a screw to death up Kirklevington . . . well that was a different matter. The alarm bells were going off in Les' empty head.

Trouble was, Fat Les, was fat for a reason.

Les was greedy. Greedy with his food and greedy with his business ventures.

He considered his options, and decided to go where the money was; besides, who was going to cross him, when his brother was the hardest man in town?

He pulled on his denim jacket, fired up his Cortina and went to see Detective Jim Hacker.

*

Within the hour, The Three Dogs were in the frame for the Morris murder.

*

Eddie opened the boot of his Mini 1275GT and gently placed the bag of items the Dogs would need for the night's business inside. The car was bright yellow with black flared arches, and was his pride and joy. Just a year old, the Mini had been in a front-end write-off. Eddie had lovingly repaired the car and returned it to its former glory. It was now worth three times what he'd paid the guy for it. He really wanted a Capri or better still a Triumph Stag, but, for now, those cars were out of his reach.

For now.

Eddie jumped into the driver's seat whilst Frankie lolled in the back. They passed a spliff, made with Fat Les' Moroccan between them, and drove to Tony's house two blocks away.

As they pulled up outside, Eddie hit the horn and waited for Tony to emerge.

The car had a brand new eight-track stereo and Eddie's favourite Northern Soul tunes blasted out. *Needle in a Haystack* and *Jimmy Mack* could be heard all along the street.

"This fuckin' music is shite!" bellowed Frankie over the din. "Have you no modern stuff?"

"Like what?"

Frankie was the epitome of the Italian gangster carica-ture. He hunched his narrow shoulders, tucked in his elbows, palms up. "Like . . . y'know . . . Blondie . . . Boomtown Rats . . . The Blockheads."

Eddie was flat, dry, northern muscle. "Anything begin-ning with 'B' then?"

Frankie leaned across the front seat and passed the spliff over. "Sometimes you are a real wanker Eddie!"

The argument over the stereo was temporarily forgotten as the passenger door opened and Tony flopped into the seat.

"What're you two shouting about? My mum can hear you in the kitchen."

Eddie handed the joint to Tony. "Sorry pal, just that Frankie has no taste in music."

Tony took a long pull and exhaled slowly. "Mmm, good shit man."

"Fat Les," acknowledged Eddie.

Tony raised his eyebrows in mock surprise, "Fat Les?"

There's a Ghost in my House filled the car.

Frankie leaned between his two compatriots.

"Yeah, Fat Les . . . grassing cunt!"

The car exploded with laughter.

*

Sunday evening was all about having fun; a few early drinks before work Monday.

This Sunday, however, was different.

Eddie drove slowly along Deepdale Road. The early summer evening was doing its best to keep the skies bright and the girls scantily clad. Frank, Eddie and Tony whistled their appreciation at the short skirts and flimsy blouses as they passed by.

The girls giggled at the three young, handsome, well-dressed boys.

Eddie had to stop Tony from waving his penis out of the window.

*

Days earlier Larry Holmes had fought for the heavy-weight championship of the world and the Army and Navy pub on Meadow Street was showing a tape of the fight. The place would be packed with boxing fans, but it was one fan in particular The Three Dogs wanted to see.

Eddie pulled the Mini up outside the pub. Tony was out in a flash and through the door. Less than a minute later, Thompson was back on the pavement. He gave the slightest of nods.

Their target was inside.

Detective Jim Hacker

When Lesley Thomas turned up at the nick that Sunday, I was ready to leave for the day. "Fat Les", as he was known, was a small-time drug dealer, who liked to think he was big time. Even so, it was still somewhat of a surprise when he told me he had information about a murder.

When he dropped the names, I instantly knew it was the Kirklevington job. I knew what he was going to say before the words dripped from his scheming fat mouth.

I should've sent him packing.

The murder that was committed in Stockton on Tees

was way out of my remit. The only evidence came from the mouth of a seventeen-year-old boy, who would simply say he was bragging to make himself look cool in front of his criminal peer. It was worthless without corroboration.

I should probably have given Fat Les his fiver, swept the whole thing under the carpet, and taken my wife out for her birthday as planned.

But I didn't.

Before I left, I sent a telex to the murder incident room at Stockton, with the details and descriptions of The Three Dogs, together with the dates they were incarcerated in Kirklevington.

I had my toe in the water and I was never going to be completely dry again.

I drove home that evening and did my best switch off cop, and switch on my best husband impression.

I remember we had a sitter for the first time in months and I was taking Marie to Angelo's on Avenham Street, her favourite Italian.

She looked lovely in her new summer dress and we had a wonderful child-free evening. Laughing and talking, just as we had ten years earlier on our first date. As I recall we even managed a dance. I'd hoped to take my good fortune back home with me as far as the bedroom, but on our return, our sitter had bad news.

*

Fat Les Thomas had been franticly ringing the CID office, in an attempt to contact me. Against my better judgement and my wife's advice, I reluctantly returned his call.

To say he was petrified was an understatement. He begged me not to use the information he had so willingly sold to me hours earlier; he even offered his fee back a hundred times over. No mean amount to a struggling cop with a growing family.

Sadly, for him, and for me, I could not undo what had been done.

*

Now, I want to be clear here. I cannot prove any of this next part of my story, as no witnesses or complainants ever came forward. It is no more than a piece of Preston criminal folklore, if there is such a thing. A tale told in hushed tones, between drunks on a Friday night. Nonetheless, this is what I gleaned from the slivers of that myth and legend.

Shortly after seven o'clock on that Sunday 18th June 1978, Fat Les' brother, Michael James Thomas was enjoying a drink in the Army and Navy public house on Meadow Street, with his two regular accomplices in violence, Jack and Steve Phillips.

Jack and Steve were Mickey's paid minders. The "king" of Preston was becoming older and slower with the passage of time and needed some protection from would-be crown stealers.

Despite Mickey's age and ballooning size, he was still a fearsome figure, and together with the Phillips brothers, ruled the streets of the town, giving no quarter, often preying on the weaker souls of the parish.

The landlord of the establishment had secured the latest in video technology and was showing the world heavyweight boxing contest between Larry Holmes and Ken Norton. Mickey Thomas and his two goons had pride of place in front of the screen.

Frankie Verdi, Eddie Williams and Tony Thompson allegedly entered the Army and Navy unnoticed. Tony and Eddie brandished what some called truncheons, some called bats. Whatever they carried, they used them to devastating effect. They struck the Phillips brothers with both accuracy and fearsome force, directly behind their knees. Both men dropped on their backs winded and shocked. Before they could recover, Eddie and Tony began raining blows down on the heads of their victims. Legend has it, the noise of Jack Phillips' skull cracking could be heard across the street.

In all the carnage, Frankie Verdi stood defiantly in front of Mickey Thomas, the hardest man in town. Verdi was dressed in a black suit, white shirt and black tie. People say his staring eyes were the devil's own.

He calmly pulled two knuckle dusters from the pockets of his jacket, slid them on his hands and set about a man seven inches taller and seven stone heavier than himself.

They say, that within seconds, Frankie stood over his

foe, as he lay unconscious in a pool of blood, glass and beer.

How accurate the story is, only a handful of people truly know. What I can say as fact, is Mickey Thomas and the Phillips brothers were all hospitalised that night. Thomas received a fractured eye socket, burst eardrum and several broken ribs. Jack Phillips still walks with a stick to this day.

*

After visiting his brother in hospital that night, Fat Les "gave" Frankie Verdi, Eddie Williams and Tony Thompson his ice cream van, and with it his cannabis business.

Frankie, generous to a fault, gave Fat Les his job, in his father's kitchen.

Les never came to me with information again.

*

It took Stockton Police six days to react to my telex, but on Saturday 24th June 1978, two burly red-faced detectives finally arrived at Preston nick with the intention of arresting The Three Dogs for the murder of Prison Officer Morris. They also held search warrants for their family homes.

In a new development in the case, a petrol attendant at a Shell station, just off the A67, close to Kirklevington prison had reported fuelling a bright yellow Mini car, with three young men aboard it, on the day of the murder.

My descriptions of The Three Dogs matched the three in the Mini. This, and the fact that Morris had worked on the same Kirklevington wing that the boys were housed, was enough for the detective superintendent in charge of the murder inquiry to spare the two Jacks to travel south, and a magistrate to issue the warrants. After spending ten minutes with the knuckle-dragging detectives, I instantly knew that they would be no match for Frankie Verdi and his crew, and indeed, I was found to be correct.

*

The house searches revealed nothing except Eddie Williams' yellow Mini car; a great find you may think; except the Stockton officers duly drove it back to the station. As the less-than-professional detectives had both visited the murder scene, this effectively ruined any chance of a forensic find in the car due to possible cross-contamination.

As I said . . . no match.

After three hours of questioning and receiving "no comment" answers, the boys from Stockton reverted to type and decided to beat a confession from The Three Dogs.

The result . . . sore knuckles and silence. Frankie, Eddie and Tony were bailed eight hours later . . . no charges.

*

On Monday 26th June 1978, three battered and bruised faces were plastered across the front page of the *Lancashire Evening Post*. The headline boasted *"Cruelty to Animals"* The same crime reporter that had branded the fifteen-year-olds with their nickname now seemed intent on immortalising the seventeen-year-olds as wounded, working class heroes.

The timing of the Army and Navy incident, the arrest for the Morris murder and now the newspaper article, projected The Three Dogs to another level. Frankie Verdi's plan had worked a treat.

It announced the arrival of a criminal gang, of an age never before seen in a Northern town.

*

Despite my minor involvement in the Kirklevington case, I had never even spoken to any of The Three Dogs, let alone arrested or interviewed them.

I'd spent my time working other cases, and simply looked in on their lives from the outside with a quizzical morbid interest. My only contribution had been that one telex. How Frankie Verdi knew about that, I still have no idea; but when I got home that Monday night, my wife was arranging a bouquet of flowers in a vase.

They had been hand delivered and came with a card.

It read, *"To my dear Marie, Sorry I missed your birthday, Frankie."*

I cannot describe the fury that burned inside me that

day. Not even after all these years. What I do know, is that in smashing her flower display across our kitchen, I scared my wife so much, I made her cry; something I had never done before, or since.

Frankie Verdi thought he could intimidate me; scare me off, and allow him to build his criminal empire in peace. Well he did scare me. I admit that. I would have been a fool not to have felt some modicum of fear; but I have never been a coward, and he and his Dogs would never prevent me from doing my duty.

*

In the coming weeks, I continued my job as a junior detective and did my best to curb my burgeoning obsession with Frankie's flowers.

Life, as they say goes on.

I had passed my sergeant's examination the previous autumn, and my divisional commander, one Ch Supt Harrison, had suggested that a change of scenery would be good for my development, and aid faster promotion.

I was unsure about a transfer, but when Marie fell pregnant with our second child in the August of that year, I took his advice, and moved from CID, to the Plain Clothes Department.

Promotion to sergeant would mean an extra thirty quid a week and it couldn't come soon enough.

*

Plain Clothes worked from a different station and I moved away from the criminal matters that would keep me close to The Three Dogs.

I greeted this event with a mixture of discontent and relief.

Plain Clothes dealt with two particular areas of policing; vice . . . and dead people. That is not to say "murdered" people, but people who had died suddenly and unexpectedly. Each member of our small team took weeks about, acting as Coroner's Officers.

This was a terribly depressing posting for me.

Dealing with heart attacks, strokes, falls, accidents on the road and at work, and worst of all, SIDS or "cot death", were a regular part of my day.

I hated the fact that for a full week at a time, I would be dealing with bereaved relatives and attending the harrowing procedure that went along with each investigation, known as the post-mortem examination.

The remainder of my work was little better, spending many cold and disconcerting hours in gentlemen's public lavatories, attempting to catch homosexual men in the act of gross indecency.

I hoped and prayed that promotion would be swift.

*

Swift, it was not, but in September of 1980, I was indeed promoted to Detective Sergeant. Unfortunately, I still languished in the Plain Clothes Department I hated.

For reasons that will become clear later in my story, the 27th of October of that year, is a date that will stay with me forever. On that day, during the course of my duties at Sharoe Green Hospital, I met a man called Harry Strange.

Harry was as broken a man as I'd ever met. His wife had been struck by one of those new style minibuses whilst she was out shopping in Leyland, a small town some five miles from Preston. She had suffered catastrophic head injuries and had been pronounced dead at the scene.

I was to produce the body to Harry, so he may identify her as Rose Helen Strange, forty-one years.

Mercifully, Rose had suffered trauma to the back of her head, and her beautiful pale features were undamaged.

Harry walked into the chapel of rest that day, ramrod straight, touched Rose lovingly on her forehead, nodded his acceptance that she was his wife, and left the room in silence.

As was my duty, I covered the body and asked the attendant to return Rose to the chiller. After collecting my paperwork, I sought out Harry to obtain his official signature.

I found him sitting on a metal bench close to the front of the hospital entrance. He was staring onto the garden area. Unseasonably, the sun shone and two children chased each other between the hedges.

I sat, Harry signed, and from that moment, under the most awful of circumstances, we began a great friendship.

*

Harry was a military man, as was his father before him. He had a son, Jamie, who had also followed the calling, and was away completing his All Arms Commando training course at CTCRM in Lympson, Devon. Jamie would come back a Green Beret attached to 40 Commando within the week. He was just nineteen.

*

On the anniversary of Guy Fawkes, Rose Strange was buried.

It was against force policy for me to attend the funeral, as Rose was one of my coroner's officer's cases, but Harry insisted, and I went anyway.

My first recollection of the events that day, was the wind that blew thousands of brown shrivelled leaves around our feet. They twisted in ever-tightening circles about the graveside, drowning out the priest and his words of comfort.

The second, was Laurie Holland.

I was three mourners to the left of her. She held onto the hand of Harry's son, Jamie Strange. He was a hand-some strapping lad and wore his full Royal Marines uniform, standing steadfast and apparently emotionless, as his mother's coffin was lowered into the grave.

The stunningly beautiful Laurie wiped a tear away with a black-gloved hand.

*

Cops are notoriously good at remembering faces, I was no different. It had been a few years, she was taller, more elegant, but it was her.

Probably a year before The Three Dogs had been sent to Kirklevington jail for the stabbing of a schoolboy, I had arrested Laurie's mother, Margaret for soliciting. A strip-search revealed Margaret had secreted two wraps of brown powder inside her brassiere. These were later identified as heroin.

Possession of any amount of a Class A substance, back in 1975, got you sent to prison.

*

That night, I visited what was laughingly called the family home. As a very junior detective, my purpose was to check for more drugs and maybe a notebook or diary with the name of her dealer.

The poky, two-bed Grange Park maisonette was, as expected, a disaster area.

I entered with Margaret's own key, announced myself, got no reply and began a search of the grubby lounge, disgusting kitchen and filthy bathroom.

Margaret's own bedroom was in a similar condition to the rest of the house, with the addition of used needles, condoms and sex toys.

The final room was the spare bedroom. The door, firmly closed, was painted a different colour to the rest of the house. I knocked, announced myself again, and pushed the door open.

Laurie Holland was standing in the corner of the tiny, but pristine room, tears rolling down her cheeks and a crowbar raised above her head. It was definitely not the first time strange men had come knocking on Laurie's door in the middle of the night.

She was intent on caving my head in with the bar, swinging it wildly and thankfully missing. When I eventually took control, throwing the weapon into the hall and gripping her tight, she begged me not to hurt her.

As she broke her heart, even this detective felt a lump in his throat.

Once she was convinced I was a policeman and not one of her mother's "friends", she produced two spotlessly clean cups from her bedside cabinet and made tea. I listened to her story, hardened my heart, and called social services.

She was just fourteen, and that was the last time I saw her . . . until this day.

Laurie wore a tight black sixties-style mini dress, the sort made popular a second time around by the pop stars of the day. Unfortunately, the dress insisted on revealing more than she'd intended, due to the blustery wind. She held it in place by the hem and whispered apologies to Jamie. I noticed an engagement ring and thought they both looked far too young.

As the final words were being spoken and earth was being ceremoniously dropped on the coffin, I studied the seemingly confident young woman who had once been that frightened fourteen-year-old.

Laurie was indeed gorgeous. She was tall and still assumed the coltishness of youth. Her copious blonde curls fluttered across her pale, perfect complexion.

However, as I gazed, somewhat in awe, at her beauty, her expression turned to one I would not expect to see at a funeral. It was one of pure sexual desire. Laurie released the hand of her beau, and cocked her head seductively. She then deliberately released the hem of her skirt. There was the briefest of smiles as the wind caught it and revealed her thighs. Those cobalt blue eyes were gazing directly across the graveside and I followed them quizzically.

Staring back at her from across the cold darkness of the grave, wearing the broadest of grins, was none other than Frankie Verdi.

Chapter Three

Jamie Strange spotted Frankie Verdi the second he strolled to the grave. He knew all about him and his villainous reputation. Jamie had attended the same school as The Three Dogs, but they had failed to notice the quiet and studious boy at the front of the class, who had now become a Green Beret.

Jamie could feel Laurie shiver at his side. She had chosen not to wear a coat, but Jamie knew deep down, that the reason for her attack of the shakes was not the stiff breeze, but the swarthy handsome man opposite.

A month earlier, on the evening of their engagement, Jamie had chosen Paco's Italian restaurant for their celebration meal. His parents had recommended the intimate Italian eatery owned by the Verdi's. They themselves had used it for many years, and had become friends with the honest and hard-working owners.

Frankie Verdi had attended to them that night.

It was supposed to be so special, but as Jamie concealed the engagement ring nervously in his hand, he was forced to watch on, helplessly, as Laurie shamelessly flirted with Frankie.

On the way home, they fought and Jamie had left for camp the next morning without reconciling their differences.

Both had spoken over the telephone since, and Laurie had seemed distant, yet Jamie convinced himself that everything would be fine and that his fiancée's behaviour was a one-off.

He worshipped her, she had agreed to marry him, and that was enough.

*

Today, the day of his mother's funeral, was the first time they had been together since that night.

Jamie just wanted her next to him. After all, her occasional indiscretions could be easily forgiven considering the circumstances.

Those circumstances being that Jamie had just completed thirty-two weeks of basic training, and had spent fewer than fourteen days at home during that time. Where Laurie was concerned, Jamie's forgiveness came as standard.

His friends had warned him about Laurie long before

their engagement. She had always been a flirt and she had a reputation for being hard and unpredictable.

Those things he could cope with.

Frankie Verdi was another matter.

Jamie walked to the edge of the grave, drew himself into his own world and looked down at the shiny coffin that contained his mother.

The small gathering started to slip away, and around him there were handshakes and kisses, hugs and condolences. For that moment, Frankie was forgotten and Jamie's tears fell for his mother.

"Are you bearing up son?" It was his father Harry, damp-eyed but smiling.

Jamie nodded wiping his cheeks. "Yes Dad, I'm okay . . . could do with a beer now though."

"The car's waiting son, we're all back to Saint Joseph's club for the wake. We'll send your mum off proper." Harry looked around. "Where's your Laurie?"

Jamie looked along the narrow gravel path that led from the graveside to the road.

Laurie was in deep conversation with Frankie. Her body language told a story anyone could read. Jamie felt a twinge of jealousy.

"I'll go get her," he said quietly to his father, and strode toward the pair.

As he closed in on them, their conversation halted abruptly. Laurie looked surprised to see him, Frankie smiled.

"Hey, it's soldier boy."

Jamie ignored the remark and took his girl gently by the arm.

"Come on Laurie, the car's waiting to take us to St Joe's."

Frankie stepped in close. He was much smaller than Jamie and he was forced to look upward as he spoke. His black eyes, shark-like, showed no fear.

"The lady and I were having a conversation," he said. "And you're interrupting us."

Jamie locked eyes with Frankie, but spoke to Laurie.

"Go to the car honey, Dad's waiting for you."

The girl hovered for a second, strangely excited by the threat of violence in the air. The thought of two men fighting for her favours stimulated her. Then she felt Jamie's grip tighten and knew it was time to make her exit.

Frankie watched appreciatively as Laurie deliberately swayed her hips as she walked to the waiting transport.

Jamie didn't take his eyes from Frankie's. His voice, no more than a whisper.

"You made a mistake here today Verdi. You think you're so clever . . . some big-time gangster now eh? Think everyone is scared of you? Well let me you something, you're just a nasty little boy from a shithole council estate. I'm not scared, not one bit lad. So, let me give you some free advice . . . stay away from Laurie."

Frankie snorted a laugh.

"Or what . . . soldier boy? Or fuckin' what?"

Jamie nodded toward the two men filling in his mother's final resting place. His grey eyes narrowed, the veins in his powerful neck bulged.

"Or those boys will be digging one just like it for you." He pushed Frankie hard in the chest with his forefinger, causing him to stumble backward. "And I'll be here to spit on it."

*

Frankie prowled around the back room of St Josephs, like a wounded animal. He thought his heart would burst it pounded so hard.

No one speaks to Frankie Verdi like that, no one. And that soldier boy fucker will pay . . . oh yes, he will pay.

From where Frankie stood, he could see through into the main lounge where the wake was taking place. He could see Jamie Strange with his arm draped around Laurie Holland. He could see them smiling at each other, sharing private conversations. He downed a third whiskey and water, slammed the glass on the bar and barked at the barman.

"Another!"

The guy was balding, fifties. "You need to find some manners young man. If you ask me, you don't even look old enough to be drinking."

Frankie leaned over the bar, teeth bared, voice barely audible.

"Maybe I'm not, but I am just in the mood to do you some fuckin' serious damage fat boy." He dropped one of his now trademark knuckledusters onto the bar and raised both eyebrows quizzically.

"I think you'll just serve me and shut the fuck up."

Frankie watched the man pour, scooped up the offensive weapon, dropped it back into his suit pocket, smiled sarcastically and turned. He flopped down into a seat and brooded. Halfway down his fourth drink, Tony Thompson appeared from the main room with mountains of buffet piled on a paper plate.

He stuffed two mini sausage rolls into his mouth as he sat.

"Fuckin' top food in there Frankie . . . loads of it . . . free too."

As he spoke he spat flaky pastry over Frankie's new black suit.

Frankie brushed the food from his sleeve and gave Tony a scornful look. "Be careful there Tone, these threads cost me near on a hundred quid."

Tony found an egg sandwich and added it to his mouth. "Sorry Frankie, just sayin' like."

He offered the mountainous plate.

"You not hungry Frank? You must be starving' mate."

Verdi sat back, his heart rate returning to something approaching normal. He turned to his lifelong friend, picked up a mushroom vol-au-vent, sniffed it and took a reluctant bite.

"Where's Eddie? Thought he was coming here once he'd sorted the ice cream money?"

Tony shrugged, "Dunno," then remembered, ". . . oh yeah . . . he said he was going looking at some warehouse or somethin'."

"A fucking warehouse?"

"That's what I think he said . . . somethin' about more vans."

Frankie shook his head, then stood and looked back through the bar into the main room. He couldn't take his eyes from Laurie Holland. He watched her move between guests, playing dutiful host. He loved her graceful movement, the way she smiled. She was class, real class.

I'll have you Laurie, make no mistake. Nothing and no one will stop me.

Frankie, back in the land of the living, turned to Tony.

"More fuckin' vans? What are you going on about now Tone, more fuckin' vans?"

"That's what he said."

Frankie grabbed his coat.

"Let's go find him, see what the big fucker is up to with our cash."

Tony looked down at his plate. "Aw, I ain't finished me grub Frankie, I'm starved."

Frankie made for the door. "Come on. I'll treat you to a Kentucky after."

Chapter Four

6th November 1980

Laurie Holland had always been beautiful. Living with her whore of a mother, it didn't take her long to realise that her looks were both her best asset and her worst enemy.

Up to age fourteen, she had done her best to hide her beauty; no make-up, jeans rather than skirts, vests to flatten her breasts. It had worked for her . . . most of the time.

She had learned when to keep quiet, when to fight and, tragically, when to give in.

Then that cop, Hacker came to her house, and her mum had finally been sent down. Her life finally changed.

A care home, then foster parents gave her a fighting chance.

Laurie wasn't stupid either; her teachers described her as a hardworking, above-average student. She never used that card to get what she wanted. Laurie didn't need to play dumb, and by age seventeen, she'd realised all she needed to do was smile, or better still cry, and the majority of men did exactly as she wished.

Laurie also had the brains to understand, that being a beautiful tart was not an option that had any longevity.

She'd seen girls her age plough their way through dozens of sexual partners. The men chased them for sex, but dropped them as quickly as their hurried performances. Laurie had seen enough lecherous blokes to last her a lifetime.

Now, she used her sexuality the same way she used her looks; to get what *she* wanted.

Walking up the steep gangway from Preston railway station, Laurie pulled her engagement ring from her finger and dropped it into her purse.

She thought for a moment, she may cry, but she did not.

Laurie had planned on writing to Jamie when he got back to his barracks, but that was the coward's way out, and she was no coward.

So, whilst holding him tight on the windswept Victorian platform, the day after he'd buried his mother, she told him that even though she loved him, she would never marry him.

The thought of waiting months at a time for her husband to come home; living in a dreary military-owned house and moving from place to place, was not the future Laurie envisaged for herself.

No more slums for Laurie Holland. No more scraping a living. She wanted a man with power and money.

She had offered Jamie his ring back; after all, it had cost several months of his wages. But as she had expected, he refused it. He'd simply shaken his head in disbelief, lifted his kitbag from between his feet, tossed it over his shoulder and boarded his train in bemused silence.

Laurie knew he suspected her actions had something to do with Frankie Verdi, and he was right. Frankie intrigued her. He had respect, he was going places.

Laurie strode into the tiny jeweller's shop on Cheapside, dropped the ring on the counter and began her tale of desertion and woe to the owner.

Minutes later, the transfixed middle-aged shop owner, ensured she exited with seven hundred pounds in cash, her two-year relationship with Jamie Strange over in an instant.

Whilst Laurie was giving Jamie his marching orders, Frankie and Tony had finally caught up with Eddie Williams.

He was at his work, lying under a Bedford ice cream van that had seen better days.

He slid his bulk from under the vehicle, wiped his hands on a rag and nodded at his two friends.

"All right?"

Frankie walked around the aging vehicle wearing a frown.

"Tell me we ain't bought this heap Eddie."

Williams rested a hand on the bonnet and tapped it gently with his fingers. "This and two more like it."

Frankie raised an eyebrow. "What? Are you taking the piss mate?"

Eddie shook his head and smiled. "Walk this way boys."

He strode along Ripon Street, before turning left into Villiers Court, fumbled in his coveralls for a solitary key, found it and walked to a rusty metal shutter door. After some grunting, he managed to raise it, to reveal a two hundred square meter industrial unit.

"Three fully fitted vans, the unit, the walk-in deep freezer; all ours for eight and a half grand."

Frankie stepped inside and examined the building. He began to see the sense in Eddie's thinking.

"Eight and a half you say?

"This is a good space; we could build an office in here, a meeting room, something secure."

"I can do all that Frankie," chipped in Tony, tapping the walls with his knuckles. "Some block to make a room at the back, bit of stud walling to make a separate office, make it look all legit, like a proper ice cream business eh? Few hundred quid and my time is all it'll take."

Eddie was in there too. "Yeah Frank, the vans are all mechanically sound, I'll spray them all matching, even our old one we got from Fat Les, make 'em look all . . ." he searched for the word, "corporate, that's it mate . . . corporate . . . I even thought of a name for us, '3D Ice'. Cool eh?"

Tony furrowed his brow, "3D?"

"Three Dogs," said Frankie wearily.

Tony smiled, "Oh yeah . . . cool man . . . 3D. Three Dogs . . . I like it."

Frankie could see the value in Eddie's scheme. He liked it too, and he trusted Eddie with his life.

Williams had recently brokered a deal with a local pharmacist. The guy had an amphet problem that Eddie "helped" him with. In return, the guy opened a seemingly endless supply of prescription drugs, Diazepam, Temazepam and Valium.

Those pills, alongside cannabis and speed, were then sold from the van Fat Les "gave" them. They even sold the odd ice cream.

That solitary vehicle, working four hours a day on Moor Nook and Grange Park, was pulling near on a grand a week.

Frankie strode around the unit, hands in pockets. He stopped, pulled out his cigarettes and shared them between The Three Dogs.

They all smoked in silence for a moment, before Frankie broke it. He placed a hand on the shoulders of each or his comrades in arms.

"We are going to be fuckin' rich boys."

The laughter could be heard streets away.

Chapter Five

Friday 5th December 1980

Laurie Holland hadn't considered it would take her long to find Frankie Verdi. Indeed, she firmly believed that he would have sought her out himself by the turn of the month.

This, much to her disappointment had not happened, and had caused her to rethink her strategy.

It came as a further surprise, when she visited Paco's restaurant with a friend, to find that Frankie no longer worked for his father. Indeed, Mario explained proudly, that none of the boys worked for anyone anymore. They had their own business, selling ice cream out of a unit in Plungington.

Mario did, however, go on to say, that all three boys enjoyed a drink in the Red Lion pub on Church Street, most Fridays.

The Lion had a reputation for being "rough". It definitely wasn't a place Laurie would normally consider visiting. As she pushed open the heavy wooden entrance door, she was greeted with ear-shattering music and eye-watering levels of cigarette smoke. The sickly-sweet smell of cannabis resin filled her nostrils as she pushed past two black girls on the way through to the bar. They eyed her suspiciously.

Laurie suspected that they'd made some derogatory comment as she passed, but hearing anything was close to impossible as David Bowie's *Fashion* gave way to Blondie's *Tide is High*.

The music was apt really, as Laurie had opted for the full Debbie Harry look. She wore a four-check black-and-white mini dress, white patent leather knee boots and the same shoulder-length messy bob of blonde hair that the American star sported.

By the time she reached the bar, Laurie had the attention of almost every man in the pub, including the one she wanted.

Frankie sat at the back of the bar by the pool table. He lolled in his chair, smoking a joint. His spare hand was fondling the breast of a pretty, but overly made-up bottle-blonde to his left. She giggled drunkenly and made eyes at him.

The second he saw Laurie Holland, Frankie stood, roughly pushing the girl to one side.

She pulled an ugly face. "Fuck's sake Frankie . . . what's that about . . . spilled my fuckin' lager there."

Frankie didn't even turn to acknowledge her. He simply made his way through the crowd, eyeing his prize as he went.

Laurie saw him move closer and felt her stomach flip.

He squeezed himself next to her, pulled out a wad of cash and looked her in the eye.

"I take it you're here to see me . . . so I best buy you a drink."

Laurie held his gaze. She was forced to shout over the music.

"I'm waiting for a friend actually, so thanks . . . but I'll get my own."

Frankie beckoned a barman and shouted back.

"Yeah right . . . course you are . . . an' I'm Margaret Thatcher . . . white wine and soda, isn't it?"

She raised an eyebrow. "Maggie would approve of you, I hear you're in business now . . . an entrepreneur . . . an ice cream man."

Frankie darkened, his inability to take a joke getting the better of him.

"Four vans and a warehouse is a bit more than an ice cream salesman darling."

Laurie ignored his mood. She'd seen plenty of hardmen come and go. Many of Preston's criminals had knocked on her mother's door late at night in search of solace. She picked up her drink, sipped it and nodded in the direction of the pool table.

The girl Frankie had so unceremoniously ditched on Laurie's entrance was staring over, drunk and very unhappy.

"Your girlfriend wants you."

"Not my girlfriend."

"So, you always feel the boobs of random women sitting next to you then?"

"We're just friends."

"Who have sex?"

"You don't like sex?"

Laurie looked straight into those black eyes and purred.

"I *love* sex Frankie."

She dropped her glass on the bar.

"But right now, I'd like to go somewhere nice."

It was time for Frankie's stomach to turn over. He'd never seen anything or anyone so beautiful.

He pulled out a set of car keys and nodded toward the door.

"I got a sports car outside . . . MG."

"Will it take me somewhere nice?"

"Or my name isn't Frankie Verdi."

She took his arm and they forced their way to the exit. Laurie looked over her shoulder to the pool table where the drunken blonde was giving grief to a well-dressed curly haired guy.

"She still isn't happy."

"Fuck her," said Frankie flatly . . . then laughed and added, "actually, Tony can fuck her."

Stepping outside into the cold night, Laurie couldn't help but think that she hadn't seen the last of the drunken blonde.

Tony Thompson was his usual jolly self. He didn't care

for the taste of alcohol, so drank Coke or Fanta. He liked the odd joint, but stayed well away from Eddie's white powder and funny pills.

Tony may have struggled at school, and it took him a little longer than most to grasp situations, but girls found his relative innocence appealing. He was a tall handsome lad, with a natural eye for fashion. All this, together with the rumour that he was particularly "big down below", ensured he always had a girl on his arm.

Problem was, Tony always attracted the younger girls; some far too young to be sharing his well-used bed.

Eddie Williams stood gripping his pool cue so hard he almost snapped it. He hadn't been able to take his eyes from Frankie as he pushed at the exit door and held it open for Laurie Holland.

He hadn't even said goodbye.

Tony noticed Eddie's mood and prized himself away from Frankie's disgruntled date.

"Hey Eddie, you okay pal, you look pissed off?"

Eddie dropped the cue on the table and rummaged in his jeans.

"I'm fine Tone, just leave it eh?"

"I was just sayin' Ed that's all mate."

"And I said leave it."

Tony held up his hands and stepped away. He may have been a little slow, but he knew when to avoid his lifelong pal. When Eddie was in this mood, he was as dangerous as a rattlesnake.

Williams found what he was looking for in his pocket, opened the folded square of paper, licked his forefinger and covered the tip in amphet. He dabbed his tongue, and finished the process by rubbing the remainder of the drug on his gums.

Eddie felt the hit instantly, his heart raced, he felt sharp, king of the hill.

"You got any of that for me?"

Eddie looked down to see the blonde Frankie had left behind.

"What's your name love?"

The girl managed a smile. She staggered slightly and pushed out her ample breasts.

"Cheryl . . . Cheryl Greenwood . . . you're Eddie ain't yer . . . Frankie's right hand?"

Eddie sneered, feeling his anger rise again. "I ain't nobody's right hand darlin'."

Cheryl felt the tingle of first nerves. "I . . . I didn't mean . . . you know . . . anythin' by that Eddie . . . I meant you're one of them Dogs everyone talks about, like."

Eddie turned from the girl.

"You're the fuckin' hound darlin'."

Cheryl was not so easily dissuaded.

"Oh, come on Eddie, sort us out with some sniff eh?"

He turned back; the whizz working overtime. It was a casual, stupid remark. Eddie knew it the second he opened his mouth.

"Okay, what do I get if I do?"

Cheryl blushed slightly. Even in her drunken state, she knew exactly what Williams meant. She looked briefly at her feet, found her brash confidence somewhere down there and looked Eddie in the eye.

"I'll give you a blow job."

Cheryl had shouted her offer above the music, so loud in fact, that two Jamaican pool players turned and laughed, even shouted encouragement.

Eddie looked down at Cheryl with a mixture of regret and repugnance. What was she? Sixteen, maybe seventeen? His mouth had run away with itself, and now he was in deep shit. He didn't think he could ever bring himself to have sex with a girl. So far, he'd managed to bluff his way through his teenage years with snogs outside pubs, fake girlfriends in Wigan and pretend visits to brothels in Blackpool.

He had to get through this with his reputation intact.

Putting on the biggest grin he could muster, he grabbed Cheryl by the hand and turned to the pool players. "See yer boys."

Five minutes later, Eddie found himself sitting nervously in the back of his Capri with his trousers around his ankles.

Cheryl worked on his flaccid penis. She bobbed up and down faster and faster. Eddie did his best to get an erection, but it wasn't happening.

Cheryl had got past her embarrassment. Once she

had her handsome blonde muscular boy in the back of his smart new car, she wanted a lot more than a quick fumble.

She lifted her head and wiped her lips. In her drunken and now drugged state she waggled his flaccid member in her hand and shot her mouth off.

"It won't get hard Eddie. Everyone gets hard on my blow jobs . . . you queer or what?"

Eddie struck with terrifying viciousness. He grabbed a handful of Cheryl's hair in his right hand snapping her head backward. With his left, he clutched the girl by the throat and slammed her against the side window of his car.

She cried out in a mixture of surprise and fear. Eddie pushed his face so close that Cheryl could feel his breath.

"What the fuck did you just call me?" he spat.

Cheryl was finding it hard to breathe. "Look . . . Eddie . . . come on man . . . you're hurting me . . . I didn't mean nothin' . . . you've just had too much whizz that's all."

Eddie's temper was up, he gripped Cheryl's throat harder. Her eyes bulged; she made a gagging gurgling sound as she fought for breath. He used his massive strength, pulled her head forward and slammed it back against the window a second time.

Cheryl's nose started to bleed.

"Please . . . please, don't," she managed.

Eddie's flaccid member had suddenly become hard.

He punched the now terrified girl in the face, once, twice; there was more blood, lots of it; he was so excited he thought he may explode there and then.

Cheryl was barely conscious as Eddie tore at her panties.

It was over in seconds.

Eddie climbed off the girl and sat back sweating and breathing hard.

Cheryl sobbed. "You bastard Eddie . . . you fuckin' bastard . . ."

Eddie didn't feel anything.

Remorse had never been in his vocabulary.

"I'll take you home," he said.

Detective Jim Hacker

In April 1981, I attempted my promotion board, which I promptly failed.

The feedback I received from the panel stated that I . . . "lacked departmental experience". This was cop talk for "you need to go back in blue for a while".

So, much to my wife's annoyance, I transferred back into uniform as a section sergeant, covering Preston's Southern Division.

This meant returning to the crippling three-shift system of early, late and night turns, often with just eight hours' rest between.

Having two growing girls, who found it almost impossible

to keep quiet at any time of day, ensured that my levels of sleep deprivation were considerable.

On the plus side, the constabulary had given me permission to buy our own house, something that had been against police regulations before.

That, coupled with Lord Edmund Davies' review into police pay, ensured our standard of living had improved dramatically.

We could finally afford a holiday.

As with all good things, the bad is never very far away; the Ying and Yang of life is always close by.

Despite my new role, I couldn't help but keep a watchful eye on the force intelligence bulletins for news of Frankie and his crew. However, the information coming through was sporadic and at times, non-existent.

In late 1981, Tony Thompson was fined for possession of a small amount cannabis resin and given a three-month sentence for assaulting the arresting officer; but if The Three Dogs were going about their villainous business, they were doing so quietly and out of sight of the Preston CID.

In my darkest moments, I imagined Verdi's burgeoning criminal empire growing steadily under the noses of the sluggish detectives in town. I knew how clever and scheming the Dogs were and couldn't help but feel that the powers that be were simply underestimating their propensity for villainy.

Was I obsessed with Verdi and crew? Well if so, as with

most obsessive behaviour, it is chronic. It creeps up on you and slowly eats away at your organs until you can't stand the pain anymore.

I somehow knew my fixation would catch up with me eventually. But in the early eighties, I had it under control . . . just.

*

If news of The Three Dogs was infrequent, the same was not to be said about Jamie Strange. I had regular drinks with his father Harry, found him to be good company and a great friend. He kept me abreast of his son's progress with a mixture of military pride and a parent's concern.

Jamie had returned to camp after Laurie had ditched him for Frankie Verdi; something incidentally that Harry was not too unhappy about, confiding that he had never really taken to the girl.

His son had travelled with 40 Commando to Cyprus and had enjoyed almost five months of sunshine and tactical training, before returning home for a fortnight's leave.

Once home, he'd met up with old friends, but had never mentioned Laurie. Harry was keen that this remained the case, his son seeming happy again.

Harry had been concerned that Jamie would be posted to Northern Ireland soon after, but his son somehow avoided this difficult and dangerous job. Instead he returned to Norton Manor, 40 Commando's new home, to train as a sniper.

As the new year dragged itself from winter to spring and with Thatcher in real danger of losing the next election, we declared war on Argentina, over a group of islands no one had ever heard of.

On 6th April 1982, Jamie Strange, along with three hundred and forty-nine other Royal Marine Commandos set sail from HNMB Davenport, for the Falklands.

They were aboard the troop carrier RFA Sir Galahad.

On 24th May, the ship entered San Carlos Water, the area that had become known as "bomb alley".

The captain's intention was to deploy twenty-five SBS troops, supported by Royal Marines from 40 Commando onto the shore. They would engage the Argentine forces made up from combat team Güemes, located at Fanning Head.

The land battle was unremarkable; the Argentines having no stomach for the fight.

It was the clash in the air and from the sea that grabbed the headlines. As the troops were returning to ship, the air war raged and The Sir Galahad was struck by a 1000 lb bomb. Miraculously, it failed to detonate.

40 Commando removed the lethal device and floated it away on an inflatable boat packed with cornflakes packets for extra ballast. Bravery seemed to come as standard.

Even today, I remember vividly, the pictures and video of the battle for San Carlos Water that cost so many British lives.

It seemed that we became ghoulishly entertained by the

news bulletins. Cops, civvies, traffic wardens, all huddled around the small television in the canteen watching the Harriers take off and land.

*

I recall 6th June like it was yesterday. My eldest had broken her wrist at school and they had called me to the hospital.

I had been drowning in work and felt truly exhausted. Starting my car, I tuned the radio to hear the news.

Jamie's ship, The Sir Galahad, had been preparing to unload soldiers from the Welsh Guards in Port Pleasant, off Fitzroy. The troops were to support the Para's and Commandos in the push to take Port Stanley.

She was attacked by three Argentine Skyhawks, each loaded with three 500 lb bombs. This time, The Sir Galahad was not so lucky. She was hit, the bombs exploded, and she was alight. The newsreader had no more information.

My heart went out to Harry. I thought of my girl, I could only imagine what he was going through.

A total of forty-eight soldiers and crewman were killed in the explosions and subsequent fire that day.

Reports later told us, that her captain, Philip Roberts, was the last to abandon ship.

He received a DSO.

It was four days before Harry received confirmation that Jamie was alive. He had been aboard during the attack and suffered shrapnel wounds to his back.

As the fires burned out of control, the remaining marine

detachment began the evacuation of the injured and wounded.

Despite his considerable pain, Jamie helped organise the launch of life rafts from the bow of the ship. The actions of the few Royal Marines undoubtedly saved lives that day, though none were mentioned in dispatches.

I met Harry at his home on the night he got the news Jamie was safe. We drank toasts of Navy Rum to units and regiments I had never heard of.

My wife said she had never seen me so drunk.

Jamie was first airlifted back to Cyprus where his wounds were treated. Two weeks later, he was back at home on sick leave. I didn't get the opportunity to see him. He didn't leave the house and didn't want visitors.

Harry later told me that the screams of the soldiers and sailors trapped below decks where the fires raged, haunted his son. Jamie blamed himself for not being able to rescue more of his comrades.

Harry, himself a veteran of the conflicts in Malaya and Aden, knew what war did to a man, and knew his son would never be the same.

Jamie returned to camp on 9th August, and as September brought autumn and darkening skies, his father's worst fears were realised. Jamie Strange was to be posted to Crossmaglen, South Armagh; also known as "bandit country".

Chapter Six

Tuesday 11th January 1983. 40 Commando Fortified Observation Tower, Crossmaglen, South Armagh

"Hey Jamie! Look at the tits on that one."

Dick, "The Birdman" Valance, was Jamie's spotter. Snipers work in pairs, and Commando Richard Valance, was the cross that Jamie had to bear.

They were almost three months into their six-month tour and the tedium of life in bandit country was starting to get to everyone concerned.

Despite the atrocious weather, Dick had taken to spotting anything vaguely female, as opposed to members of the Provisional Irish Republican Army, who were intent on killing them.

Jamie had a quick glance through his scope. The rain

lashed the roof of the tower, making conversation difficult and spotting even harder.

"She's sixty if she's a day you fuckin' moron!"

Dick lifted the powerful binoculars for a second look.

"I reckon fifty-five . . . she's still got massive norks though eh?"

Jamie shook his head and smiled. Dick was a funny guy. He was a born and bred Londoner, but his parents had moved to Australia when he was seven. Bird therefore considered himself an Aussie. He was built like a rhino and had the same temperament. The two shared a mutual respect and toughness.

They also had plenty of banter about prison ships and cricket.

It helped pass the time.

Since their arrival at XMG as it was known amongst the lads, their days, and nights were split pretty evenly between the observation towers and patrolling.

The towers were designed to ensure that the PIRA boys didn't leave any IEDs in the ditches around the police station and main roads leading in and out of town. The home-made devices being responsible for the deaths of dozens of soldiers and police officers.

Not that 40 Commando were allowed to use the roads for patrolling. Oh no, this was not an option. Soon as a Green Beret's boots touched tarmac, the very friendly locals would be on the phone to the PIRA snipers.

Getting hit anywhere on your body by a .762 or .556 sniper round was not an option. It got you dead instantly. That or you bled out within minutes.

So, when patrolling, the Commandos were shipped out by helicopter to some godforsaken location in the middle of bandit country. Each marine carried somewhere between sixty and eighty pounds of kit and rations. Add weapons and ammunition, and you can imagine how cumbersome and slow a process it was.

Being unable to use even the roughest of dirt tracks or gateways, the units were forced to yomp through muddy fields, climb stone walls or push their way through fearsomely sharp hawthorn hedges.

Jamie and Dick normally returned from these often-pointless expeditions, knackered and with more scratches than an alley cat.

The freezing wind howled through the open slots in the tower. The rain had seeped into both marines' uniforms. Jamie checked his watch. "Another hour and we're out of here."

Dick sat back and rubbed his eyes. "Thank fuck . . . I hate the tower. I'm piss wet through and frozen solid. My legs get all cramped up, and this time of day, your eyes start to play tricks."

Jamie examined his colleague; his sharp grey eyes flashed as he grabbed the binos from him, "What tricks?"

Dick snatched them back and scanned the horizon. "Calm down Strange Brew, I didn't see anythin'. I was just sayin' that . . ."

Dick worked the focus wheel, "Motherfucker!"

Jamie instantly gripped his L96 sniper rifle, pushed in the magazine and slid the action forward, making the weapon ready to fire. He exhaled slowly, lowering his heart rate the way he had been trained. "Tell me the story Dickie boy."

The spotter dropped his voice. No more comedy for today.

"Three hundred meters . . . two o'clock . . . the woman with the titties . . . ain't no lady Strange Brew."

Jamie moved slowly, deliberately. The weather would make any shot almost impossible over the distance. The wind howled left to right and the rain fell in sheets. He made minute adjustments to the Schmidt and Bender 6 x 42 telescopic sight.

"You sure it's male?"

"Or my name ain't Bird."

The suspect had doubled back away from the tower and was walking toward a vehicle checkpoint, set up by the RUC five hundred yards along the road. The target passed an aging cart, seemingly abandoned at the side of the lane, casually removed his wig and pushed it inside his coat. As the suspect climbed under the green tarpaulin covering the cart's cargo, it would have been obvious to a blind man he was male.

Dick found the pretzel on his comms.

"Zulu Zulu nine-five, we have a suspected target concealing himself in an old hay cart three hundred and fifty meters north-east of tower. Suspect is facing the VCP and will have a clear shot of RUC officers . . . over."

Jamie exhaled again. He felt his muscles relax.

The suspect wiggled himself into cover; he was lying flat under the tarp, facing away from the tower. Slowly he pushed out the barrel of a rifle from under the green shiny cover.

Jamie didn't wait for control to answer. He'd seen enough.

Safety off, one last slow exhalation, wait for the wind, wait . . . wait . . . If a doctor had checked his vital signs, Jamie would have been considered close to death. All he could see was his sight picture. The crosshairs sat where he assessed the target's head would be. He squeezed the trigger, and felt the rifle kick. The empty cartridge rattled on the floor.

James Stuart Strange had his first PIRA kill.

*

Marine Jamie Strange and Marine Richard Valance were airlifted from Crossmaglen to Belfast and were in the middle of a blow-by-blow debrief within the hour.

This, often unpleasant process, was part and parcel of Northern Ireland's standard operating procedure.

Jamie's rifle had been confiscated and his hands swabbed for traces of the usual accelerants associated with a man who had just pulled the trigger. For a good couple of hours he was made to feel like he was about to be charged with murder, as opposed to a man who had just saved the lives of several Irish cops.

Thankfully for the two Green Berets, the dead suspect was a well-known PIRA player, and the long black tube sticking out of the hay cart, was indeed an ArmaLite rifle.

The investigator eventually stopped asking stupid questions, and left Jamie alone in his interview room deep inside the heavily guarded RUC station.

Some fifteen minutes later, Jamie was joined by a plain-clothes officer of indeterminate rank. The man didn't look much older than Jamie himself. His somewhat scruffy appearance, collar-length curly hair and droopy moustache, were in contrast to his green eyes that were so sharp, they disconcerted the young marine. From the smell on his clothes, he was a smoker, something Jamie hated. A shoulder holster dangled loosely under his arm, weighted down by a 9mm Browning SLP.

"Stand up Strange!" the man barked.

Jamie did as he was commanded without a second thought and looked straight ahead.

"Sir!"

The officer pulled up a metal chair, sat, and as Jamie had suspected, opened a pack of Rothmans. His manner softened, as did his voice.

"At ease Marine . . . do you smoke?"

Jamie relaxed slightly. "No sir; never used them."

The mystery officer lit up and exhaled. "Good for you Strange, save you a bloody fortune it will."

"Sir," was all Jamie could think to say.

The man eyed Jamie for a moment; his green gaze unsettling the young marine for a second time. He took another long drag and pointed his cigarette forward.

It was all so matter of fact. "After topping a player," he said, "the SOP is that the shooter goes home for a little jolly. You okay with that Strange?"

Jamie did his best not to eyeball the man back. After three months in XMG, any leave was welcome. "Sir, yes sir . . . that would be nice sir."

The man looked for an ashtray; when he couldn't find one he flicked the end of his fag into a teacup.

He managed a wry smile.

"Nice . . . yeah . . . I suppose it is . . . Anyway . . . five days leave . . . from today. Then maybe we'll find you a different way to annoy the shit out of the paddies. You . . . and that daft Aussie you were teamed with."

He stubbed the remainder of his cigarette out under his foot. "That was some shot son; just shy of four hundred yards in a howling gale and pissing rain. Maybe only half a dozen guys in the country could make that kill."

He stood and got in Jamie's face. "Be prepared for a visit while you're home son."

Jamie wanted to ask who might be going to visit him at his dad's house, considered he wasn't going to get an answer and stayed silent.

The mystery man made to leave. He shouted as he walked.

"Travel warrants will be with the crap hats upstairs . . . Oh and don't get in any shit back home either . . . no late-night tear-ups with the local scallys, or you'll be back tabbing through hawthorn bushes before you can say Jack Robinson."

Within the hour, Jamie and Dick had changed into civvies, and were being driven at a scary rate of knots through the streets of the city. They were en route to the port and the awaiting ferry to Liverpool.

The car was driven by another plain-clothes guy. This one didn't speak at all until they reached the dock gate. As the car pulled to a screeching halt, he looked over his shoulder, raised both eyebrows and said, "Well . . . fuck off then."

The lads kept their wits about them as they found seats in the boarding area. Dozens of surly looking characters mingled with businessmen and the odd brave tourist. Belfast was hardly holiday destination of the year 1983, and despite their casual jeans and sweats, the pair may as well have had *"British soldier please blow me up"* tattooed on their foreheads.

"You want a beer Strange Brew?" asked Bird, rummaging in his pockets for cash.

Jamie nodded. "Why the fuck not pal, we're on holiday."

Dick was gone a good ten minutes. Jamie made sure his back was pressed firmly against a wall and he kept his eyes peeled.

When the beer finally came, it was warm and flat. Jamie grimaced as he took the first mouthful.

"This is shite!"

"This," pointed Bird, "was two pounds a fuckin' pint!"

The two marines shook their heads ruefully, drank their expensive brew and kept a close eye out for anyone leaving rucksacks about.

Once aboard the ferry they relaxed a little, and finally grasped the fact that they were on leave.

Dick managed to find a comfortable chair and slouched down on it. He made a pyramid with his fingers and gave Jamie a quizzical look.

"I got two questions for yer Strange Brew," he said quietly.

"Go ahead, shoot, so long as it ain't Mastermind standard."

Bird leaned forward. "Okay, question one . . . what was it like to kill that guy in the cart . . . y'know . . . to actually drop one."

Jamie turned down the corners of his mouth, considered his response and spoke coldly. "Better than pulling burning Welshmen out of The Galahad pal. That paddy . . . he was going kill them RUC lads, weren't he? Bastard got what was coming I say."

Bird found a Marathon bar in his carry-on, opened it and took a large bite, spitting chocolate and nuts onto the table as he spoke.

"Okay, question two . . . Who were them fuckers that turned up after the debrief then?"

Jamie jumped forward, snatched the remainder of Bird's

chocolate from his hand and quickly pushed it into his own mouth.

"22 SAS," he managed through a mouthful of Marathon. "The fuckin' top men Birdie boy, the fuckin' dog's bollocks."

Dick nodded. "I thought you was going say that . . . so what do they want with us then?"

It was Jamie's turn to sit back and ponder.

"That's three questions Bird. I only got answers for two."

Chapter Seven

Tony Thompson swept plaster dust from the floor and barked at the sparks working above his head.

"Hey you two! You should've sheeted up if you was gonna make a fuckin' mess."

Tony may not have been too sharp when it came to social skills or the written word, but he knew his way around a building site. He was approaching twenty-two years old, and cut a formidable figure. His lanky frame had filled out and his naturally muscular arms and shoulders were close to bursting from his sweat-soaked T-shirt. The two middle-aged electricians fitting the last of the spotlights above his head, had no desire to argue with him.

The Three Dogs had worked tirelessly for over two years. Their "ice cream" business had flourished. The four vans had become six and were now manned by trusted employees rather than the Dogs themselves. That said, the three still kept a close eye on proceedings with regular visits and checks. It was always one of the Dogs that delivered the drugs to the vans and later in the day, collected the cash and balance of the goods. Anyone considering rolling one of the vehicles would feel the wrath of the crew, and several beatings had been dished out to remind the locals just who was in charge.

In early 1981 they had moved into the east side of the town and had encountered some issues. The Jamaicans had taken exception to their cannabis dealing business being eroded by The Three Dogs and a turf war had ensued.

One of the 3D Ice vans had been attacked and robbed. The driver, Fat Les' cousin Freddie suffered a broken arm.

Frankie returned the favour by tying one of the Yardie players to a lamp post outside the Red Lion and smashing his kneecaps with a lump hammer.

Eventually, a truce was called. The Dogs kept their vans away from Callon and Avenham, but in return, supplied the Jamaicans with speed and prescription drugs.

Peace was restored and even more money was made.

On the 8th of July 1982, Frankie brought Tony and Eddie to an eight thousand square feet derelict building just off Church Street.

In just twenty-four weeks Tony had transformed it, on time and in budget, into "Toast", Preston's newest and most exclusive disco.

It boasted three bars, two dance floors, ten thousand watts of state-of-the-art PA, and a lighting rig to make

Wembley proud. Just as importantly, Frankie had insisted on one more special touch. It was the only club in the north of England to possess a VIP area.

And tonight was opening night.

The total cost of the building and refurb was twenty-nine thousand pounds. The three had put in equal amounts, but Tony, not wanting to use his saved cash, had sold his flat in Ingol, and used that money for his share.

He knew he wasn't as bright as the other two, but there was method in this madness. He had built smart, modern living quarters at the rear of the club and intended to live on the premises for a while.

The money he'd saved was earmarked for a piece of building land in Fulwood. Tony's dream was to build houses, lots of houses.

In addition to 3D Ice, all three now had their own businesses, Tony's building firm, Eddie's sports car sales, and since the death of his father Mario, Frankie had inherited the family restaurant and opened a second. The club would be another piece in the jigsaw. All of it paid for by violence and people's need to get high.

The two electricians were done and started to fold away their ladders. Tony counted out a hundred in twenties and pushed them into the top pocket of the eldest man.

"Good work Sid," he said. "Frankie will be very happy."

Sid Kershaw would like to have said, he never wanted to see any of The Three Dogs ever again. He wanted to point out that the "favour" to wire the club had just about bankrupted his family business, but he didn't. Instead he kept quiet and, like a frightened child, looked at the pathetic bunch of crushed notes in his pocket, picked up his toolbox and carried it to the exit.

Tony locked the door behind the men and walked through the main bar to a private office at the rear of the club.

Inside was a working space, safe, desk and the club's CCTV system. Everywhere, barring the toilets and the VIP area were covered.

At the back of the office was another door, which led to his living quarters. He strode to his small bathroom, stripped, stepped inside the shower and let the hot water cleanse and revive him. He dried himself and changed into Levi jeans and a plain white T-shirt. As he pulled on a pair of Reeboks, he checked his watch.

One o'clock.

Just nine hours to go before opening the doors. Laurie had been pivotal in the interior design of the club. She had a great eye for detail and had picked all the furniture, along with the interior fixtures and fittings. Probably more importantly, she was the figurehead of the business and would control the front of house. The Three Dogs all had serious criminal records, and were unable to obtain the necessary paperwork for the club. It was her name that was over the door. It was her liquor licence.

Tony's role in the club was security. He had used a local firm, headed by Frankie's cousin Paulo, but it would be nine o'clock before his team of seven bouncers arrived.

With Eddie away in Liverpool on some mystery business, it was down to Frankie and Laurie to organise the rest.

He switched on the TV and listened to his stomach rumble.

Rooting in the kitchen revealed nothing of interest. Fitting the cupboards had been one thing, but Tony had neglected to fill them.

Chastising himself, he strode toward to front door, dreaming of a burger.

The moment his hand reached the lock, he heard knuckles rap from the other side. It was a sharp insistent knock, but not one from someone with great strength.

He stood there in silence, considering whether to open the door, or ignore whoever was standing in the rain outside. He wanted food, not a conversation with some irate joiner searching for a payout.

The knocking continued. Whoever it was wasn't going away. Tony muttered a few expletives under his breath and pulled the heavy door open.

"We're closed!" he shouted, poking his head into what could only be described as a deluge.

Tony had to look down to see the source of the knocking. He didn't recognise Cheryl Greenwood at first. After all, the last time he had seen her, had been over two years earlier in the Red Lion. The night Frankie had got with Laurie.

She had been blonde then.

The girl looked up at Tony, her now natural, mid-brown hair, plastered against her wet face. The unrelenting rain had soaked her flimsy coat through at the shoulders and she shivered. He couldn't tell if tears or raindrops ran down her cheeks. The girl was holding the handles of a buggy. A clear plastic cover protected a small child of indeterminate age.

Tony screwed up his face and attempted to work out what to say.

"Cheryl?"

The girl nodded fiercely. Rain dripped from her nose.

Tony leaned out of the doorway to inspect the child and was immediately drenched.

"Yours?"

More nodding, "Mine and Eddie's," she said.

Tony's voice raised an octave. "Eddie's! Bloody hell Cheryl . . . does he know?"

Cheryl was losing patience.

"Of course he doesn't fuckin' know! Now are you going to let me in before we both fuckin' drown!"

Tony looked up into the black January squall and suddenly seemed to realise it was raining.

"Oh, yeah . . . err . . . I suppose so."

He grabbed the bottom of the buggy and lifted it up the steps. Cheryl followed, holding on tightly to the handles.

Standing in the entrance of the club for a moment she tried to take in the opulence that greeted her. Rainwater puddled around her feet. Her jeans were soaked from the pavement upward and the only pair of shoes she owned had let in water. They made squelching noises with each embarrassing step. The tot stirred and she shushed it.

"Is this all yours then Tone?" she said quietly.

Tony shook his head. "Mine, Frankie's and Eddie's."

Cheryl gave a wry smile.

"I should've known that eh? None of you do anything without each other, do you?"

Tony shrugged; it was the most natural thing in the world to be in business with his lifelong partners. He couldn't consider an existence without the other two.

Cheryl rolled the buggy forward and back to comfort her toddler. She was wet, cold and shivering as she looked at the furniture.

"Very nice indeed. This must have cost Eddie a fortune."

"Not just Eddie, we all put our cash in; we all work bloody hard love."

She stopped rocking the stroller and turned to face him. Her almond eyes were close to tears, yet she managed to jut her chin defiantly.

"Where is he?" she asked. "Where's Eddie?"

Tony Thompson was perfectly capable of dealing with an angry violent man, but a female, close to tears, pushing a child in a buggy, was a completely different ball game.

He studied his Reeboks and scratched his curls. "He's erm . . . he's away on business."

Cheryl stepped closer and craned her neck to look into Tony's eyes.

"Give us a break Tone eh? We had some laughs, didn't we? Me, you and Frankie? Got pissed together in the Lion back in the day eh?"

Thompson managed a half smile and nodded. "I suppose we did girl yeah."

Cheryl placed her small hand on his chest. "Where is he then? I wouldn't ask if I weren't desperate Tone . . . I managed as long as I could without him. I'm on me own; I'm nineteen for fuck's sake!"

She pulled the plastic cover from the stroller and revealed her blonde, blue-eyed boy.

"Look at him Tony . . . look at him . . . William . . . I called him William . . . but he needs stuff mate, stuff I can't give him . . . I just can't manage . . . there's the fuckin' gas bill an' the electric . . . he needs a coat . . . an' . . . an' . . ."

Her voice fell, and with it silent tears. Her quiet weeping became uncontrolled hacking sobs. Finally, her legs gave way, buckling beneath her. There was no fight left and she sat on the deep pile carpet gripping the stroller, with the last of her strength, for support.

Tony was at a loss. He stared for a moment.

Finally, he used his huge strength to help Cheryl back on her feet.

"Come on love. Let's get you in the warm and get you dried off. I got a flat in the back here. You bring the little one inside; I'll put the fire on."

Cheryl wiped her tears away with an already wet sleeve. "Thanks Tone . . . thank you."

Thompson came from a large Catholic family. He was the only boy, but had five younger sisters. Babies were not alien to him and he'd changed more nappies than he could care to mention. He sat Cheryl on his small sofa, lit the gas fire and comforted the child in front of the warmth.

"You got any grub for the little one?" he asked.

Cheryl nodded. "I got a jar for him in me bag under the buggy."

"Well," he said. "Why don't I give it him? You can jump in the shower; I got a dressing gown behind the door, and we'll get your wet clothes on the maiden."

Cheryl was in no place to argue, she was frozen and exhausted.

"Okay Tone . . . thanks mate . . . I'm sorry about before . . . it's just that everything has come on top, you know what I'm sayin'?"

Tony found a kind smile. "Look, just get yourself sorted, I'll give Billy here his bottle, then I'll nip and get us both a burger."

Cheryl raised a pink finger. "William," she said. "His name's William, not Billy."

Forty minutes later, William was fed and asleep in front of the fire. Tony and Cheryl had wolfed down double cheeseburgers, fries and Cokes. The television played quietly in the corner.

"Where you living then?" asked Tony as he wiped the dishes.

Cheryl sat on the sofa, feet tucked under her, drowned by Tony's huge towelling gown.

"I got a flat in the high rise off North Road . . . Westmorland House."

"Oh yeah, I know it."

"It's no good for a kid. The bloody lift only works half the time, and I'm twelve floors up."

"Keep yer fit," joked Tony.

Cheryl ignored the quip. "When I first got the place, I left William's buggy at the bottom of the stairs and carried him up. I'd still got my stitches in from havin' him and couldn't manage a baby and the pram. When I went back down, some fucker had nicked it."

"Bastards!"

"Yeah, never got it back . . . bet they wouldn't have nicked it if they'd known William was Eddie's kid."

Tony finished drying the last plate and joined Cheryl on the sofa.

"Why'd you not tell him about the baby love?"

Cheryl crossed her arms and tucked her hands under her armpits. What should she say?

I didn't tell him because he raped me? I didn't tell him because I think he's gay? I didn't tell him because he's a violent psychopath?

"I thought I could manage on my own," she managed. "Let's face it . . . it was a one-off eh? We were both pissed and on the whizz; it was a fumble in the back of his car."

Tony nodded. "Suppose . . . but I reckon I'd want to know."

Cheryl looked him in the eye. "You ain't Eddie Williams, though are you?"

He considered that information, and let it sink in.

"No," he said. "I'm not."

She took a deep breath.

"And I've decided, if you can keep a secret from him, I ain't gonna tell him either. I made a mistake, I shouldn't have come."

Cheryl stood and checked her clothes were dry. "I'd better get dressed; time's gettin' on."

She took her jeans and top from the maiden and stepped into the bathroom.

Within minutes she was back, her hair brushed, looking human again.

Tony thought she looked very pretty.

He pushed his hand in his pocket, pulled out two hundred pounds and held it outstretched.

"Keep you going for a week or two I reckon," he gestured toward the buggy. "Get him a coat as well."

He thought Cheryl was about to cry, but she did not. She took the money and slipped it in her jeans.

"You're a good bloke Tone," she managed.

"I'll drive you," he said with a smile. "Make sure that lift is working."

Tony took hold of the stroller and pushed it toward the door.

As he reached it he stopped and turned. He seemed troubled, as if struggling with a major dilemma in his head. Eventually he blurted out what was his quandary.

"I won't tell Eddie. I mean, I'll keep your secret if you like."

Chapter Eight

Harry Strange poured strong tea into large mugs and stirred two spoons of sugar into each. He checked the bacon and sausages under the grill, before cracking half a dozen eggs into a large frying pan. Baked beans and tinned tomatoes were simmering on the hob.

The lads had slept the clock around. Harry decided they needed it. There were only two possible reasons Jamie and Dick were home in the middle of a tour; they were in the shit, or they'd had a kill. Worse-case scenario, both.

Harry hadn't asked questions when the two knocked him out of bed around three a.m. They both looked all in, and there was no rush. Harry knew all about taking a life for the first time. And if that was the reason Jamie was home, he knew, from experience, it would stay with his son forever.

At a time like that, the last thing he would need was an old hand giving him grief.

At forty-seven, Harry was still a very fit man and he vaulted the top three stairs on the landing before pounding on Jamie's bedroom door.

"Come on lads, breakfast is ready . . . if you can call it that at this time of day!"

There were groans and the sounds of stretching before Jamie managed, "Smells bloody marvellous Dad . . . two minutes."

Harry set the small kitchen table. Jamie's mother, Rose had always insisted they eat at the table together and he had kept up that routine. Even in the long and lonely periods when Harry was now alone, he still sat at the table to eat; old habits and all that.

The two marines sauntered into the kitchen, yawning and scratching as young men do.

"Morning Mr S," said Bird. "You've cooked up a serious breakfast there sir, enough to choke a horse."

"Sit down lads," said Harry. "I know how shit the food is in the NAAFI."

Jamie picked up a slice of bread and butter from a mound in the centre of the table, tore off a corner and dipped it in an egg. "The rations are the worst Dad, it's a wonder we don't starve to death on a patrol."

Harry gave both lads the once-over. They were both built like houses. "You don't seem to be going short of anything lads. In my day . . ."

"Oh, here we go," laughed Jamie. "We ain't been up ten minutes and the old war stories are coming out."

Harry smiled and pointed a sausage-filled fork at his son. He was full of pride and delighted to have his boy home.

"You are not too big to be pulled down a peg," he joked.

The table erupted into a mixture of Rocky Balboa and Bruce Lee impressions.

There was laughter, tea was spilled and a mountain of food consumed.

Finally, the three men sat back satisfied.

"I'll get the pots," offered Dick.

Jamie gave his friend a knowing look. "Cheers Birdman, me and my old fella got a few things to talk about in the parlour, give us ten eh?"

Bird gave the briefest acknowledgement and began clearing.

Harry sat in his favourite chair with the remnants of his tea for company. Jamie found the sofa, perched himself on the edge of his seat, clasped his hands in front of him, and began the story of how he had killed another human being.

When Jamie had finished, Harry moved from his seat and sat next to his son, the way he had done all his life when he needed him.

"To take a life," he began, "is a terrible thing. But sometimes, in conflict, we have to kill, we have no choice.

You shot that man to save the lives of others. Maybe one day, you will have to kill to save your own life. In the heat of battle, you rarely know if you have killed or not; just that you are still alive. Either way son . . . that is the most important thing . . . you . . . are still alive."

The two remained silent for a moment before Jamie broke it.

"Thanks Dad," he said.

Harry smiled and patted his son's leg. "No worries son . . . now . . . let's go and get a beer eh?"

The kitchen door flew open and Bird stood in the opening, a tea towel in his hand. "Did I hear someone mention the demon drink?"

"You were listening, you Aussie bastard!" shouted Jamie.

Bird shrugged. "It's these walls pal . . . so thin . . . not like Aussie walls . . ."

Harry stood between the two powerful young men.

"How about we start at the Legion, I need to show the old dodderers what real marines look like."

Jamie nodded. "Okay by me Dad."

Bird tapped himself on the chest. "They'll be lookin' at the Aussie marine then Mr Strange."

Bruce Lee and Rocky made a triumphant return to the parlour.

Harry couldn't stop laughing.

*

By the time the three men left the Royal British Legion, the town centre was awakening to its usual Friday night antics.

They walked along Friargate until they reached the junction with Ringway. Harry's love of real ale, as opposed to modern beers and lagers drew him into the Black Bull.

Jamie pulled a face. "Aw come on Dad . . . not another old man's pub. Me an' Birdman here are looking for a bit of life."

Harry stopped in the doorway. "By 'life' you mean girls, I take it?"

Both lads were dressed in shirt, tie, trousers and shoes. No jeans or trainers meant only one thing, a club. Harry wagged a warning finger. "And I'm not going clubbing at my age Jamie. I'd feel like the oldest swinger in town, so you can forget that."

Bird was in there, "Aw come on Mr S, you're still a fine-looking man, look at De Niro and Pacino, they still pull 'em."

Jamie noticed his father's face fall and his hand move unconsciously toward his wedding ring. This was not a conversation Harry wanted to have. Jamie saved him the embarrassment.

"Tell you what Dad, we'll have another couple in here, and you can jump a cab home. Me and Birdman are quite capable of looking after ourselves eh?"

Harry smiled knowingly at his son. "Good shout . . . come on then . . . my round."

*

The couple of beers turned to three, before Harry finally wobbled outside and found his cab. Jamie and Bird stood on the pavement and watched the car drive away, the streets now packed with revellers; groups of girls and lads heading for the cattle markets of northern nightlife. As the pair strolled toward the centre of town, a pretty girl in legwarmers thrust a leaflet into Jamie's hand.

She gave her practised spiel.

"Here you go boys, three bars, two dance floors, lots of girls, only a fiver in with this flyer. Three minutes' walk away."

Bird pulled the leaflet from Jamie's hand and examined it.

"Toast? You ever heard of it Strange Brew?"

"Nah, I was thinking of Squires."

"It's new," interrupted the PR girl, "opening night tonight."

Bird looked at the address. "Church Street . . . where's that?"

"Keep walking," gushed the girl. "Turn left at the junction and it's on your right next to the Con Club . . . can't miss it!"

Bird pushed the leaflet in his pocket. "Let's give it a go eh Strange Brew? It's only half ten; if it's shit we can fuck it off and go to Squires after."

Jamie smiled. "Yeah, why not?"

As they approached the club, the boys' hearts sank. The queue for entrance was huge and snaked over fifty yards.

"Oh, for fuck's sake," said Jamie. "I'm not waiting half the night to get in. We might get our visit tomorrow, and then fuck knows what will happen."

The Aussie gave a wink. "Have no fear, Bird is here," and strode to the front of the line.

Jamie followed and shouted. "Don't do anythin' stupid now Birdman. Remember what the man said about gettin' in shit with the locals."

At twenty-four, Marine Richard Valance (yes, his father was a Teddy Boy) was two years older than Jamie, around the same height at six foot, three inches and weighed in at a similar weight, just shy of sixteen stone. Where Jamie had managed to keep his face in good condition, Bird's love of fighting had ensured his dark-skinned features had been damaged both in and out of the ring. He looked a proper handful.

He stopped, looked at his friend and pointed a finger at his own face.

"Now who could resist a handsome boy like me?"

Before Jamie could answer, Bird had turned and was talking to one of two very surly-looking bouncers at the door.

As Jamie got close, he could hear the doorman explaining that there were no special privileges for Falkland's veterans.

Bird was not so easily dissuaded. He grabbed Jamie around the shoulders, stabbed him in the chest with his index finger and began his pitch.

"This man here . . . is a hero mate; a bloody hero. This man . . . this man here in front of you . . . rescued dozens of men from the Sir Galahad . . . remember it on the TV? Eh?"

The bouncer still wasn't impressed and was shaking his head. Jamie's embarrassment was rising.

He was about to pull Bird away when he saw her.

Laurie Holland stood in the doorway. She wore a black off-the-shoulder dress that hugged every curve. Her mass of blonde tresses, pulled up onto the top of her head with just a single spiral allowed free to rest on her pale cheek.

She locked eyes with Jamie and gave him the broadest smile. For a second, he was convinced there was static in the air.

Laurie rested a graceful hand on the shoulder of the doorman.

She spoke quietly to him, but never took her eyes from Jamie. "It's okay Malcolm these two gentlemen are my guests. Let them pass please."

The doorman raised his eyebrows, stepped to one side and the boys were in.

Bird was open-mouthed. He managed a hurried whisper in Jamie's ear as Laurie sashayed down the corridor ahead of them.

"Who the fuck is that?"

Jamie was about to try and explain when Laurie turned, dropped a manicured hand on her hip and purred. "I'm his ex . . . and this is my place."

Laurie's mood switched, instantly businesslike, she pointed to the ticket booth. "Now don't get too excited Jamie. I did you a favour for old time's sake, nothing more. You pay there, this isn't a freebie. Bars and dance floors are this way, but the VIP area is out of bounds . . ." she gave Bird a cheeky wink, ". . . even to war heroes."

And she was gone. Just like that. Jamie could feel his heart beat in his chest. He'd never stopped loving her. He doubted he ever would. Even Bird was silent for a moment.

Finally, the Aussie found his tongue. "You . . . now just tell me the truth here . . . you used to f . . . I mean, you two were together?"

Jamie shook his head, his heart breaking all over again. "We were pal . . . once."

*

Laurie pushed open the office door to find Frankie sitting behind the desk studying the CCTV monitor. He wore his trademark black suit, white shirt, black tie. Laurie thought he was taking the gangster thing a little too far.

"We're about full Frankie." she chirped. "We're going to have to let the doormen know soon." She walked to a small table and poured two shots of Jack Daniels.

"Drink?"

Frankie shrugged. She handed him one anyway. He took it in silence.

Laurie was desperate to lighten the mood, after all,

come on, this was a special night. "I think we should toast
. . . 'Toast' Frank, what do you say?"

Verdi reluctantly chinked glasses.

He downed the liquid and tapped the screen in front
of him with his finger. Laurie noticed he was shaking.
"Was that soldier boy I just saw you with?"

Laurie's stomach turned. There was ice in the room. In
the two years they had been together, she had witnessed
Frankie's ferocious jealous moods on several occasions;
each time they had ended with Laurie nursing injuries.

She did her best to placate him. "He's just another
customer Frankie, nothing more love; come on, don't spoil
the opening night. We're making a fortune out there."

Frankie stood and walked around the table. He stopped,
fists clenched, knuckles white, his voice barely a whisper.

"We . . .? We are making money? What's this fuckin'
we business?"

Fear began to creep into Laurie's voice. "Come on
Frankie, you know what I meant. We're in this together,
you and me."

He came closer, his nose almost touching hers. "Who
the fuck do you think you are?"

Laurie cowered expecting the worst. Frankie pushed
her backwards slamming her against the wall, banging her
head. Before she could move, he was completely in her
face, his sour breath hot on her cheek.

"I'll fuckin' tell you who you are," he sneered. ". . .
What you are . . . You're a fuckin' whore that's what you

are . . . been fucked by half the town ain't yer? Your mother sold you . . . didn't she . . . pimped you out to the highest bidder so she could stick a fuckin' skank needle in her arm!"

Laurie began to cry.

"Please don't Frankie, I wish . . . I wish I'd never told you about my mum. It weren't my fault what she did Frank . . . I was a kid for fuck's sake."

He grabbed Laurie's hair and pulled her head to one side. She cried out in pain.

Frankie was losing it. "I've heard it all before sweetheart, all the fucking sob stories, all the excuses. Well I'm not fucking interested. What I want to know is, if that soldier boy is 'just another fuckin' customer' how come he gets to jump the queue eh?"

Frankie drew back his fist and punched Laurie in the stomach. The blow was so hard, she was instantly sick.

As she writhed on the floor in agony, Frankie Verdi wiped specks of bile from his suit. He eyed Laurie, full of disdain and hate-filled jealousy. He pointed to the pool of vomit on the floor.

"Clean that up," he spat. "And get your shit together . . . you look a mess."

*

Verdi stepped out into the main bar. The place was packed. The DJ played Kool and the Gang, *Ooh La Let's Get Dancin'* and it seemed pretty girls in revealing clothes writhed in every corner of the room. The club was a success, no doubt, but Frankie couldn't enjoy it, not right now. He couldn't get Jamie Strange out of his head. He pushed his way through the crowd until he reached the VIP area.

Eddie Williams was in deep conversation with a bullish-looking black guy he'd brought over from Liverpool. Tony was surrounded by four teenage girls, one of whom looked far too young to be in the place.

Frankie caught Eddie's eye and beckoned him over.

Williams was high as usual. He sniffed as he spoke. "What's up Frank? You look stressed mate."

Verdi shook his head. "Never mind that. Who you got dealing in the club tonight?"

"Joe Madden, the lad who does the Grange Park van, he's cool, good lad."

"You trust him?"

Eddie nodded. "Yeah, like I said, he's a good lad. What d'you need Frank?"

Verdi leaned in close and covered his mouth.

"There's a guy in the club tonight, a soldier, I want him followed; I need to know where he lives; but I want it done on the quiet."

Williams shrugged. "Just point the fucker out Frank. Consider it done."

*

As two a.m. approached, the floors filled with couples for the final slow dances. Jamie had drunk his fill and held onto a raven-haired girl, more for support than romance.

From the safety of the office, Laurie Holland watched her ex-boyfriend's every move. She felt her stomach flip. And for a change, it filled with butterflies rather than bile. How had she let it come to this?

As she panned the camera left, she saw Frankie and Eddie in the crowd. Frankie was pointing, Eddie acknowledging. Laurie didn't like the look of it.

Not one bit.

*

Joe Madden had worked a 3D Ice van for seven months. It was easy money. Work four hours a day selling dope, and get a decent bung out of it. He'd just made an extra fifty, dealing in the club. Eddie told him it would be a regular thing, so long as he kept it low key and didn't attract attention to himself. Joe had done exactly that. Why fuck up a good number? As far as Joe was concerned it was a perfect situation. He didn't even bother skimming any speed for himself. He earned enough to play it straight. Besides, who wanted to mess with The Three Dogs? Better to have a cushy number than broken kneecaps any day of the week.

Just as the night was coming to an end, Eddie had come up with a different kind of job for Joe to do. He needed a couple of squaddies followed home to find out where they lived.

It was a bit of a pisser, as he had pulled a right little darling of a bird from Penwortham who had her own car and flat. That said, the task paid another twenty quid so the bird could wait till next week.

Why Eddie wanted to know this information, was none of Joe's fuckin' business. He was just glad he was the one doing the following, rather than being the object of The Three Dogs' interest.

Madden had done a bit of time for his crime. Nothing he considered serious, just some burglaries and a bit of football violence. As he shuffled out of the club, five or six bodies behind his two targets, he didn't feel like a criminal at all. He felt like James fuckin' Bond.

Jamie was drunk, and on more than one occasion, Bird had to grab his arm to keep him upright. Joe kept well back as the two marines staggered toward the main road in search of a cab.

The night was freezing, and as Madden's car was only a few yards away, he reckoned it would be far more comfortable to watch the pair from the driver's seat.

Moments later, sat in the relative warmth of his Ford, he watched Bird vainly attempt to flag down any vehicle that looked vaguely like a taxi, whilst stopping Jamie from falling into the road with his other arm.

A light came on in Joe's head. *Why follow a cab, when I can be the cabbie myself?*

Starting the engine and crawling toward the pair, Joe pulled up alongside and his plan worked a treat.

"Taxi?" he shouted through the open car window.

Bird instantly took the bait, grabbing Jamie with both arms to prevent a certain nosedive. "Whoa there, Strange Brew, come on now . . . cab's here . . . our carriage awaits!"

Jamie closed one eye and tried to focus on the car. "Fuckin' marvellous . . . hey . . . Birdman . . . any chance of stoppin' at a kebab house pal, I'm Lee Marvin here?"

Joe played helpful cabbie and concentrated on Bird who was slightly the soberer.

"Just get your mate in the back pal. If I find a place open, I'll stop for you."

Bird half carried, half pushed Jamie's bulk into the back of Madden's Sierra. The second he hit the back seat he was out cold.

Bird shook him. "Oy! Come on! Aw look at the state of yer! You fuckin' English twat! You're all the same . . . can't hold your beer . . ." Then Bird turned to Madden. "Sorry pal if you're English . . . no offence to Pommy bastards an' all that."

Joe needed to take control and play the pissed-off taxi driver.

"Look, where we goin' lads?"

Bird rubbed his face with his hands and got himself together as best he could.

"Well there could be a problem there me old mate. As you can tell by the accent, I'm not a bloody local, and Strange Brew here is sparko. What I do remember is it's off a place called Ribbleton Lane; get us there an' I'll probably be able to direct you eh?"

Joe shook his head. This was not what he had planned.

"Okay pal, Ribbleton Lane it is, but it's a fuckin' long road."

A light came on in Bird's head. "It's near a pub . . . The Villa . . . if that helps?"

Joe pulled away smiling to himself. "Yeah, that helps a lot pal."

Despite the early hour, progress was slow out of town. The flood of taxis and drunken revellers walking in the road saw to that.

Bird was doing his best to rouse Jamie, whilst watching the route. He didn't often ride in taxis. They were an expensive option in London, so the tube was his preferred mode of transport. Not only that, he was sober enough to know he didn't want this scally-boy driver trying to rip off an obvious out-of-towner.

The fact was, the last time he's been in a taxi of any kind was in Belfast.

When you got a night off from XMG, the lads always had it drummed into them to use particular cab companies, and not just climb into any old vehicle. It wasn't unknown for the PIRA to go cruising for drunken soldiers in fake taxi cabs, and for those soldiers to end up dead.

Bird looked over the driver's shoulder at the dashboard. No meter.

He scanned the windscreen.

No badge.

The car crossed the ring road and took the right fork at the prison entrance. Street prostitutes stepped forward into the headlights, looking for punters.

Madden tut-tutted as he swerved to avoid one.

"Skanks," he muttered.

Bird ignored him and concentrated on waking Jamie. He grabbed his mate's thumb, found the base of his cuticle with his own thumbnail and delivered some pain.

Jamie jumped up. "What . . . what the fuck?"

Bird placed his hand at the back of Jamie's neck and pushed his head downward.

"Driver!" he shouted. "Driver . . . he's gonna throw up mate . . . he's gonna be sick."

Joe looked over his shoulder and saw Jamie with his head between his knees.

He was getting paid to get an address for Frankie, not spend it all trying to get the smell of puke from his carpets.

"Just a sec, hold on pal, don't throw up in here, just let me pull over!"

The car swerved to the left and screeched to a halt. Bird was out in a flash and ran around the car to open Jamie's door.

He grabbed at his mate's shoulders and kept up the charade. "Come on pal, be sick out here, I don't want to pay to clean the fuckin' cab."

Jamie was coming around. His brain was telling him something wasn't right. He followed Bird's lead, staggered into a cobbled alley and started to cough violently. Bird played the concerned friend and rested a hand on his back.

"It's not a fuckin' cab," he hissed.

"Who is he then, a moonlighter?" whispered Jamie between pretend retches.

"Dunno, but the more I look at the fucker, the more I'm sure I saw him in the club. He was talkin' to some big blonde guy in a suit; looked a proper bad boy."

Jamie straightened and wiped his mouth with the back of his hand.

"Let's find out then eh?"

Bird sauntered to the back of the car.

No taxi plate.

No surprise.

Madden sat in the driver's seat unconcerned and confident his twenty was coming his way. He rolled a fag, head down concentrating on his task. As he raised the paper to his lips to lick it, Bird almost ripped the door from its hinges.

"Wha . . .!"

Joe was cut short as Bird's massive fist caught him square on the jaw.

Madden felt dizzy and sick in equal proportions. He was pulled from the car and out into the cold. His legs wouldn't work, but he was conscious enough to see cobbles on the floor. They were dragging him down the alley.

"Hey lads," he managed. ". . . Come on . . . Come on, stop this eh? Look . . . you can have me takings."

"You ain't got any takings," growled Bird. "You ain't a fuckin' taxi."

Madden did his best. "I am . . . I'm new is all, I just ain't picked up my badge and stuff yet."

Bird slammed him against the wall, knocking the wind from his body. As he fell forward Jamie stepped in, grabbed him by the hair, lifted his knee with thunderous force and smashed it into Madden's face.

This time they let him fall. Blood poured from Madden's ruined nose dripping black onto the shining cobbles as he tried to clamber on all fours.

"Now . . . what are you up to?" asked Bird flatly.

Joe spat blood from his mouth. "Fuck you."

Bird lifted a leg and penalty-kicked him in the ribs. There was a sickening snapping sound as Madden fell sideways.

Jamie stood over him as he fought for breath. "That's your ribs broke, to go with your nose pal. What else do we have to break before you tell us what you're up to?"

Joe Madden was a tough lad; well known in town as a hardman. He'd had kickings before.

He lay on his back and found a smile. His teeth were covered in claret. He turned his head and spat a second time.

"Like I said . . . fuck you!"

Jamie grabbed at Madden and tore off his jacket, dragging him around the floor like a rag doll and sending rivers of pain through his ribcage.

He swiftly searched the pockets, found what he was looking for, opened the wallet and pulled out a driving licence.

"Joseph Francis Madden," he pronounced, throwing the wallet to Bird and rooting elsewhere in the coat. "What do we call you then eh? Joey . . . Joe? . . . Frank . . . Frankie?" Jamie leaned in, the influence of drink fazing his judgement and fuelling his anger; a dangerous combination. His voice was cold, menacing. "No . . . not Frankie . . . They won't call you Frankie, will they? Coz that's who you work for isn't it? Frankie Verdi?"

Madden remained tight-lipped.

Jamie managed a snort. "Of course, how stupid of me . . . Toast isn't Laurie Holland's gaff at all is it? She's Frankie's girl now eh? It's all a front for the Dogs!"

He pointed, "And Bird here . . . well he tells me, he saw you in the club talking to a big blonde gangster in a suit . . . let me think Joey . . . Joe . . . would that be Eddie Williams? Am I warm?"

Jamie checked the last of the pockets in Madden's coat and removed a clear plastic bag with several smaller packages inside; some in foil, some in paper.

"Oh, this just gets better and better for you Joey . . . Joe eh? How much is in here, a good couple of hundred? What will happen if you don't tip up to Eddie eh?"

Madden again remained silent. Jamie was impressed, but not beaten. He grabbed him by the hair a second time and delivered another vicious blow to his face. Madden cried out and scrabbled on the floor helpless.

Jamie dropped on his haunches, his voice flat, matter of fact. "Joey . . . Joe . . . let me explain something. I am going to beat you to death in this piss-filled back alley if you don't tell me what that fucker Verdi is up to. I mean it sunshine. It's a promise . . . on my mother's grave, you will die tonight. Do you understand me?"

Madden managed a deep breath despite the agony from his ribs.

"I don't . . . don't . . . know anyone called Verdi."

Jamie cocked his head to one side so he could look into Madden's face.

"That's a shame Joey." He stood and turned to Bird. "Okay, let's do his ankles first, find two house bricks."

"No!" shouted Madden.

Jamie grabbed Joe's leg and started to drag him further into the alley on his back. Every bump was agony; he found it hard to breathe. He tried to kick Jamie's hand with his free leg, but the marine simply stamped on his groin causing him to dry retch.

Bird found what he was looking for, rested one brick on the cobbles and held the other in his massive hand.

Madden's face was etched in fear. "No . . . no . . . please . . . look . . . no . . ."

Jamie rested Joe's ankle joint on the edge of the brick.

Madden tried to wrestle free, but his opponent was just too strong.

Bird raised the other brick in his fist.

Jamie halted proceedings. "Just a minute Bird; this fucker's gonna scream the place down when we do this. You got a rag or somethin' for his mouth?"

Bird shook his head. "Stuff his jacket sleeve in there."

Jamie raised an eyebrow. "Good idea pal."

Madden raised a hand. "Stop . . . okay . . . just . . . please . . . okay . . . Frankie . . ."

"Frankie what?" spat Jamie.

"He . . . he . . . wanted to know where you lived . . . he asked me to follow you . . . that's all, I swear, that's all."

The two men strode from the alley leaving Madden to scrabble about for his drug stash in the dark.

"He won't mind us taking his car, will he?" asked Bird.

"Nah," said Jamie.

*

The boys had dumped Madden's car and left it for the kids to destroy.

Bird stood in Harry Strange's kitchen and dropped sugar into instant coffee.

Jamie set down his cup as quietly as he could and poured washing powder into the sink where his trousers were soaking. He only hoped his dad stayed firmly asleep. The last thing he needed was Harry catching him trying to wash blood from his clothes.

Bird read his mind.

"Bloodstains or not, you're gonna have to tell your old man, Strange Brew. We can't have Frankie Verdi turning up on the doorstep when we're away. Harry needs to know what the crack is."

Jamie felt slightly sick. He couldn't comprehend Frankie hurting his father. He shivered slightly.

"I'll deal with it."

Bird leaned against the fridge and studied his friend.

"So, Frankie Verdi stole Laurie from you?"

Jamie shrugged.

"Not exactly Bird. I think she left because I was going to be away so often. That was the main thing. That and money."

"Ah, that old chestnut . . . money . . . the root of all evil; funny how women that look like Laurie Holland always seem to be driving around in Range Rovers and Jags eh? Rich men and beautiful women always go together."

Jamie screwed up his face.

"Don't talk about her like that."

Bird held up his hands. "Apologies to the wounded there blue, but come on pal, it's been two years and not so much as a phone call. She's moved on . . . so should you."

"Yeah . . . I know what you're sayin Birdman, but I tell

you, she didn't have the best of starts in life mate. Her mum was a druggie and Laurie had to be taken into care. She didn't talk about it too much, but I reckon she had a bad time. Maybe the thought of struggling on a marine's pay didn't appeal. Maybe once you've had so little, the appeal of a lot is too good to turn down."

"Maybe," countered Bird. "But I don't see taking up with a psychotic gangster as the preferred option. I mean, she ain't stupid. I only caught a glimpse of her . . . and what a glimpse it was by the way . . . and from what I saw, she seemed to have a clever head on that absolutely perfect body."

Bird cupped his hands in front of his chest and stuck out his lips in mental appreciation of Laurie's assets.

Jamie couldn't help but smile. That's what Bird did for you, made you laugh when things were shit.

"You don't need to remind me how beautiful she is Bird. And I don't have an answer when it comes to Verdi. The moment she set eyes on him, I knew I'd lost her. It was like some kind of animal attraction. She probably dropped me without a second thought. In fact, I know she did. She even sold her engagement ring the same fuckin' day she dumped me . . . like we'd never even existed."

Jamie jutted his square jaw. "But there was something going on there tonight, I reckon her and Frankie may be wearing thin."

Bird shook his head. He'd seen this kind of blind love and false hope from soldiers and sailors before. Being away from home for months at a time was not conducive to good relationships and he'd heard many a tale of woe from devastated young men as a result.

"Oh yeah, and what super power did you suddenly obtain, that enabled you to read the mind of the beautiful Laurie?"

"Come on Bird, give me a break here . . . Yes, I admit, it was partly the way she looked at me and . . . *Yes* . . . I know she could be just playing with me, but . . . but . . . look . . . we saw her at what . . . ten forty-five, eleven at the latest yes?"

"Affirmative."

"Well immediately after she saw us, she walked straight to the office, and never came out."

"You certain of that?"

"Pretty certain."

"Go on, I'm listening."

"Ten or fifteen minutes after she entered the office, Frankie came out looking like a bulldog chewing a wasp and wiping something from his suit."

"They had a row."

"Two points."

"You're good Strange Brew. You should be on some cop show."

"Bird!"

"Okay . . . go on."

"Frankie went straight to the VIP area to meet with Eddie and Tony. Then he asks Eddie to get Joe, the unfortunate drug dealer, to follow us home and find out where I live."

". . . and your point is?"

"Frankie could have just asked Laurie, couldn't he? She knows exactly where I live. So, I'm thinking, maybe he *did* ask Laurie . . . and she refused to tell him."

"Hence the row."

"Hence the row."

"Because she still loves you."

"Exactly."

"Oh, Jamie mate . . . come on . . ."

Jamie held up his hand. The conversation was over, his point made. He examined his trousers soaking in the kitchen sink.

"This blood isn't coming out."

"Bed time," said Bird.

Jamie almost had the chain of events nailed.

*

Frankie nearly took the office door off its hinges; it slammed against the wall punching a hole in the plaster.

Laurie was still sitting behind the desk. She'd emptied the bottle of Jack and was drunk. The alcohol coursed through her veins and gave her courage; but the sight and sound of Verdi charging into the room like a marauding bull, still made her jump.

He stormed to the desk and pointed a finger. "I want to know where your soldier boy lives, and I want to know now!"

Laurie sat back in her chair and took a sip from the last drops of whiskey.

"Oh dear," she mocked. "What's happened? Has poor Frankie not got his own way?"

Verdi's eyes were pure jet. "What the fuck do you know about it?"

The alcohol had done its job. Laurie was feeling no pain, no fear. Her head fell forward and she snorted a laugh.

"I saw what you did." She waved an arm at the television monitors in front of her. "On here! It's all on here. What you did; you and your silly little . . . Dogs. You sent out a boy to do a man's job Frankie."

Verdi took a wild swing at her head, but he was equally inebriated and missed. "Bitch!" he shouted, staggering backward to retain his balance.

Laurie was unfazed. She stood up with some help from the desk.

"I saw you arrange for Joe Madden to follow Jamie home, and I've just seen him fall back in the door with a face like a burst tomato. What's happened Frankie? He get sussed? He's had a beating, that's for sure; he's a real mess; took a proper kicking eh?"

Frankie faced Laurie, fists clenched, just as he had hours earlier. "It's none of your fuckin' business. Now, like I said before, give me the fucker's address."

Laurie smiled sarcastically, and despite the danger, taunted him.

"He's got one over on you ain't he Frank; stuck one up you. He's a hard lad is Jamie y'know. I wouldn't mess with him if I were you. He's not some fat has-been street fighter isn't Jamie Strange.

"What you gonna do, gang up on him three on one? It'll take all three of you Frank . . . he'd eat you for fuckin' breakfast."

Verdi thought his head would explode. The bitch was goading him; standing in his office, in his fuckin' club and fronting up to him.

He drew back his fist.

Instead of shying away Laurie stuck out her chin.

"Go on Frankie, fuckin' hit me! Punch me! Go on, show what a big fuckin' hardman you are!"

Verdi stood stock still; he shook with anger, his mouth turned down in a vicious sneer.

"I'll . . ."

"You'll what?" countered Laurie. "Kill me? Is that it, you're going to kill me?"

She raised her arms out. "Go ahead Frank, do your best. Come on, no witnesses!"

Laurie had suffered enough. She hadn't escaped one brutal household, just to exchange it for another, no matter how plush. She moved even closer to Verdi, her lips touching his cheek; her voice a flat, low whisper.

"The next time you hit me Frankie, you better had kill me, or so help me, I'll cut off your cock as you sleep and laugh as you bleed out."

She took a step back. Walked to the desk, and picked up her bag.

"I'm going home. I suggest you get your head down here at the club. Tony's off with some little tart and I want my bed to myself."

Making for the door, she turned as she opened it.

"Oh, and as for Jamie's address. I won't need to tell you where he lives. After what you and your bozos did tonight . . . he'll come find you himself."

She gave one last false smile. "Good luck with that."

Detective Jim Hacker

On 17th July 1983, I was promoted to inspector and took up my posting with Lancashire Constabulary's Regional Drug Squad based in Hutton. It was just two miles from where we had bought our house in Penwortham and life was good again.

I had two detective sergeants and seven detective constables working under me. Together, we covered a massive area which included Blackpool and Fylde, Preston, Chorley and Skelmersdale, the new town built to accommodate the overspill of people in need of social housing in Liverpool.

I had a small party to celebrate my promotion. Nothing major, just a few close colleagues, their wives and of course, Harry Strange.

I hadn't seen much of Harry since Jamie had been

posted to Northern Ireland. Other than a quick pint or two one night before Christmas, we'd hardly spoken.

As we tucked ourselves away in the corner of Headquarters Social Club, it turned out I'd missed some interesting times.

Jamie had been given leave back in January after an "incident" in Crossmaglen. The way Harry described it, I presumed it involved a shooting. He remained tight-lipped about the details, and I didn't pry.

Whilst Jamie, and another marine, Richard "Birdman" Valance, were at Harry's house, they got a visit from a very hush-hush type.

Harry described him as "Firm". It wasn't a term I was familiar with until Harry enlightened me that "The Firm", aka MI5, worked hand in hand with the SAS in running covert intelligence operations in Northern Ireland.

In addition to the Secret Service, and a fully deniable squadron of Special Air Service soldiers, another little-known intelligence unit, called the Det or 14th Intelligence Company worked undercover, in three locations in the Province.

The mystery man wanted to recruit Jamie and Bird to the ranks of this company.

I had never heard of the Det, but Harry had.

Unknown to me, sometime prior to 1973, Harry Strange had worked in a unit called the Military Reconnaissance Force. The MRF ran informers and lived undercover in some of the worst areas of Belfast.

Harry explained that, after months of painstaking

work, his team had managed to turn two IRA players and were receiving regular intelligence from them. Unfortunately, the operation was somehow compromised. The men were discovered by the Provos and interrogated. During the horrific beatings they endured, the men gave up the MRF operation, which was based in the rear of a coffee bar, in north Belfast. The IRA ambushed an MRF van leaving the plot. Harry was wounded, and his partner was killed.

The powers that be decided that the MRF had reached the end of its useful life and established a highly trained undercover, plain-clothes surveillance unit in its place.

14 Intelligence Company, or the Det, was born. Its personnel were selected from all parts of the armed forces, and were trained by a specially set-up wing of 22 SAS. Additionally, SAS officers formed the unit's command.

Much to Harry's concern, Jamie and Dick had been whisked away by the man from MI5 in the middle of the night. And other than one quick call in late February, he hadn't heard from his son in five months.

Harry was adamant, something wasn't right.

I was in no position to know any different or offer solace to my friend. My contact with the Secret Service was limited to watching *Tinker Taylor Soldier Spy* on the box. All the same, if it had been my blood, I'd have been worried too.

I was also very concerned about what Harry had to say about Frankie Verdi.

Apparently, on the boy's first night home, they went to the opening of a new disco in town called Toast, where they ran into Jamie's ex, Laurie Holland.

Now, I'd known about The Three Dog's involvement in the club quite early. Frankie'd even had the nerve to apply for the licence in his own name. Eventually, even he conceded that he would never pass the fit-and-proper-person criteria and Laurie had taken the helm.

To the casual observer, Toast was just another 1980s yuppie adventure. I knew differently.

On their way home from the club, the marines were picked up by a guy purporting to be a taxi driver. The boys sussed out the fake driver and managed to escape from the car. Harry told me he suspected they had dished out some serious summary justice, before one Joseph Francis Madden, had given up the name of Frankie Verdi, and how he'd been given the job of discovering Harry's address.

I'd known Joe Madden since he was a knee-high. I couldn't help but give a wry smile when I found out he'd had a thump or three. I hadn't heard his name since I'd been a Jack on CID at Preston, but I made a note to make some further inquiries about young Joe on my return to work.

He was a connection to Verdi and that was just what I was looking for.

The fact that Verdi was looking for Harry's address really concerned me, and I offered to speak to the local station. Harry refused gracefully, explaining that you never really knew who may be in a gangster's pocket.

Least said, soonest mended.

*

By 1st August, I had settled into my role as DI and had quite a file on The Three Dogs. I pieced together all the intelligence that had been gathered by the force over the last three years. Associates, girlfriends, drinking establishments, vehicles, houses, business ventures, anything and everything that may lead me in the right direction.

I ensured that every car and every associate was flagged on PNC. I needed more detail, and this was the best way to achieve my goal.

My team got on with just about everything else, whilst I was left alone to brood and feed my obsession.

Part of my role was to contact financial establishments and obtain copies of the bank accounts and financial transactions of known drug dealers, particularly international importers. This was far from straightforward, offshore banks being particularly unhelpful. As Verdi, Williams and Thompson had just one minor possession conviction between them, I could hardly tag them as international drug smugglers, and so, for the time being, this avenue was a non-starter.

Despite this, I did some sums of my own.

I looked at the average expenditure involved in the purchase and refurb of Toast; the quantity of cash needed to buy the goodwill and fixtures and fittings of Frankie's second, rather plush Italian eatery in Broughton; what Eddie Williams Car Sales would have paid to boast Sierra Cosworths, Audi Quattros and Astra GTEs on its new, modern forecourt; and how Tony Thompson's building firm had managed the purchase of a plot of land in Fulwood, large enough for six detached properties.

An accountant, I was not, but I estimated that The Three Dogs would have needed an income of one thousand pounds a week each, every week for the last two and a half years to fund their set-up costs.

Not bad eh?

To say people were reluctant to come forward with any information on Verdi and his cronies, was an understatement. People still talked, and people still listened, but I needed facts.

My starting point was what I myself knew.

I knew that the Dogs had taken control of Fat Les' cannabis dealing business after the attack on his brother in the Army and Navy pub back in 1978.

That single ice cream van had become a well-known ice cream business around the town.

I believed that the business unit on Plungington and the six vans that scurried around the council estates of Preston were an integral part of the crew's funding.

After much desk beating, I finally persuaded my DCI to fund a five-day surveillance on the 3D Ice unit and their vans, beginning Monday 15th August 1983.

Chapter Nine

13th August 1983

Colin Whittle had worked as an intelligence collator at Lancashire's Regional Drug Squad for almost three years. It was a very important role that had once been taken by a police officer. But in the days of wage restraint, some posts had been given to civilian employees to lower costs.

He was a married man, and a good Catholic, with six children. Due to his ever-expanding family, his wife Maureen had insisted they move, as their three-bed semi was too cramped. She was correct, of course, she always was, and his two eldest girls constantly reminded Colin that they were well past sharing a bedroom.

Hence, he now had a crippling mortgage to go with his loans and credit cards.

Maureen Whittle had also taken a shine to the thought of a holiday abroad in October. Their regular one-week jaunt to a caravan in Tenby was as equally unsuitable as their old home. After all, the Jameson's at number seventeen were going to Tenerife, and now Maureen was dreaming of a villa in Torremolinos. As a deft reminder, the brochures were scattered across the living room, when Colin had left for work that morning.

He felt sick.

Colin pulled his battered Escort to the kerb, took out his wallet and strode to the cash-point.

The machine asked for his PIN, and then what he wanted to do next. Colin pushed the button to check his balance.

With three days to payday his account held eleven pence. He was broke.

"Fuck," he muttered under his breath, before pulling his card and stomping back to his car. He sat in the driver's seat and pondered the fuel gauge.

Red.

"Fuck," he repeated.

Colin dropped his head. He wasn't a bad person, it was just that he wasn't good with money; well actually, his wife Maureen wasn't good with money. And now, after all her bleating about foreign holidays, the kids would be looking forward to Spain, to some sun on their backs. He hated himself for what he was about to do. But what choice did he have?

He fumbled in his pockets and pulled out shrapnel, then started his car and drove to the nearest phone box.

*

Frankie sat at the old family table. Since the death of his father Mario, his mother had taken to visiting her sister in Bologna. During these long visits, Frankie used the house for meetings, the way The Three Dogs had done in the early days.

He felt safe in the small parlour, the familiar smells, the tablecloth, the teapot all banded together to calm him. And today of all days he needed to be calm.

Tony sat with his headphones on. He'd just bought the latest Walkman DD and was listening to New Order.

Frankie left him to it as he waited for Eddie to arrive. He checked his Rolex.

Any minute now.

On the stroke of two p.m., Eddie padded into the room. He pulled out Tony's earphones as he sat. "Switch that shit off Tone, fuck me, can't you listen to some decent stuff?"

Tony smiled. He knew Eddie was just jibing him. "Better than that old-fashioned soul you still listen to . . . innit Frank?"

Verdi poured the tea into green cups.

"We're not here to talk about music boys . . . We have a problem."

Eddie stirred sugar into his tea. "What kind of problem Frank? It's not them niggers again is it?"

Frankie shook his head. "Don't talk like that Eddie; you know I don't like it."

Eddie rolled his eyes, "Sorry Frank."

Verdi took a gulp of tea. "It's the cops; they're onto the 3D Ice vans. They're starting surveillance soon . . . Monday . . . for a week."

Tony screwed up his face. "What's surveillance?"

"The coppers are going to be watching the vans," said Eddie.

"Oh . . . right," mumbled Thompson. "Why's that then?"

Frankie shrugged. "'Cos someone somewhere has been talkin' I reckon. Some low-life grass bastard has tipped 'em off."

"Well let's sort 'em out," said Tony. "Like we did with Fat Les."

Eddie shook his head. "It's a bit late for that now Tony. More important, we need to sort out where we're gonna trade from. The vans are fucked."

Frankie nodded. "True, the vans are finished. Even after the cops stop snooping, they'll still have them in their sights. The first time one gets turned over, we'll have to sell up anyway."

Eddie's bright blue eyes were flashing. His temper was up. This was going to cost the business, big time. "How'd you know about this Frank? How good is the tip-off?"

"The best . . . straight from the horse's mouth."

Eddie sat back. "You got a copper in your pocket Frank? When did this happen?"

"Not a copper, but as good as; he's a civilian what works with 'em; gathers all the information that comes in. He's what they call a collator . . . Anyway, he called me today; gave me the good news. It cost a few quid like, but he's worth keeping sweet . . . he's in the Drug Squad office see?"

Eddie rubbed his face with his palms, "This is not fuckin' good guys. We got the new product arriving from Liverpool at the end of the month; a big fuckin' invest-ment. I worked fuckin' hard to get that deal."

Frankie held up an arm. "I know you did Eddie, and we will still go ahead, don't flap. The fact is, we were never going to sell the cocaine from the vans. No fucker on Grange or Brookfield can afford eighty quid a gram. The vans were always going to service the lower end of the market; the weed and the whizz. The club, and a select few dealers will move the coke; that VIP room will be a goldmine. The question is, how do we keep our other markets open without the vans?"

Tony Thompson played with the buttons on his Walkman. "Taxis . . ." he said, ". . . use taxis . . . No one bothers them, do they? We can even deliver, just buy a cab business."

There was silence in the room for a moment as the other two absorbed Tony's words.

Suddenly Eddie grabbed Tony around the neck and knuckled the top of his head. "Don't ever let anyone tell you you're thick again Tone . . . that's a fuckin' brilliant idea!"

Frankie poured more tea.

He wasn't so sure.

*

Tony Thompson sauntered across Preston's flag market in the warm August sunshine.

He'd driven his van from the house on Moor Nook, into town and visited Action Records on Church Street.

Tony had bought himself a few new cassettes for his Walkman. Spandau Ballet, Paul Young and KC and the Sunshine Band were stuffed in a bag together with an Al Pacino T-shirt.

He'd slipped in the Spandau the moment he left the shop and *Gold* blasted in his ears as he passed the Cenotaph toward his favourite clothes shop, Duncan's.

He was about to step inside when he felt a gentle tap on his shoulder. Pulling out his headphones, he turned.

Cheryl Greenwood was wearing white pedal pushers and bright smile. William was plastering himself with ice cream in his buggy.

"Hi-ya Tone," she chirped. "How's tricks?"

"Hey, Cheryl . . . yeah good . . . I'm good."

He knelt to get a closer look at William. The boy's bright blue eyes sparkled. "And how are you little fella, enjoying your cornet eh?"

Cheryl looked on, bursting with parental pride. "He's gettin' big now Tone; he's into everything he is."

Tony ruffled the tot's hair. "He's a fine boy sure enough Chez."

Tony stood and looked Cheryl up and down. "Not looking too shabby yourself girl."

Cheryl blushed. "I suppose I were a bit of a mess last time I saw you eh?" She tapped her tummy. "Finally back to my fighting weight too."

Tony eyed her appreciatively. "Aye you're looking tidy Chez, I'll say that."

For a moment, an awkward silence slipped between them as they both thought of Eddie.

Cheryl broke it.

"I'm glad I never bothered tellin' Eddie about William . . . thought it were best all considered."

Tony nodded. "I never said anythin' to him Chez . . . told you I wouldn't eh?"

She smiled.

"Thanks Tone, that cash you slipped me really helped me out." She rubbed her thumb and forefinger together, "And I got a part-time job now. Only in the Bull and Royal, three afternoons like, but it's all right money."

"So, you're managing then?"

"Getting by, yeah."

"Still in Westmorland?"

Cheryl nodded and turned down the corners of her mouth. "Yeah, bloody shithole it is, no place for a kid, but the council won't move us." She looked into Tony's face and her smile returned. "What about you Tone, you still in that little flat at the club?"

Tony couldn't help but smile back.

"Not for much longer love. I've been building myself a house up Fulwood, be finished for Christmas."

Cheryl was in awe. "Your own house? Bloody hell Tone, you done well for yourself mate, I'm so pleased for you."

Tony puffed out his chest. His mum was always telling him how clever he was and how well he had done, but Frankie and Eddie never mentioned his business or how much money he put in the pot from his building work.

"I'll show you if you like," he blurted.

Cheryl pursed her lips and gestured toward two heavy-looking bags balanced in the handles of William's buggy. "Aw Tone I'd love to, but I've got all me shopping here an' I've no car seat for William like so . . ."

Tony lifted the two plastic carriers from the pram. "I'll sort these, an' we'll nip to Halfords in the precinct and get Billy a chair, he'll need one anyway."

Cheryl knocked the brake off the pram with her foot and followed Tony as he strode toward St George's centre.

"Tone . . . erm . . . look mate I didn't mean for you to be buyin' a chair for him."

"No worries," said Tony over his shoulder.

Cheryl lengthened her stride and made it alongside him. "An' it's William," she said. "Not Billy . . . William."

*

With William safely ensconced in his new seat, Tony drove mother and child toward his development of six detached houses, situated in Sharoe Green. It was a prime location, almost equidistant between Preston's two major hospitals, within a mile of the motorway network, and the location of some of the town's most desirable properties.

Tony had bought the land cheap from a local developer, Brooks and Sons, who had fallen on hard times after overextending themselves with the bank. The Brooks family were not the only victims of the Thatcher "revolution".

1983 saw over three million workers on the dole and interest rates at fifteen per cent.

Times in the building trade were hard, but Tony knew that wasn't the case down south, and his mum always said what happened in London one year, would happen in Preston the next.

So far, the old girl had been spot on.

Interest rates didn't matter to Tony of course. He didn't even have a mortgage. And the fact that there were plenty of lads out of work, only too willing to work cash in hand, was good news for the entrepreneurial young man.

As he pulled his van into the semi-circle of partly constructed houses, Cheryl let out a gasp.

"Oh, my word Tone. Is this all yours?"

He nodded. "Kinda, yeah. I suppose it is. I share my profits with the lads o'course."

Cheryl looked puzzled. She may have grown up in a

council flat, never travelled further than Blackpool, and had certainly never been inside a house as big as any that she saw this day, but she was no fool either.

She knew all about Tony's history, how people called him "slow" or worse behind his back and couldn't help but feel a twinge of concern at the revelation that he would give the lion's share of his hard-earned profits away.

"You don't just give Eddie and Frankie your cash do you Tone?"

Thompson turned, his face suddenly menacing, threatening. "We all put in Cheryl . . . all of us, Frankie and Eddie have watched out for me all my life. Whenever I was in trouble, they always knew what to do. I wouldn't have nothin' if it weren't for Frankie and Eddie . . . So remember, it's not your business, and don't ever talk that way again . . . not ever."

William stirred in his seat, something primal, something subconscious, telling him the atmosphere around him had turned dangerous and dark.

Cheryl locked eyes with the burly young man, her tone conciliatory. "Okay, mate. You're right, it isn't. It's none of my business. It's just you . . . well you looked out for me and William. I thought we was mates like, that's all."

Someone turned a switch. Tony produced a smile from somewhere and he stroked Cheryl's face with his thick fingers. Even so, venom still lurked in his eyes, hiding there, waiting for the opportunity to be released. She had dared to criticise The Three Dogs, and made a note never to repeat the action. She shuddered at his touch, part fear, part fascination.

Thompson's voice was calm, low. "Course we are Chez, course we're mates. I like yer. I like yer a lot. But, don't ever try and get between Frankie, Eddie and me eh?"

Cheryl nodded and bit her bottom lip.

"Yeah," she said. "Course not. Why would anyone do such a thing eh?"

Managing a smile, she took a deep breath and said, "So . . . which one's yours? Yer gonna show me around?"

Chapter Ten

The news that the cops were onto 3D Ice was a major blow for the Dogs.

Tony's idea of changing the selling point to cabs was a good one, but how long would it be before some other grassing bastard gave CID the word on the taxis?

Frankie drove a little too fast from his house in Broughton. He'd returned there after the meeting to find Laurie still in bed, nursing another hangover, and the place a mess. They'd argued, again, and she'd tested his temper, again.

Things weren't at all rosy between the pair. Laurie had started to make noises about weddings and children. Frankie was more interested in making money.

Right now, he needed to go and see Fat Les at the 3D Ice depot, give him the bad news, and make sure there wasn't going to be anything for the cops to find come Monday.

He drove his Jaguar onto the forecourt of the unit. It had an 'A' prefix on the number plate, telling the whole town it was just days old.

Two 3D vans were parked outside having been loaded with goods to take out for the evening run. After all, it was August, and folks did actually buy ice cream from them.

Frankie pulled open the door to find Fat Les had company.

Les was sitting on a solitary chair he'd dragged from the office, whilst his company sat on the bonnet of another 3D Ice van, swinging her legs and eating a cornet.

Frankie took a good look at the girl on the bonnet before turning to his employee, who appeared very uncomfortable indeed.

"Giving our stock away?" he asked, with more than a hint of rancour in his tone.

"Erm . . . Hiya Frank," spluttered Les. "No mate, I erm . . . well I paid for it mate, honest I did. I mean . . ."

Frankie had lost interest in Fat Les' meanderings and was taking an even greater interest in his visitor.

"And who might you be?" he asked, removing his aviator sunglasses to reveal his most powerful weapons.

The girl stopped swinging her bare legs, cocked her head to one side and smiled. Before she could answer, Fat Les was in.

"This is Maisy, Frank. Our Margaret's eldest. She lives next door see. She's just nipped in to drop off me sandwiches. I forgot them when I left this mornin'. She ain't doing no harm, I . . ."

"Shut the fuck up Les," spat Frankie, turning to the girl.

"Maisy eh?"

Frankie walked closer to her. She had fine shoulder-length blonde hair, sparkling blue eyes and a full petal-lipped mouth. She licked her ice-cream seductively, knowing exactly the effect it would have on the well-dressed hand-some man in front of her.

"That's me," she offered. "But who are you?"

Frankie presented Maisy with his best smile that didn't reach his eyes. "You don't know who I am?"

Maisy licked her lips and shook her head. "Nope," she lied, and began swinging her legs again.

"I'm Frankie Verdi, I own this place. I own that van you are sitting on, and I own that ice cream you are eating."

The girl raised her eyebrows, stretched out her arm and offered the cornet to Frankie. "Would you like a lick?" she said, raising the sexual odds even further.

Frankie locked eyes with the girl but spoke to his employee.

"Why don't you step outside and have a fag or two Les? Take a look at my new Jag whilst you're at it."

Les shuffled in his seat, knowing exactly why Frankie wanted him gone.

"Erm . . . well, Frank, look mate, Maisy's just nipped in to . . ."

Verdi spun on his heels, eyes blazing, fists clenched.

"I fucking know what you said, you fat bastard . . . now piss off!"

Les went pale, stood, and shuffled outside, shaking his head as he closed the door behind him.

When Frankie turned back, Maisy had stopped her leg swinging, and had crossed them, revealing her tanned thighs in all their splendour.

Frankie admired them.

"That's a very short skirt Maisy," he offered.

"It's my tennis skirt," she said, gripping the hem with her free hand and lifting it even higher. "I like to play on Saturday morning."

"And then come here to steal my ice cream?"

The girl took the whole head of the cone into her mouth and twirled it around. She pulled it out with a "plop".

"Les pays for them," she said, tossing it into a nearby bin. "Anyway, if you can afford a new Jag, you can afford an ice cream."

Frankie got in close. The girl had full breasts that strained against her white T-shirt. He traced his finger across them and for the first time, Maisy's confidence seemed to waiver.

"I can buy anything I like, Maisy . . . anything, or anyone."

Maisy pushed his finger away.

"You can't buy me," she said.

"No?"

"No."

Frankie gave up on her breasts and traced patterns on Maisy's thighs with his nail. "Do you have a boyfriend Maisy?"

"Kind of."

"Kind of?"

Maisy nodded.

"And do you let him touch those nice big titties of yours?"

The girl giggled at his brashness, leaving Frankie to suspect that she wasn't as old as he'd first thought.

"Maybe," she said.

Frankie could smell her perfume. Laurie hadn't touched him in weeks. He felt he may burst.

"And what else do you let your boyfriend do?"

Maisy was excited too. Scared, but excited. She'd known exactly who Frankie Verdi was, the second he walked through the door; knew he was one of The Three Dogs, the most powerful gang in town. Her fear was surmounted by her desire to get close to such a powerful and handsome man.

"Stuff," she said. "I let him do some stuff, you know?"

Frankie grabbed the girl's hand and placed it on his crotch.

"This kind of stuff?" he panted, planting his mouth on her neck.

Maisy thought to pull her hand away, but Frankie held it in place, rubbing himself against her palm.

"Come on," he whispered. "Stop teasing Frankie now."

Maisy had never gone all the way. She knew her virginity was a prize many of the boys on Moor Nook estate coveted. She also knew that to lose it to this man would mean something different . . . something maybe very special.

"I . . . I . . . don't know," she managed.

Frankie pushed Maisy further back onto the bonnet of the van and buried his face between her bare thighs.

"Oh, I know honey . . . Frankie Verdi always knows best."

*

Frankie stepped out to his car, flushed with exertion. He wiped sweat from his brow with a white handkerchief, before straightening his tie and replacing his aviators.

Les' guts churned with hatred. He hated Frankie Verdi almost as much as he hated himself.

Les knew what Frankie had just done, and knew he'd allowed it to happen. He'd been too scared to stop it.

Les cursed his cowardice and cursed The Three Dogs.

Frankie didn't notice Les' distaste or feel an ounce of regret at taking Maisy's virginity.

"The cops are onto us Les," he said flatly. "Make sure you clean the unit and vans up good. There'll be no gear sold until further notice. I'll take the stash with me now. I don't want so much as a fuckin' roach found inside the gaff. Understand?"

Les nodded.

Frankie studied him for a moment.

"What's up with you? Fuck me Les, it should be me that has a face like a wet weekend. You should be fucking grateful you still have a job."

Les was scared of Verdi, he was scared of all the Dogs, but he had to say something.

"You shouldn't have done that Frank."

Verdi turned instantly, his voice the embodiment of savagery.

"What'd you say fat boy?"

Les jutted his chin toward the unit.

"That . . . to our Maisy . . . she's just fifteen for fuck's sake."

Verdi let out a callous laugh. He grabbed Les by the chin and squeezed hard, his voice a mere terrifying whisper.

"Listen you fat lazy prick. Old enough to bleed, old enough to butcher . . . that's what they say eh? She wanted it right? She was begging me for it. She's inside there now, with a big fucking smile on her face, twenty quid in her knickers and two complimentary tickets for Toast. And I'll tell you this too fat boy, she'll be back for more of the same . . . but . . ."

Frankie increased the pressure on Les' jaw.

"But if anything should ever come on top over what happened here today, I'll know exactly where to come looking eh?"

Verdi slapped Les across the cheek hard enough to knock him down.

"Now, take my new little plaything home to mummy, and get this place cleaned up."

Detective Jim Hacker

The operation on 3D Ice was to be completed in two stages. The first, a surveillance operation on the vans, followed by a fingertip search of the 3D depot and eleven other addresses identified as being used by The Three Dogs and their associates, including the nightclub, Toast.

As I stood before my team on the morning of Monday 15th August 1983, I recall my stomach churned with anticipation, and no small amount of concern. I had put myself out on a limb, in the hope of netting The Three Dogs, and I was fully aware should a positive result not be forthcoming, that my fledgling career as a DI, could be over before it had begun.

I had been allocated seven additional officers to assist my department with the operational side of matters.

These were made up of just three fully fledged detectives, the remainder being uniformed constables who had been earmarked for a possible future in the CID branch.

These, mainly junior constables, were willing to don plain clothes and sit in the back of a roasting van for hours on end, in the hope it gained them brownie points with the powers that be, when it came to their final CID interview.

I had also requested further support in our intelligence gathering, and a very attractive young lady by the name of Candice, had been drafted in from HQ control room, to work alongside our dedicated collator, Colin Whittle.

As I completed my briefing, I was confident that the complicated logistical issues of such a critical observation had been overcome, and within hours, rather than the five days I had been assigned, we would have enough evidence to move on Frankie Verdi, Eddie Williams and Tony Thompson.

I was, at best, over-optimistic.

*

By the end of day three, not one gram of cannabis had been sold, nor a single wrap of amphetamine sulphate recovered. My officers, however, did report and record the visits of dozens of known drug users to the vans, yet all appeared to walk away either empty-handed, or with nothing more than an innocent ice cream.

At 0800 hrs on Thursday 18th August 1983, I was summoned to my DCI's office and given an ultimatum.

Either execute the search warrants issued by Preston Magistrates to search The Three Dogs' premises, or call off the operation altogether.

I had often felt alone in my role as a policeman, but never so much as that morning. I walked to the canteen, bypassed the mountain of bacon and sausages on the grill, took refuge in a lone cup of over-brewed tea and pondered my fate.

If I executed the warrants on The Three Dogs and found nothing, I would be an even bigger laughing stock than I already appeared. Should I call off the operation without undertaking the searches, I would save the taxpayer a few thousand pounds, but look as if I lacked both leadership, and the courage of my own convictions.

I was, as they say, between a rock and a very hard place.

As I stirred two cubes of sugar into the dark abyss that was my tea, I was joined by our newest recruit to the team, Candice.

Her presence didn't alter my mood in any way, but she did brighten my view.

Candice, however, was far more than a pretty face, and after four more cups of frankly awful Typhoo, she had convinced me that some of Lancashire Constabulary's most stringent vetting procedures had failed us, and that we had a bad egg in our unit. By lunchtime that day, Candice had been able to collate enough circumstantial evidence, to point out a potential suspect.

Colin Whittle.

Colin would be described by most as a nice man. Average in almost every way, he went about his duties in the most studious manner, leaving me in little doubt of his competence. As a result, I'd had no reason to even notice him, or his rather obvious personal issues.

A casual chat around his closer colleagues revealed that Colin had major money worries, an overbearing wife and daughters, with not only ideas above their station, but Colin's meagre wages.

The family had recently moved to a house that came with a mortgage payment that would cripple most detective inspectors, let alone a civilian worker, and with the recent hike in interest rates, Colin had intimated to some in the office he was struggling.

When one rather vicious sort from the typing pool commented that the Whittle family had just booked a foreign holiday for the coming October, I'd heard enough.

Much to my irritation, at 1400 hrs, I called off our operation and invited Colin Whittle into my office for a friendly chat.

It didn't take long before Colin admitted his crime. Frankie Verdi had given him a thousand pounds for his tip-off. He had approached Verdi months earlier, because he was broke and couldn't live with the demands of his wife and family.

Now you could say that Colin was as much a victim in this case as anyone else, and I would concur with that, to a point. Yet Colin had cost the taxpayer eleven times the fee he had solicited from Verdi.

Worse still, he had risked bringing the good name of Lancashire Constabulary into disrepute, and allowed The Three Dogs to survive another investigation.

As is the way in most embarrassing scenarios involving large organisations, Colin wasn't formally charged.

He simply went quietly.

As for me, I remained in my post, even more convinced that I should concentrate on bringing The Three Dogs to justice. My seniors, however, had different ideas and I was instructed to leave well alone, unless further corroborated intelligence was forthcoming.

On a far more positive note, just a month later, on 12th September, my wife announced that she was once again pregnant. As time progressed, we were to find we were expecting a boy. With two fine girls in the household, our family would be complete. Although the news didn't totally rid me of my obsession with Verdi and friends, it went a hell of a way to it.

*

Some three weeks later, I met Harry Strange for a beer or two in the British Legion. He'd finally gotten to see Jamie, who had been home on leave after his somewhat mysterious absence from planet earth. Harry shook his head as he described his son as looking like a layabout.

It appeared that the 14th Intelligence Unit worked totally undercover, and Jamie had not only been forced to let his hair grow, but now sported a full set. The bad news was Jamie had only been home a day or two when he'd been called back over the water. Things, as they say in our line of work, had gone pear shaped.

*

The Maze Prison escape took place on 25th September 1983.

The Maze, sometimes referred to as Long Kesh, was a high-security prison that held prisoners convicted of taking part in armed paramilitary campaigns during the Troubles.

Thirty-eight PIRA prisoners escaped from the infamous H-Block. During the daring escape, one prison officer died and twenty others were injured, including two who were shot.

The escape was major news and was all over the TV.

Harry told me it was no coincidence that this event coincided with Jamie's early recall to duty.

I followed the story with great interest.

Of the thirty-eight that escaped, fifteen were recaptured on the first day. Four more escapees were held over the next two days, including two men who were apprehended following a two-hour siege at an isolated farmhouse.

What I wasn't aware of at the time, was out of the remaining escapees, most ended up in the republican stronghold of South Armagh.

Most, but not all.

Chapter Eleven

28th September 1983. Coalisland, County Tyrone, Northern Ireland

Jamie Strange and Richard Valance had been briefed by a surly suit with a London accent. He didn't give a name, or department, he simply gave out their orders with brusque efficiency. The two marines, now fully fledged members of 14th Intelligence Unit, Belfast, had gotten used to meeting new faces with each operation. It seemed that the workings of the Secret Service and Special Forces needed lots of people in suits, but only at the blunt end.

These officer types appeared to be flown into the Province, have a single meeting and be instantly whisked away again back to the relative safety of Whitehall.

Their briefing completed, the pair collected a car from the pool of Det vehicles parked in the yard. Bird had a quick check of the log to ensure it hadn't recently been used in the area they were about to visit, whilst Jamie took a quick sniff inside to ensure a certain other member of the crew hadn't been using it. Happy neither was the case, they threw in their kit and made for Coalisland, a town in County Tyrone that was over ninety-eight per cent Catholic and where the SAS had shot dead two PIRA players some months earlier.

British soldiers, were as popular as a fart in a spacesuit in Coalisland.

An hour's drive found the lads sitting a couple of hundred yards away from an address that had been identified by today's suit, as a PIRA safe house.

Recent intelligence had suggested that one Sean Calloway, an escapee from the Maze, and known terrorist, was on his way to this very terrace. It was Jamie and Dickie's job to sit on it, wait for the said Irishman to show up, and give the nod to the awaiting team, made up of army and RUC, parked out of town, before fucking off, quick sharp.

It was never in the interest of members of the Det to be identified as security service personnel.

These jobs were political hot potatoes. The fallout from the Maze breakout had been massive and ministerial heads were about to roll.

To make matters worse, the allegation that the two players slotted in Coalisland by the SAS, weren't given a verbal warning before the undercover unit opened fire, only added to the dogma that there was a "shoot to kill" policy prevailing in the elite units of the British Army serving in the Province.

Not for the first time in recent days, the suit had reminded the boys of their responsibilities, and their terms of engagement whilst operating undercover. All very well, but he of course, would be at home with his missus when the lads were at the sharp end.

Bird sat in the passenger seat of their Cavalier, struggling with a packet of custard creams, and complained bitterly about the Irish deluge that made it almost impossible to see out of the car windows.

"Do you think it always pisses down here Strange Brew?"

"I reckon, Bird yeah."

"Well I think that if the weather was better, they'd not be so keen on slotting each other all the fuckin' time . . . I mean, give 'em a dose of good old Aussie sunshine and the fuckers would be a lot happier eh? What d'you say blue?"

Jamie shook his head, snatched the packet of biscuits from his partner and sliced the pack open with his nail.

He stuffed two in his mouth before Bird retrieved them.

"I think," spluttered Jamie through a mouthful of biscuit, "if you love Australia so much, you should fuck off back there with the rest of the jailbirds and kangaroos."

Bird pointed a half-eaten custard cream.

"Jailbirds we may well be my English and inferior friend,

but because our country has seasons, as an Australian citizen, you know what you are going to get, as in, during summer the fuckin' sun shines . . . we Aussies, even the most bad tempered of us, are more chilled out."

Jamie just shook his head, stole another two biscuits and waited for the inevitable rant.

"I mean, look, us Aussies don't worry if you are a Catholic or a Prod eh? We don't give a monkey's if you have potatoes to eat, salute King Bill, or dance the fuckin jig, diddly-hi-doe . . . because . . ."

"Because you have sunshine," added Jamie.

"Exactly."

Bird zipped his bomber jacket and pulled on a black woollen hat. The lads couldn't have the engine running as it would identify the car as being occupied. This ensured the pair were cold, damp and struggling with the misted windows of their chosen vehicle.

"This guy ain't going to turn up here blue," shivered Bird.

"Why's that?"

The Aussie pulled his Browning from his shoulder holster, checked the safety and stuffed it in the door pocket to his left.

"Because my old mate, if you had just pulled off a miraculous escape, from one of the most secure prisons in the world, after spending four years inside, getting your little botty banged by big hairy paddies, you would want some better fucking weather than this!"

Jamie couldn't help but laugh.

"You're a fuckin' case, I'll give you that pal."

Bird peered through the windscreen that ran with rivers of rainwater.

"This boy's a case here Strange Brew . . . The lad with the Parka . . . two o'clock."

Indeed, striding purposely down the narrow street toward the undercover Cavalier car, was a skinny youth, dressed in jeans and a three-quarter Parka. The coat itself was only wet at the shoulders, suggesting that the boy had just slipped out of a parked car or a house further up the street.

"Off to the bookies?" suggested Jamie, pulling his own BAP from its holster.

As the boy drew closer, Jamie's question was answered. The player ripped open his coat, pulled a long-barrelled pistol from his jeans, and instantly opened fire on the stationary Cavalier.

"Jesus fuckin' wept," bawled Bird, grabbing his radio. "Contact, contact, contact!"

Jamie stamped on the clutch and fired up the car. Small calibre rounds began to slam into the bonnet and grill of the Cavalier.

Thankfully, although Det cars looked like old sheds, there was at least some modicum of protection offered to the occupants. This took the form of a reinforced windscreen and some Kevlar stuffed in the two front door panels, enough to stop a .38 or 9mm round.

They were also tuned to the maximum of their capabilities.

Jamie floored the accelerator and the car lurched backwards. He was driving blind, but he didn't care. They clipped another parked car, as the Cavalier gained pace, slewing first left then right in an attempt to avoid further small arms fire.

"Shit," spat Jamie as he corrected the car back to the centre of the road, putting further distance between them and the shooter.

Bird was back on the blower. "Romeo Alpha six-nine, we have contact, contact, contact. Anderson Road, junction Smithfield. White male, early twenties, six feet, wearing green Parka coat, jeans, armed with handgun, weapon discharged, repeat contact, contact, contact."

Once Jamie had the Cavalier out of range, he screeched to a halt. The boy simply stood in the centre of the road, gun in hand, being drenched by the rain, and seemingly unsure what to do next.

Jamie and Bird made his mind up for him, rolled from the Cavalier and set off running toward their target.

The boy turned on his heels and was off like a scalded cat.

Now there was always a chance, that in these circumstances, the skinny kid with the little gun, was not the main issue. The Provo's had a nasty habit of leading undercover personnel into ambushes, where bigger guys, with bigger guns lay in wait.

There was no time to worry about that.

Jamie and Bird were big lads, but had only recently completed a selection process close to the equivalent of the SAS regime.

They were gaining on the boy with each stride.

"Security Services," bawled Jamie, over the deluge of rain and wind. "Stop or we'll shoot."

If the boy heard, he wasn't going to stop, that was for sure, and did a sharp right down a narrow ginnel.

"Shit," shouted Bird. "I'm gonna have this little bastard."

The pair reached the junction, and had a quick look-see before following their target. They were getting so close, Bird could hear the lad blowing hard just up ahead.

At the end of the ginnel, was what appeared to be some roadworks; a cement mixer and a hole in the ground cordoned off with bright orange tape.

If the lad kept on his course, in twenty yards, he would be in open ground, and a sitting duck. Bird knew it, and so did the kid. As he reached the mixer, he did a sharp left, and the boys heard the telltale sound of a pair of tired legs climbing a metal fire escape that ran up the gable of the end property.

Bird stopped at the corner, back to the wall, Jamie at his side. They were soaked to the skin and steam rose from their clothing as their body heat dissipated into the Irish cold.

The kid on the fire escape was desperately trying to open the door at the top, that would lead him into the upstairs flat of whatever shop this was.

The boy was out of luck.

Bird tried again. "Security Services," he shouted. "British Army . . . throw down your weapon, and come down with your hands on your head."

Silence.

Jamie tried the same script and got nothing.

Finally, the lads heard the first of the sirens in the distance.

"Hear that?" shouted Bird. "That's the RUC boy . . . them and a couple of pigs full of pissed off Para's who will shoot you down like a dog if you're still holding that peashooter of yours . . . Come on mate, throw down your gun."

The boy coughed "I will not," he said, a definite tremble to his voice, part fear, part cold. "You'll fuckin' shoot me anyways." Jamie was surprised to hear he had a Southern Irish accent.

"Don't be stupid lad," countered Bird. "Don't believe what you hear in the papers. Come on lad. Throw it down . . . you'll be fine."

There was another long silence before finally both men heard the clatter of the pistol as it hit the bottom steps and slithered under the nearby concrete mixer.

"Good lad," shouted Bird. "Now . . . come down all nice and steady like, with your hands up, and you'll be fine."

A pair of unsteady boots started their descent.

"Don't shoot me now," said the unseen voice.

"Just come down, and do as we say," reassured Jamie. "No one has been shot today, no one is dead . . . you'll be fine."

As the boy neared the bottom steps, Bird spun to his left and put two rounds in the boy's chest.

"Fucker," he spat.

The young lad had fallen on his back and slipped down the last metal steps. Jamie knelt next to him. His eyes were open, pupils fixed, no pulse.

Jamie shook his head, rainwater dripping from his nose onto the face of the dead boy.

"Fuck me Bird, what you go and do that for?"

The Aussie pushed his Browning into his shoulder holster, grabbed Jamie by the collar and lifted him to his feet. He was nose to nose with his friend.

"Listen here Strange Brew. That little fucker just tried to slot us both yeah? Given half the chance, he'd have another go. You know the script, this way, is the only way . . . this isn't a fucking game . . . this is war."

Jamie's temper was up. He pushed Bird away from him.

"Even in war, you don't shoot a surrendered man you stupid bastard. He was just a kid! He'd thrown down!"

Bird rummaged under the cement mixer with his boot and kicked the Irishman's weapon over toward his corpse. It stopped inches from the body.

Again, he got in close to Jamie to make his point.

"The kid came down the stairs with the gun in his hand, ignored our warning and got himself dead."

Bird poked Jamie in the chest.

"Are we clear on that Strange Brew? I mean, you won't be letting the side down, now will you?"

Jamie glared at Bird, there was real venom in his tone.

"I'm a marine. I took the oath. I know the rules."

Bird cocked his head to one side, teeth bared, violence in the air.

"And what does that mean exactly?"

"It means, I owe you Bird. I owe you from The Galahad. Otherwise . . ."

There was a screech of tyres behind the pair and shouts from armed RUC officers. Jamie and Bird held up their hands, and declared themselves as Security Services. They were pushed roughly against the wall, disarmed, and held at gunpoint until they were properly identified.

An RUC detective of indeterminate rank pushed his way through the melee of cops and soldiers who were organising cordons to protect the scene. He was a short squat man for a cop and wore a full-length black raincoat. Kneeling by the body, the detective pulled a photograph from his pocket and held it against the face of the boy.

Happy he'd identified the corpse, he turned to Jamie and Bird. He seemed tired, either through lack of sleep, or maybe just tired of the Troubles. His quiet Belfast accent was barely audible over the torrential rain.

"Who's the shooter?" he asked.

"That will be me sir," said Bird, flashing a glance in Jamie's direction.

The cop nodded, took a long slow breath and said, "Okay, you know the script boys. Any more weapons in your vehicle?"

"There's a Sterling under the driver's seat sir," said Jamie.

"Fired?" asked the detective.

Both boys shook their heads.

"Right then," offered the cop. "The lads here will take you separately back to Palace Barracks for the usual swabs and debrief."

Jamie jutted his chin toward the dead player.

"Who is he sir?"

The cop pushed his hands in his pockets. "Not yer man Calloway, that's for sure. Much too young. He's a new one, recruited in the South . . . Barry McGuire . . . he's seventeen, or was."

Jamie and Bird were led away whilst the detective returned to the scene. As they reached the end of the alley, a crowd had begun to gather. Both marines pulled their jackets up over their faces and pushed through the line of squaddies protecting the ginnel.

As he stepped across the road to the waiting car, Jamie noticed a young girl standing off to his right. She was maybe eight or nine years old. She was totally drenched, her jet hair stuck to her red cheeks. The girl looked directly into his eyes.

"I saw what you did," she said.

Chapter Twelve

30th September 1983. Amsterdam, Netherlands

It had been just six weeks since the police had completed their operation on the 3D Ice vans. They'd come away empty-handed of course, and that meddling Detective Jim Hacker, that Frankie hated so much, had been humiliated.

Despite this, it was a hollow victory for The Three Dogs. No drugs were being sold and income had dropped.

The day after the operation had ended, Frankie had called Eddie and Tony to his mother's house on Moor Nook and had challenged the gang to find new ways to sell their narcotics.

Frankie had dismissed Tony's earlier idea of taxis and so, as usual, it had been down to Eddie.

It had always been Williams that had been at the fore-front of the gang's drug trade. From the early days of

Wigan Casino's all-nighters, it had constantly been his contacts, his concepts, his guile, that had kept the Dogs out in front. He sourced the cannabis resin from the Pakistani in Blackburn. He bought the amphetamine from the Mancunians and it was his chemist contact that was so invaluable for the supply of Valium and Temazepam. Even the most recent deal with the Liverpudlians for the cocaine that was sold inside Toast was his doing.

At the meeting, Eddie had persuaded the gang to think bigger than selling a quarter-ounce of resin to potheads on council estates. It was time to farm out the lower end of the market, to disassociate themselves from the street deals that had once been the backbone of their business, but was now a thorn in their side.

If you were going to deal drugs, it was time to deal big.

*

It had been whilst Eddie had been in Liverpool buying the gang's regular four ounces of cocaine from his contact Arron Tower, that he had been invited to a party. It was at this booze, drugs and sex-filled romp, that he had found the ear of Luuk De Jong.

The Dutchman had taken a fancy to Eddie, and although, Williams was most definitely of the homosexual persuasion, there could never be any other man in his life than the one he already had, Frankie Verdi. And as Verdi was one of the most homophobic men Eddie had ever met, Williams was destined for a life of frustration, violence and celibacy.

The Park Plaza Victoria Hotel was located in an historical building just opposite Amsterdam Central Station. Eddie had arrived the previous evening and had taken full advantage of the luxury the Plaza had to offer.

Today, however, was a different matter. As he walked from Dam Square toward Herengracht and the home of Luuk De Jong, Eddie felt wire in his blood. If this deal came off, he knew it would mean two things.

Big money, and big trouble, and Eddie was very fond of both.

De Jong's home was situated in the most luxurious part of the inner city. Herengracht means "Gentleman's Canal" and the homes that rose skyward either side of the arterial route, once owned by wealthy Dutch ship owners, were now valued in their millions.

Eddie found the door he was looking for and pressed the intercom. To his surprise, it was answered in English, by a very cultured female voice. Williams simply stated his name and he was buzzed inside.

The Three Dogs had come a long way since their humble beginnings on Moor Nook council estate, but nothing had prepared Eddie for the sheer opulence and statement of wealth that greeted him.

Polished oak floors gleamed like pure honey under his feet. The ceilings soared to over twice his height, with ornate plaster roses and huge chandeliers announcing affluence and power. Paintings of times when Holland was a great sea power, adorned the delicately painted walls.

If the surroundings were stunning, the source of the female voice outshone it all. Eddie may well have been gay, but he could appreciate true female beauty when he saw it.

Standing at the end of the hallway, was a willowy creature with porcelain skin and hair that surpassed the gloss of the oak beneath him.

"Mr Williams," said the beauty striding along the hall, hand outstretched. "So nice to meet you. I'm Hanna, Luuk's sister."

Eddie swallowed hard. For the first time in his memory, he was lost for words, his mouth full of cotton.

He managed a smile and took Hanna's hand.

"My brother is taking an international call, Eddie," purred Hanna. "I can call you Eddie, can't I?"

Williams shrugged his massive shoulders. "Why not, it's my name."

"Quite," added Hanna with a practised smile. "Of course it is. Come this way please."

Williams followed her along the hall, into the living room overlooking the canal. Eddie guessed he could have fitted his whole flat into the space.

Hanna waved a manicured hand toward an oxblood Chesterfield. "Please, sit down Eddie. Luuk won't be long . . . can I get you anything to eat or drink?"

Eddie had used the hotel's fitness suite that morning

and had consumed enough eggs and bacon to satisfy a small army. He took off his suit jacket and draped it over the arm of the sofa, conscious not to crease his latest designer purchase.

"I've had breakfast," he said. "But a cup of tea would be good . . . three sugars."

Hanna brought out that smile again.

"Three sugars . . . of course."

Finding himself alone, Eddie took to examining Luuk's Bang and Olufsen Hi-Fi.

A voice emanated from behind him.

"It's a Beomaster 2000 system Eddie. Do you like it? It's brand new."

Williams turned to see Luuk De Jong standing in the doorway holding his tea.

"It looks like something out of a spaceship," said Eddie.

Luuk walked over, handed Williams his cup and waved his hand over the unit. Instantly, classical music played quietly from unseen speakers.

"Do you like Vivaldi, Eddie?" asked Luuk.

"Never heard of them," countered Williams naively.

Luuk issued the same smile as his sister, considered correcting his guest, decided against it and sat.

He was a tall man, lithe and tanned with seemingly perfect teeth. His homosexuality didn't show. There was no hint of femininity or camp about him. Just like Eddie Williams, De Jong did an excellent job of hiding his sexual preferences. In private however, this was a different matter.

He patted the sofa.

"Come and sit Eddie, it's so good to see you again," he flirted.

Eddie didn't move. Instead, he took a gulp of his tea. "I'm okay standing thanks."

Luuk looked slightly hurt, but it was brief.

"Of course . . . business before pleasure eh Eddie?"

"That's why I'm here."

"Yes . . . that's why you are here . . . indeed."

Luuk leaned forward resting his elbows on his knees.

"Before we go any further Eddie, I think we should lay our cards on the table, don't you?"

Williams found a suitable spot for his cup. "Fair enough . . . shoot."

Luuk's smile returned. "I like your directness Eddie, and I like your innocence, it's . . . how should I put it . . . refreshing."

Eddie was not amused. He may not have been as sophisticated as the Dutchman, but he had a business brain and was as tough as any man.

"I'm not here for your refreshment pal. I'm here to do a deal . . . the deal we talked about. What's the problem with that? Do you think we ain't got the coin? Is that it?"

Luuk raised a hand.

"Easy Eddie, that infamous temper of yours will be your undoing. This is exactly what I'm talking about . . . Look, I can supply all your needs, the cocaine, the amphetamine sulphate, the cannabis and more, at prices that are very attractive in comparison to what you have been paying . . . but there are issues."

"What are they then?" asked Eddie sharply.

"The issues are twofold. First, you need outlets for such large quantities of product. If you are to climb the ladder, so to speak, you need the customers."

"We have those, no problem. We have a plan in place . . . so . . . the second?"

"The second, my dear Eddie, is that if you climb this ladder, there are people on the rungs above you. People that do not wish to move from their high position. People who will fight with everything they have to stay in this lofty place."

"You mean that Scouser Tower? The Paki Mahmood?"

Luuk nodded. "You have been their customer, and now you want to bypass them. My concern is that these people will go to war with you for this slice of business."

"We won't be taking their custom. We have other options."

Luuk shrugged. "They may not see that as a good enough excuse."

Eddie's eyes flashed. "We may not give a fucking shit."

De Jong's manner transformed from jovial host to hard-nosed drug dealer. He'd seen hundreds of Eddies over the years. Seen then come with big ideas. Seen them end up floating in the canal too. Especially ones who crossed Arron Tower.

"I want twenty grand, up front," he said. "In English

pounds. I want the money washed before it comes to me and I want you to deliver it in person. When I have the cash, I will ensure your goods are delivered to the Kent coast. Once they land on English soil, my part of the deal is done. These terms are not up for negotiation. If the big boys come and take your toys away, it won't be my problem. Are we clear?"

"Clear," said Eddie.

Chapter Thirteen

Palace Barracks, Holywood, County Down, Northern Ireland

Jamie Strange lay on his bed unable to sleep.

During the debrief, he had stuck to the tale that Bird had asked him to. He'd told the officer that despite repeated warnings, the Irishman had refused to surrender his weapon. Corporal Valance had turned the last corner in front of Jamie and, although, he hadn't actually witnessed the final events, he believed that the lad had started back down the fire escape, weapon in hand leaving his partner no option than to engage him.

The officer who had conducted the proceedings had seemed unconcerned with the fine detail. The boy had shot at members of the British Armed Forces and he'd been killed as a result of his own actions.

His instant verdict was one of a righteous kill.

Once the weapons had been checked and swabs and alcohol tests had been completed, Jamie had expected to be issued with a travel warrant and to be sent on leave.

Except he hadn't.

He lay on no more than a bunk in an eight-by-four room with no other furniture. He couldn't call the room a cell, as it wasn't. It was situated on the top floor of a single man's accommodation block. However, all the other rooms were empty and there was a guard at the end of each corridor.

Jamie wasn't going anywhere, not just yet.

Forty-eight hours after Richard Valance had shot dead an unarmed teenage boy, a very serious-looking officer arrived at Jamie's door.

"Get up son," he said sharply. "The RUC wants a quiet word."

After a considerable walk, the angry officer pushed open the door to an interview room. Jamie stuck his head inside and found the obvious.

A metal table, bolted to the floor, with full matching accessories.

"Take a seat," said Angry.

He did as he was ordered, and waited.

An hour passed. Jamie knew what the game was, he'd had all the training, but this was different. This was for real.

Finally, the interview room door opened and in walked

the detective he'd spoken to at the scene of the shooting in Coalisland.

In the starkly lit room, Jamie could see that the guy was much older than he'd first thought. The man still wore the same long black overcoat that contrasted his pale lined face and drinker's nose.

He shrugged his mac off his shoulders, sat and lit a cigarette without offering one to the marine.

"I'm Detective Chief Inspector Kierney," he said allowing the smoke to simply fall from his mouth along with his words.

"Sir," acknowledged Jamie.

He leaned in closer and locked his watery green eyes on Jamie.

"I want a wee word with you about the boy McGuire . . . understand?"

Jamie nodded.

Kierney took another long drag, this time he blew smoke toward the ceiling in a long plume. "I'll tell you this son," he began. "There's not many in here are too concerned about young Barry lying there in the morgue . . . know what I'm sayin'?"

Jamie remained impassive. The guy wasn't telling him anything he didn't know. There had been a lot of back-slapping going on over the shooting.

The RUC's insistence on further questioning, would cause political fallout upstairs and operational irritation down.

156

The DCI didn't appear to care about either.

"You want to run the whole thing by me again there Strange?"

Jamie took a deep breath and began his rehearsed response.

"We were parked just off the junction of Anderson and Smithfield when we spotted McGuire walking toward our vehicle. As he got close, he opened his coat, pulled a long-barrelled handgun and opened fire on us."

"How many times did he fire?"

"Four, five maybe."

"It was four, son. We pulled all of them from the grill and bonnet of your car . . . there were two left in his gun. Not the best shot, was he?"

Jamie stayed quiet.

Kierney stubbed out his fag. "Why do you think that was?"

"What? Why he was a bad shot?"

"No son . . . why do you think he didn't fire the last two?"

Jamie shrugged.

"Did he fire one-handed, or two?"

"Two, it looked like he'd had some training."

The DCI cocked his head and managed a smile. "So, what happened then?"

"We . . . well I, started the car, and reversed down the road away from the danger area, whilst Bird . . . I mean, Corporal Valance, called in the contact."

"And then?"

"Well . . . then the lad sort of just stood in the road."

"He didn't run away?"

"Not . . . not straight away, no. He only ran when he saw me and Bird get out of the car."

"Did you not consider it a trap?"

"We never mentioned it, but it crossed my mind."

"But you ran after the boy anyways?"

"We did."

Kierney found a second cigarette and lit it. "Bit reckless wouldn't you say? Out of cover, running down the middle of the fucking road, in a dangerous part of town. After all, despite all your Secret Service antics, you'd obviously been bubbled eh?"

"Obviously," managed Jamie.

"I'd've been thinkin' that the wee boy was a decoy," pointed the detective. "A means for the Provo's to drag me away from the relative safety of my car and my comms . . . down that dark alley . . . to shoot me down, or worse still capture me alive. But you didn't think that did ye boy?"

"Like I said it . . ."

"Aye it crossed your mind . . . so you weren't just following Valance's lead?"

"He was ahead of me . . . so I suppose . . ."

Kierney nodded and examined the end of his fag.

"So ye chase him down the alley. Young Barry turns left at the end and runs up the fire escape . . . correct?"

"Correct."

"And how close to him were ye when he started his climb?"

"Close enough to hear his feet on the metal rungs."

The DCI managed a smile. "Aye they do make a row now don't they?"

"They do."

"Was that when you issued your first challenge?"

"Yes . . . erm . . . no . . . we challenged him as soon as he ran off."

"You challenged him?"

"Yes, I think it was me."

"You think?"

"Yes . . . yes, it was me, I issued the standard challenge."

Kierney ran his tongue between his teeth and top lip. "Then what?"

"Well once we got to the end of the alley, we could hear the lad rattling the door at the top of the stairs, trying to get away. When no one came to open up from inside, it was pretty obvious he was caught."

The DCI eyeballed Jamie. "Like a rabbit in a snare eh?"

"We gave him every opportunity to surrender."

"Did ye now?"

"Yes, we did, we both challenged him, both did our best to persuade him to throw down."

"But he refused?"

"He did . . . yes sir."

"Then what?"

"Then we heard the boy making back down the fire escape. Bird had point, he was right at the corner of the building, his back to the wall in front of me. If the boy had made the bottom, we would have been in the open."

"So?"

"So . . . he did what anyone would have done . . . he spun left and double-tapped the boy."

"You saw this?"

"No sir . . . heard it. I was still in cover."

Kierney rubbed his chin. He needed a shave.

"And the boy fell down the steps to the bottom, gun in hand?"

"Like I said sir, I only heard the shots and heard the boy fall. As soon as he was down, I went to him, to see if we could save him, but he was stone dead."

Another fag was pulled from his packet, before Kierney began again.

"I want you to think carefully now Corporal Strange. I want you to tell me how many steps the boy took down that escape, before Valance turned and fired."

Jamie was well aware that Kierney would be an expert in the interrogation of suspects. He hadn't banked on this question.

"I'm not sure," he offered.

"Not sure?"

"No."

"Well let me offer you this information son. That escape has twenty-two treads. It was pissing down and they would be slippery . . . agree?"

"I suppose . . ."

"Well suppose this. Young Barry is shitting himself. Let's say he's a little on the fucking reticent side. Wandering down the escape into your arms is not high on his list of priorities. His best chance of survival is to get halfway down the stairs, vault the rail and run like fuck toward the village."

"His best chance of survival would have been to surrender his weapon."

Kierney gave a sardonic smile. "Of course, how silly of me . . . but he didn't."

"No, he didn't."

The detective nodded and turned down the edges of his mouth.

"I reckon, the young boy, standing there in the pissing rain, had no idea if he had any rounds left in his gun. Even an experienced soldier as yourself . . . even you, were unsure how many he'd fired eh? It's the adrenaline you see. A professional shooter should never pull the trigger on an empty weapon . . . but wee Barry was no professional."

"He was a terrorist, nonetheless."

Kierney sat up at that one.

"Oh aye, lad . . . no doubt about it, he was one of those . . . but I'll come back to that in a moment."

Another fag was lit.

"Let's say," started the DCI. "That the boy starts down the steps, clunk . . . clunk . . . clunk . . . how many steps before you two highly trained individuals realise that he's either about to do a runner, or he's coming for you?"

"Like I said . . ."

"Yes, I remember, you aren't sure . . . but just hazard a wee guess for me. Five . . . six . . . seven?"

"Six maybe . . ."

"Six, and did you hear him open the revolver as he negotiated the steps, maybe a turn of the cylinder to see if he had enough bullets to kill you both?"

"No, the rain and wind wouldn't have allowed . . ."

Kierney held up a hand to stop Jamie.

"So, at six steps, your partner Valance has heard enough, he spins to his left and double-taps Barry in the chest. Barry falls down dead, and it's over."

"That's about it, yes."

The detective stood and beckoned Jamie.

"Stand up for me there Strange."

The marine did as he was asked.

"Now," said Kierney. "Put out your hands, the way Barry had them when he was shooting at you in the street."

Jamie stretched out both his powerful arms and cupped one hand with the other. Without warning, Kierney shoved him in the chest. Jamie was far too big and strong to be pushed over and simply stood his ground.

Kierney smiled that smile again. "Now put your hands on your head son. As if you had been ordered to do so by an armed officer."

Jamie didn't like the sound of this one bit, but did as requested.

Kierney gave him a second shove in the chest and Jamie was forced to take a step back to keep his balance.

"Thank you," said the detective. "You've been a great help."

"Can I go now?" asked Jamie, relieved at the prospect.

Kierney held out a hand and twisted it, first palm up, then palm down.

Jamie was growing irritated.

"Look, I've told you all I know."

The DCI leaned over the table and got in Jamie's face.

"No, you fucking haven't son . . . You haven't told me why, if that boy was shot six rungs from the top of the stairs, some thirty feet from Valance, why there are powder burns on his clothing, consistent with him being shot at point-blank range."

The cop pointed a nicotine-stained finger in Jamie's face.

"Also, McGuire was found on his back, with his head resting on the bottom step. As I have just demonstrated, if he'd been treading down the stairs holding his gun out ready to fire, the force of the shots to his chest wouldn't have knocked him backwards, the weight of his outstretched arms would mean he would have fallen on his face, or his legs may have simply given way. On the other hand, if he'd done as ordered . . . had thrown down his gun, put his hands on his head, and walked down the stairs, he would have fallen backward as the rounds hit him, and slid the remaining couple of treads, just as we found him eh?"

Jamie shook his head. "You're making this up. I've had enough."

"Am I? Have you?"

Kierney found his briefcase and removed a plastic bag. Inside was a long-barrelled pistol. He lay it on the table and smoothed out the bag to make the weapon easier to see.

He pointed his little finger at a substance smeared on the sight on the top of the barrel.

"See that?" he said.

Jamie peered. This was not going well.

"I can't see anything," he mumbled.

"Well let me help you Corporal Strange . . . It's cement powder."

Jamie shrugged.

"It's the same cement, that was underneath the mixer at the end of the alley some fifteen feet from the bottom of the stairwell. Now how'd you reckon that got on there?"

Jamie thought his heart may burst. His palms were sweating, his stomach lurched.

"I don't know."

Kierney slammed the tabletop with his fist. Jamie jumped in surprise at the detective's sudden change of mood. His tone was vicious.

"Well I fucking do, Corporal. I know exactly how. It's there because when Barry McGuire surrendered to you, he threw down his pistol from the top of the stairs and it slid under the mixer, leaving traces of cement on the barrel and inside one empty chamber. He then walked down that fire escape, hands on head until he was close to the bottom, at which point, Corporal Richard Valance turned and shot him twice in the heart at point-blank range. Valance then recovered the pistol from under the mixer and placed it near the body to make it look like McGuire was armed at the time."

The DCI's voice dropped to a whisper. "I am right, aren't I Strange? Come on, what are you? A man? Or a murderer?"

Jamie stared straight into Kierney's face but didn't answer.

The DCI made a show of putting the gun back in his case, before once again lighting up. His tone had levelled again.

"You know when I said I'd come back to the point about young McGuire being a terrorist . . . well he was . . . no doubt. He believed he was fighting a war and he went by the rules of that war. See the enemy, shoot them dead . . . simple. Now we . . . we are different. We tell the PIRA that this is not a war . . . these are Troubles, and that they are criminals. Indeed, we catch them and put them in jail, just as any robber or rapist. My point is, Corporal Strange, that we cannot shoot on sight, we have a responsibility to the Crown to play by the rules, even if our opponents do not.

"Now on the evening of 28th September 1983, in the town of Coalisland, County Tyrone, Corporal Richard Valance murdered Barry McGuire in cold blood.

"He knows it, you know it, I know it.

"Most of all, Katie Harrison knows it. A nine-year-old girl who was running home from the corner shop, across the waste ground that overlooks the fire escape. She saw McGuire throw down and she saw him murdered.

"We have an independent witness, we have the forensics to back that witness up. All you have to do now Strange, is decide . . . whose side are you on?"

Chapter Fourteen

Toast was filling nicely. It was Student Night. One way to pack the club's bars with bodies midweek. Cheap entrance, cheap booze and Indie music. It had been one of Laurie Holland's many business ideas that had ensured the business remained firmly in profit.

Laurie had nothing to do with the darker side of The Three Dog's dealings. She had drawn up the business plans for Frankie's two successful Italian eateries, and designed the signage for Eddie's car showroom. She even had a hand in promoting the upcoming sale of Tony's five detached properties in Fulwood, but drugs and violence held no interest for her. Indeed, she had pleaded with Frankie to ditch the evil trade and go straight.

Her pleas had fallen on deaf ears. Frankie yearned for

the danger of criminality more than the money. The risk-taking, the constant desire to outwit the cops, the need to persecute anyone who stood in his way.

Most of all, he craved to be feared. He lived for it, and he would die for it.

To the casual observer, Laurie Holland had found her niche in life. She understood business, had a fabulous eye for detail and the customers loved her.

Yet, she desperately needed Frankie to ditch the gangster lifestyle, settle down, marry her and give her the child she so craved.

That seemed further away than ever, and she spent many sleepless hours dreaming of Jamie, and what might have been.

Since the incident on the opening night of the club, Frankie had become more and more obsessed with her ex-boyfriend. After the police had put an end to the 3D Ice scam, he'd become convinced that there was a connection between the detective leading the operation and Jamie Strange. He prowled about the house like a caged lion, accusing her of keeping information from him, information that somehow prevented him discovering the link between the cops and her first love. He'd never gone as far as to hit her since that fateful night, but sex was, at best rushed, and often deliberately violently painful.

Laurie had taken to drinking a little too much and sleeping a little too long, but her beauty was as evident as ever. One girl, who waited tables at the club, even dared to suggest she could do much better, yet Laurie knew that Frankie would never allow that. There would be no escape from his grasp. No place to hide.

As she worked the floor, checking all the staff were doing their jobs, she drew admiring glances from the young male students queueing at the bars. Not that any man, of any age, dare approach her.

Even though Frankie hardly acknowledged her presence, God preserve anyone who did.

Three weeks earlier, a middle-aged man, who was slightly the worse for wear, attempted to chat her up as she stood at the bar. Frankie had seen the man's pathetic efforts on the CCTV system, had followed him out of the venue and beaten him so badly, he still remained in hospital.

Despite four witnesses to the vicious assault, no one had come forward, and Frankie had never been questioned.

Laurie opened the door to the office, poured herself a large Jack and Coke, and flopped into her chair. She flicked through the CCTV cameras, until she settled on the front entrance. A steady flow of customers came in and out of shot.

The door staff were always under strict instructions to monitor the ages of the clientele. After all, it was Laurie's name over the door, and she had no desire to give the authorities any reason to refuse the application to renew her licence. This was a particular issue on Student Night, as the attraction of a flock young, single men, was too much to resist for younger girls who considered they may pass for eighteen.

Laurie zoomed in on one such young girl. She was tall, fabulous figure, long blonde hair and one hundred per cent jailbait.

Laurie picked up the internal phone and called the doorman who had just let the girl pass without even checking for ID.

"She's on Frankie's guest list Miss Laurie," said the burly doorman.

Laurie put down the phone and followed the girl through the club with the camera system. She was indeed a beauty. Long tanned legs, big boobs. Just Frankie's type.

Laurie felt the first pangs of jealousy flip her stomach.

"On Frankie's list, eh?" she muttered to herself.

The girl went directly to the ladies and out of shot. No cameras allowed. After all, Frankie, Eddie and Tony wouldn't want pictures of the activities in that area being available to the cops. With the demise of the 3D Ice vans, more and more cocaine was being sold in the club, and that often meant that the ladies and gents wash-rooms were used for other reasons than your standard ablutions.

She sipped her drink and scanned the rest of the club until she found Frankie. Unusually, he wasn't in the VIP lounge, rather he was at the main bar, in deep conversation with Eddie Williams. Eddie had just returned from another mysterious trip abroad. Tony had let it slip that something big was on the horizon, but other than that tiny lapse of confidentiality, Laurie was in the dark.

She kept the camera on her man, and sure enough, within minutes, along came the young blonde. Frankie instantly stopped his chat with Eddie, slipped his arm around the waist of the girl and gave her a peck on the cheek.

"More than I've had in a month," commented Laurie to the screen.

The girl looked longingly into Frankie's face and rubbed his chest with her free hand. Frankie passed the girl a glass of champagne, then rummaged in his pocket. He pulled out something small, hard to see with all the flashing lights, but to Laurie, it looked suspiciously like a wrap of cocaine.

The girl jumped up and down like the schoolchild she was and skipped off back to the ladies to powder her nose.

Laurie stood. She wanted a word.

Striding inside the washroom, Laurie found every cubicle occupied and half a dozen other girls applying make-up or doing their hair at the vanity units. She occupied herself by reapplying her lipstick. As she dabbed her lips with tissue, the mystery girl appeared from a cubicle, rubbing her nose with the back of her hand and sniffing loudly. Laurie considered she may as well have had a sign on her head. The blonde sidled up against Laurie to get a look at herself in the mirror.

She was indeed striking, lovely eyes, full mouth, great hair. Even though Laurie was barely in her twenties, the girl made her feel suddenly old.

Undeterred, she gave the child her best beaming smile.

"Hello, I'm Laurie Holland, this is my club. I haven't seen you here before."

The girl looked momentarily shocked. Whatever tissue of lies and deception Frankie had fed her, Laurie was about to find out.

"Oh . . . hi," she gushed. "I'm Maisy, I'm Les Thomas' niece."

Laurie looked confused.

"Les Thomas?"

The girl was flying, full of cocaine-fuelled confidence. She giggled. "Oh, sorry, I mean Fat Les, as in, you probably know him as Fat Les . . . he does the ice cream vans."

Laurie managed a smile. "Ah yes, I do know Les, he works for my boyfriend, Frankie Verdi. Do you know him too?"

If Maisy hadn't just put a line of cocaine up her nose, she would probably have folded there and then. But she had, and she didn't.

"Yeah, I know Frankie," she looked Laurie up and down. "I didn't know he had a girlfriend . . . and this is *his* club, isn't it?"

"We live together," hissed Laurie. "And yes, he owns

it, but it's my name over the door, so my rules . . . as in, who is allowed in and how old they are."

"Right," managed Maisy, collecting her handbag and turning. "Well, I'm old enough, and I'm on Frankie's guest list, so I suppose that makes me a VIP."

And with that, Maisy was gone. All flowing locks and swaying hips.

Laurie turned back and spoke to her reflection.

"We'll see about that young lady."

*

By midnight, every bar was packed with revellers taking advantage of the discounted drinks. The dance floors heaved with bodies as the DJ faded out *This Charming Man*, and *Burning Down The House* boomed from the PA. The odd drunken scuffle had been promptly snuffed out by the door staff as one or two of the younger crowd had just that one too many. Yet it was worth the limited hassle. The tills were full once again.

Laurie sat in her office chair and brooded over Maisy. She scanned the club for her image, but she was nowhere to be found. Just like Frankie Verdi.

She imagined them holed up in the VIP area, snorting coke and snogging each other like a couple of stoned school kids.

Laurie knew all about infidelity. After all, she hadn't been such an angel herself when she'd been dating Jamie. But then it had been her playing away from home, and the excitement of an illicit affair had given her butterflies; now the thought of her man with another woman simply made her sick to her stomach.

How could you have been so cold? How could you have been so stupid?

Finally, she clicked the camera closest to the ladies and there they were, pushing their way toward the toilets. Frankie was all over the girl like a rash, hands everywhere, fondling, groping. They were both laughing. Her man, the man she had given everything for, was openly flaunting his indiscretion, rubbing her face in his betrayal, as he pawed at Maisy's ample breasts.

Laurie downed the last of her Jack, stood and straightened her dress.

She stared at the screen.

"Oh no, you don't Frankie. Not here. Not in my club."

She was forced to push her way through the bustle toward the ladies. It seemed to take her an age. Then, as she got near to her goal, a young girl blocked her path and began to complain that the condom machine was empty. Laurie gave the teenager short shrift, shoved past her and strode to the washrooms. This was no time for customer service.

Once inside the ladies, she took a deep breath and scanned the room for her man. Other than two girls giggling in one corner, the room appeared empty. The end cubical, however, was occupied. As Laurie drew closer, she could hear exactly why the girls laughed behind their hands. It was the distinctive sounds of a sexual encounter. Moreover, the unmistakable sound of Frankie Verdi's rhythmical grunting. A sound she'd heard so many times, as he'd driven himself so painfully inside her, too impatient to satisfy himself.

Laurie thought her head would explode. She burned with anger, took a step back and kicked out at the cubical door with everything she had.

It flew open, the top hinge becoming detached, before the flimsy door twisted and fell to the floor.

There inside was Frankie, bare arsed, trousers around his ankles, thrusting into Maisy from behind, gripping the girl's naked rump as she bent over the toilet, her hands, grasping the cistern to support herself as Frankie pounded her.

He turned his head to see Laurie standing there, shaking with rage. Frankie didn't stop. Rather he threw back his head and pursed his lips with satisfaction as he slapped out an ever-increasing tempo against Maisy's naked bottom. The two giggling girls, joined the show and fell into fits of laughter at the sight of the pair. One made "dirty cow" comments as they ran out of the room desperate to tell their friends what they had just witnessed.

Frankie began to laugh, a deep guttural sound, and with each movement, his hilarity grew. It was almost manic.

Maisy began to moan with ecstasy as she came close to her climax, neither player in this game of betrayal caring who could see or hear.

Laurie felt her tears run. There was nothing she could do to stop them now.

Frankie had deceived and shamed her in one fell swoop. She turned on her heels, unable to bear the sight of her man's treachery.

As she ran from the room, all she could hear was Frankie's cackling laughter ringing in her ears.

It would be a sound she would never forget.

And at that moment, she made herself a promise.

Detective Jim Hacker

Harry Strange never rang me at work.

Throughout our friendship, he had only ever called me at home. Indeed, it was generally me that did the calling.

Harry was a quiet, solitary figure. As measured a man as you may ever meet. Therefore, during our all too infrequent visits to Preston's many hostelries, if Harry presented a rare unsolicited comment or observation, it always seemed to carry all the more heft.

I'd never heard him so concerned than on 8th October 1983.

Even when Jamie had not been accounted for after the attack on the Sir Galahad, Harry had been calm.

He'd waited four days for the official confirmation that his only son was alive, yet there had been no sense of alarm from him.

I'd witnessed Harry lay his wife to rest, and watched him carry the burden of grief and subsequent loneliness with the strength of ten men. Yet on this day, I heard his voice falter as he pleaded with me to help him.

Jamie Strange had been arrested, charged with murder, and was in military custody. It was all he knew. He didn't know who had been killed, he didn't know where Jamie was being held. Harry suspected Jamie had been working undercover across the water, but he was in the dark as to exactly where.

He'd scanned the press and TV for any possible incidents. The papers had been full of the Maze escape, but nothing more.

He was desperate.

Despite my massive workload, I dropped everything and set to work on helping a man who had become one of my closest friends.

Back in 1983, information was sent from station to station, division to division, even force to force, by teleprinter. There was no "search box" on a screen where I could start looking for RUC incidents. Everything was done manually. If the teleprinter operator saw a message was flagged for your department, a copy would end up in your in tray . . . maybe.

Checking the Irish press for anything that might be a clue meant just that, finding hard copies and reading every page.

There was no simple or quick way to find out what

had happened to Jamie, yet I had a break within an hour.

*

Lancashire Constabulary HQ, was not only the heart of the force's communication and clerical operation, but the site also boasted a world-renowned training facility.

Whilst I had been on a residential course at the school, I had met one Seamus Connery.

Seamus was a detective sergeant in the RUC, was as mad as a March hare, and we of course, nicknamed him Sean.

We'd spent a rather boozy, two weeks together and had swapped contact details before he'd returned to Belfast, promising to keep in touch, but never had.

I dug out my diary, found his telephone number and dialled.

Seamus was only too happy to help.

He worked in Cookstown, some twenty minutes' drive from a place called Coalisland. Apparently, about a week earlier, there had been a shooting incident there, where a seventeen-year-old had been killed by the British Security Services. Although there had been an enforced news blackout, the rumour was that the shooting was the work of two members of an army unit known as the Det, and that the young lad had surrendered himself before being killed in cold blood.

He didn't know any more, but suggested I contact a

DCI Tierney who he believed was the investigating officer.

Don't ask me why, but I instantly knew Jamie was involved.

Within eight hours, I had confirmed my darkest suspicions.

*

Tierney was a quietly spoken, man, with no small modicum of intelligence. Before he offered any information, he remined me that the army not only demanded a blanket news ban, but also, of my responsibilities, not only to the Crown, but also to his case.

I assured him, I had no intention of interfering with his investigation and eventually he supplied some details on the matter, most of which seemed damning in the extreme.

The evidence strongly suggested that after being fired upon, two Security Service personnel gave chase to a seventeen-year-old by the name of Barry McGuire. Barry was a known PIRA member, and indeed, there was no question that he had shot at his pursuers intending to kill them. However, a nine-year-old witness had testified that, after being cornered at the top of a fire escape, the Irishman had thrown down his weapon and had his hands on his head, when one plain-clothes soldier shot him dead. Tierney was also adamant that the forensics at the scene bore out this testimony.

When I mentioned the name Strange, the DCI reluctantly confirmed that a man of that name had been charged in connection with the shooting. However, the detective had no idea where the two 14th Intelligence Unit members were, or if any proceedings had yet taken place. It was, for now, out of his hands, and in his opinion, a massive political issue.

Due to the recent dogmatic fallout in the Province, investigating the incident had obviously given Tierney a problem in his home station. The RUC were predominantly Protestant, and had suffered many losses at the hands of the PIRA. Yet Tierney had conducted his investigation with total impartiality, much to the annoyance of his colleagues and the army.

Equipped with this information, I then followed my nose. England has only one military prison. Indeed, they don't even call it a prison, rather a "corrective training centre".

MCTC, Colchester, Essex, is known in military circles as "Colli".

What I suspected, however, was that due to the extremely sensitive nature of the incident, the powers that be had decided to throw a blanket over the matter until a decision had been made as to the fate of Jamie Strange and Richard Valance.

Therefore, just as Harry had drawn a blank with the detention centre, so did I.

No one knew anything.

This was not surprising.

Toward the end of 1982, the British Army and Royal Ulster Constabulary had been openly accused of operating a "shoot-to-kill" policy, under which suspects were alleged to have been deliberately killed without any attempt to arrest them. This alleged policy had been directed, almost exclusively, toward members of the PIRA. In November and December of that year, six PIRA suspects had been shot dead at checkpoints by the RUC. The SAS had added to that tally in an undercover operation, bringing the total to eight in a period of weeks.

Now, it would appear that Jamie Strange and Richard Valance had continued the theme.

There was already talk of a public inquiry.

The allegation doing the rounds in the press was this policy had emanated from high places and that eventually a senior police officer would be engaged to investigate the matter.

So, you can understand why I felt the need to tread carefully. After all, I had a wife and ever-growing family to consider.

I had never been a fan of the legal profession. From junior solicitors to full-blown barristers and judges, I had little time for them.

Their world, like my own, was by the book. That said, theirs was their own very special book, a book that could only be read and understood by a select few, and the clever manipulation of the "facts" contained within those exclusive pages was how they made their, often dubious, living.

I had spent most of my adult life watching the judiciary carve up people's lives, quite often to the detriment of the poor victim, so you may understand my reluctance when it came to dealing with them.

If lawyers could find a way to extricate their often-vile clients from their charges, be it on technical grounds or by influencing a jury with intelligent argument, they would.

Of course, there is always a Ying to the Yang. So, it was best not to rebuke any profession publicly. Being a cop, there was always a slim chance that at some point in your career you might find yourself in trouble with the same law you were paid to uphold.

I had long ago decided that should I ever suffer this particular misfortune and require legal assistance, I would only ever turn to one man.

Montague Kane.

It was he who I contacted regarding the case of Jamie Strange.

I had the feeling that the allegation against Jamie would interest Kane enough to drag him away from anything else he may be embroiled in. He would be unable to resist the high-profile nature of the matter. The massive press interest and alleged government involvement would pull him off the golf course and down the motorway to Colchester in an instant.

A quick and curt phone call proved me correct, and there and then Jamie Strange had one of the finest legal minds at his disposal, for free.

Chapter Fifteen

Montague Kane was a tall, lithe man. A former Cambridge blue, he'd rowed in the famous boat race three times. Since leaving the hallowed halls, he'd kept himself in trim on the squash court and golf course. He never drank and ate a balanced diet.

Indeed, everything about Montague Kane was balanced.

He'd remained single until his thirty-fifth year, before marrying twenty-seven-year-old Italian beauty Marcia, a socialite and daughter of wealthy Sicilian winemaker, Antonio Giovani. Monte, as he preferred to be known, fathered a son a year later.

The rumour was, just a day after the birth, he'd visited a private clinic to have a vasectomy.

Monte knew what he wanted.

Harry Strange knew what he wanted too. Right now, that was to see his son.

Although Harry didn't instantly take to Montague Kane, he valued his friend Jim Hacker's opinion. If Jim said the guy was the best, that was good enough for Harry.

The barrister certainly hadn't scrimped on the expenses, and had taken great pains to explain to Harry that there would be no fee to change hands. Monte would do his very best for his son, whatever the cost to himself or, as Harry suspected, the British legal aid system.

Kane had flown to London that very day to visit an unidentified man, who would allegedly grease the wheels to enable Harry to visit Jamie in Colchester. That, and for Kane to begin to build the case for the defence.

Harry, some twelve hours behind the lawyer, sat in the back of a chauffeur-driven Rover as it negotiated the M6 traffic. Alongside him was a waif of a girl wearing a two-piece outfit with shoulder pads the Miami Dolphins would have been proud of. Her name was Davina, and she was Kane's clerk.

She held a legal jotter on her lap and scribbled on it as she spoke.

"What can you tell me about Jamie, Mr Strange? I mean, what was he like as a child? What was his relationship like with you and Rose . . . Mrs Strange, you know, before her death?"

Harry was a little taken aback by the bluntness of the girl. Nobody ever spoke of Rose.

It wasn't that Harry didn't think of her every day, or visit her grave each week to tell her what had been happening in his life, it was just a shock that another person had uttered her name.

"Erm . . . well he was a good lad. A little on the quiet side when he was younger, not a lot of friends, but enough. Who needs lots of friends eh? They say you can count true ones on one hand . . ."

Harry was rambling, unnerved. Davina noticed too.

"I'm sorry to be blunt Mr Strange, but it's my job to get as much background on Jamie as possible. Your wife's death is a matter of public record. There was a coroner's inquiry. I have already read the transcripts."

She turned slightly and managed a smile. Harry suspected that Davina didn't smile too often. Nonetheless, it wasn't an unpleasant countenance, rather a pretty one.

Harry nodded. "I know, you are just doing your job love, and I'm grateful for it. Rose would be too, if she were still here, bless her. Look, Jamie *was* a good lad. Good at school, never got into trouble . . . well not with the law anyway. He was a bit of a scrapper . . . like me I suppose. He wouldn't take any messing from anyone. But he loved his mum. Doted on her. I think it hit him harder than he showed when she passed."

Davina stopped scribbling.

"Do you think he was suffering some kind of trauma then? I mean, as a result of Rose passing?"

Harry shrugged.

"There was no doubt losing his mum was a massive blow. To me and to him. She was a rock was Rose, she kept us all on the right road, you know? But the lad was wounded when the Sir Galahad was sunk last year. They were landing troops off Fitzroy for the final push to take Stanley. The ship was hit and on fire; men were trapped below deck. Jamie rescued some, but others . . . well . . . others didn't do so well.

"So, if you are looking for trauma, I'd be more inclined to say he was affected by the Galahad."

"By what he saw?"

"You never forget it love . . . never."

Davina wrote some more, then asked, "Any other recent issues? Changes in behaviour?"

Harry shook his head.

"Not that I noticed. You must realise Davina, that being a marine, and being whatever Jamie is right now, means you are away from home a lot. I only saw him for one day after we buried his mum, then for a few days when he was convalescing after Galahad, and maybe a week after the XMG shooting incident . . ."

"There was another shooting?"

Harry held up a hand, sensing the girl was on the wrong track. "Yes, but that was all above board, a totally clean kill. It's standard operating procedure for the shooter, and in the case of a sniper, his spotter, to be given leave after a shooting. They both turned up at my house and had some R and R."

"And who was Jamie's spotter?"

Harry felt his stomach churn. "Look, I know what

you're thinking Davina . . . but it has no bearing on this case . . . okay . . . yes it was Bird . . . it was Richard Valance."

Davina recorded the information on her pad. "It doesn't matter what I think Harry. It's what the jury thinks." She leafed through her papers until she came upon a blown-up picture of Jamie Strange. Harry had provided the original from his mantle.

"Good-looking boy," she muttered, almost to herself. Then, turning again, "No girlfriend?"

"No," said Harry. "There was for a while, but they broke up."

"When was this?"

Harry locked eyes with the girl. "The day after Rose was buried."

*

Montague Kane sat opposite Davina and sipped his black coffee.

His clerk had been up most of the night. She had dropped Harry Strange at his hotel and begun to draft Jamie's antecedence file, finishing around three a.m.

After just four hours' sleep, she then correlated the information Harry had given her about his son's background, with the hard facts the law firm of Kane and Drew had already acquired on their latest high-profile client.

Then, Davina produced a concise report, succinct

enough as not to annoy her very demanding boss, who now scanned the text as he sipped.

"This is good," he said, sending a wave of relief through Davina. She had been at the sharp end of Kane's infamously short temper on several occasions, when her work hadn't reached his extremely high standards, and it wasn't pretty.

"We can use this as a final throw of the dice if we need to. Handsome young marine, no prior convictions, father and grandfather both decorated. Loses his mother in a tragic accident, fiancée dumps him the day after the funeral, wounded in the Falklands, kills a hardened terrorist with a wonder shot in South Armagh before being drafted into the most secret undercover army unit of all time. The lad's a bally hero."

Davina, poured milk into her tea and added a sugar.

"He's also a liar, if you believe the prosecution. He may not have pulled the trigger on the gun that killed McGuire, but in his support for Valance, he is acting in concert with him and therefore both soldiers are guilty of murder."

Monte dropped his cup on the table. His eyes flashed with irritation. "I don't need a lesson in the legal fact Davina. I'm fully aware of what we have here thank you. I was merely stating that should we not be able to discredit the prosecution's case, then this file, that you have so kindly put together, will be useful to show mitigation. Maybe even a stress-related condition, if we can find a friendly psychiatrist."

Davina shrugged off Kane's cantankerousness, pulled a sheet of paper from her briefcase and pushed it across the table.

"Dr Irvine Kulturwort. He's an expert in stress-related conditions, particularly, post trauma. He believes servicemen and first responders can suffer from a condition called Post Traumatic Stress Disorder. It's new, but his theories have received some praise in the *Lancet* recently. So, I've booked him for a session with Strange for tomorrow at eight a.m."

Kane calmed. "Good . . . good work. So . . . what do we know about the prosecution witness?"

Davina rummaged again and pulled out a thin file. "Katie Harrison is nine years old. Parents moved to Coalisland from Belfast when she was six as the father found work there."

Kane poured more coffee. "Catholic?"

"Strangely not, no. So no axe to grind there. The Harrison family are about as religious as you and me."

Kane shook his head. "Typical. At the last census, Coalisland was ninety-eight point two per cent Roman Catholic, and we have to find the only bloody none-Catholic witness in the town. What about reliability? Does she have any issues?"

"You mean is she retarded?"

Kane shook his head. He sometimes considered that his clerk was harder nosed than himself. "No, I mean, does she wear glasses? Did she wear them on that evening? Does she hate soldiers?"

"No glasses, it was raining hard on the day but she was only fifty yards away. Anyway, there is no need for her to make any identifications as there is broad agreement that all the parties were present. All she is going to say is that one guy shot another guy after the first guy threw his gun down and put his hands on his head."

Kane pursed his lips and tapped them with a manicured finger.

"She still has to be able to see a small handgun thrown down a stairwell, in poor visibility from across the road . . . Just dig up what you can on her. Has she told lies to the police or at school before? Is she a fantasist? Any criminal elements in the family history? In fact, any skeletons at all that may discredit her or her parents."

"You think this is going to get that dirty Monte?"

"It always gets that dirty Dav . . . What about forensics?"

"Nothing as yet. The prosecution hasn't officially disclosed anything from their ballistics tests crime-scene samples, or the post-mortem on the victim, but from what I gathered from the Lancashire copper, Hacker, it was pretty damning."

Monte stood, lifted his suit jacket from the back of his chair and slipped his arms into it. "Then we'll have to see how much of that unconfirmed and undisclosed evidence DCI Tierney told our client in interview then. Coercion is a terrible thing Davina.

"Oh, and whilst we are on the subject of Tierney, get

one of our investigators on a plane to Belfast ASAP and have then do some digging there. He's going to be the most unpopular guy in the station right now. People will want to tell all manner of tales about him."

He checked his Omega. "What time are you collecting the father, Harry?"

"Forty minutes."

"Okay, it's been agreed that he gets half an hour alone with Jamie. Then we get him for another hour. Meet me in the lobby in fifteen minutes."

Chapter Sixteen

Harry Strange had been inside a prison before. Maybe not as organised and as professional as MCTC, Colchester, but a prison nonetheless. He'd held prisoners, fed them, watered them, even tried to give them solace in his own way.

Prisoners of war, prisoners of conflict, are very different from criminals, and should be treated as such.

People who are instructed to fight for their country, ordered to bear arms against a common enemy, who find themselves captured, are not criminals.

Yet the men incarcerated in MCTC Colchester were just that, criminals. Men who had either broken the criminal law, or who had breached the military code, disobeyed orders.

And then there was his son, Jamie. Where did he fit into all this?

That is exactly what Harry was desperate to find out.

Harry was shown into a small white-painted room. A polished table with four matching padded chairs took centre stage. There were no bars on the window, indeed there were brightly coloured curtains pulled half closed, to shade the room from the low October sun.

Harry sat, and waited.

Ten minutes later, Jamie walked in the room, flanked by two burly guards. They ordered Jamie to sit.

One spoke to Harry. "We'll leave you now Mr Strange, to give you some privacy, but we'll be just outside should you require us."

The door closed.

Father and son stood in unison, stepped around the table and embraced each other.

"I love you son," whispered Harry, holding his son so tight his arms ached. "No matter what . . . okay . . . no matter what."

Jamie began to weep. It was a sorry sound, and it tore at his father's heart.

"Come on Jamie," Harry led his son to a seat. "We've only got half an hour, I need you to talk to me."

Jamie wiped his tears. "I'm so sorry Dad, I've let the family down."

Harry sat opposite his son, reached across the table and gripped his hand. "Don't talk like that now lad. I know you, probably better than you know yourself. Come on, talk me through this."

And Jamie did just that. He told his father exactly what had happened, how he and Bird had been compromised, how they'd been fired upon and how they'd given chase to Barry McGuire. Slowly, Jamie talked his father through the final moments of the contact. When he had finished, there were more tears.

Harry watched his son cry. He sat back in his seat, his head full of conflicting emotions.

"And what did you tell the RUC?"

Jamie lifted his head from his hands. "That the boy came down the escape with his gun, and Bird had no option."

Harry nodded. "But the boy threw down?"

"Yes Dad."

"So, you lied to protect Valance?"

"Yes Dad."

"But there is a witness . . . a girl?"

Jamie nodded.

Harry rubbed the top of his head with his hands. He knew his son had done wrong, but he also knew the pressure he was under to protect his fellow marine. Even if the Irish conflict had been declared a war, Valance had broken the Geneva Convention on the taking of prisoners. But the Troubles were not a declared war, the soldiers deployed over the water were peacekeepers, policemen in army uniform, who must follow strict rules of engagement.

Harry considered his words carefully.

"Listen son, there is no doubt in my mind that McGuire

194

deserved to go; he'd fired on you, not knowing if you were armed or not. If you had put two in his back as he ran off after the first challenge, we wouldn't be here now. But the point is this, once a man surrenders to you, you must take him prisoner. It doesn't matter if you are fighting a full-blown war or not. A man has surrendered himself, and even though he has done his best to kill you, he had the rights of either a prisoner of war, or, in McGuire's case, a civilian criminal. Valance knew that, you knew that."

Jamie stayed silent.

"So, what are you going to tell your lawyer? This guy Kane. What will you tell him? What you told the RUC? Or what you just told me?"

"I don't know Dad. It's driving me crazy."

Harry took his son's hand again. Jamie had never seen his father so intensely serious.

"Listen to me son. Your first priority as a Royal Marine is to queen and country. To uphold the values and reputation of the Crown and the colours, to follow your orders, to do your duty, and to defend the good name of the British Armed Forces.

"What Valance did was to tarnish the good name of the Royal Marines, and with that act, disgrace the whole of 40 Commando.

"Now, I fully understand that the friendships formed in conflict, are some of the strongest bonds a man can hold, but I still believe that the reputation of the Royal Marines comes first. What Valance did was nothing short of murder. I brought you up to know right from wrong Jamie. If you don't want to listen to my advice, then that is your prerogative, you are a grown man, but you asked my opinion, and now you have it."

Jamie squeezed his eyes closed and held the bridge of his nose between thumb and finger. His tears had dried, but as he opened his eyes to look at his father they were red with salt. He bit his lip, then spoke.

"I know what you are saying Dad, but that lad didn't think twice about shooting at us. We weren't in uniform, we weren't showing arms. His whole plan was to walk up to two guys sitting in a car and wipe them out. Cold and calculated. Now, I owe Bird Dad . . . I know he did wrong, but I owe him big time. He saved my life."

"You never mentioned this lad."

Jamie nodded. "I know, he did. He . . . he saved me that day on the Galahad. I'd gone back down below to try and get some more lads out and got myself trapped in the fire. Bird pulled me free . . . protected me . . . without him, I'd be a goner for sure. Now I'm expected to hang him out to dry for some little shit terrorist?"

Harry'd had a feeling that there had been a special bond between the two lads, he'd just not realised it was one so close.

The closest possible.

Harry grabbed Jamie's hands again. "I can't tell you what to do son, but just think on this. What would your mum want you to say?"

Jamie blew out his cheeks and sat back in his chair. He was about to speak when there was a sharp rap on the door and one of the guards entered. Standing with him was Montague Kane.

"I'm sorry to interrupt gentlemen," he said sharply. "But there has been a major development in the case and we need to change our arrangements forthwith."

He sat, reached across the table, took Jamie's hand and shook it. "My apologies Mr Strange . . . Kane, Montague Kane, I'm acting as your defence barrister . . . not the best introduction, but a necessary one."

Jamie shrugged. "That's okay Mr Kane."

The lawyer shook his head. "Monte . . . call me Monte please . . . yes, anyway, as I was saying. I've just been informed that the prosecution is now looking to make a deal, and avoid a trial."

Harry screwed up his face. "Why such a swift change of heart? You led me to understand they were determined to make an example of the lads."

Monte opened his briefcase and removed a file. "And they were Harry, indeed they were, but as I said, things have changed."

Kane took a swift glance toward the door to ensure they had privacy.

"It would appear, that Valance has stated, off the record, that he did indeed shoot McGuire after he had thrown down his weapon, and that he placed your son here under duress to support his story."

Kane's eyes burned into Jamie. "Is that the truth Mr Strange? Did Valance pressure you to lie for him?"

Jamie nodded, and a wave of relief that only the telling the truth can allow you flowed through him.

Kane appeared emotionless. "Good, at least we are on the same page. Now here is the crux of the matter. The reason that everyone suddenly wants to play ball.

"Valance is adamant that if he is put in the dock, charged with the murder of Barry McGuire, he will testify to the fact that he was under orders to kill him, armed or not."

"You mean this 'shoot to kill' business on the news?" blurted Harry.

"Exactly," said Kane again looking directly at Jamie.

Jamie shook his head. "Not to my knowledge sir . . . in fact we were briefed just prior to deployment, and our rules of engagement were spelled out in no uncertain terms."

Kane jotted on a pad. "And who gave this briefing?"

"I'm sorry Mr Kane," said Jamie, "but in our line of work, real names and ranks are rarely used. We are briefed by different faces all the time."

"So, this 'face' couldn't be named?"

"No sir."

"So, Valance is lying?"

Jamie considered his words carefully.

"There has been a . . . a mood around the barracks for some time Mr Kane . . . I mean Monte . . ."

Kane pushed. "A mood? What kind of mood?"

"Well the lads are fed up with having their hands tied behind their backs. I mean, we all know who the terrorists are, we know where they live, where they drink. They come and go almost at will, and our side are losing good blokes to snipers and car bombs."

The brief scribbled some more. "So, there is a policy."

"I didn't say that," said Jamie flatly.

"No," muttered Kane. "No, you didn't. But the fact that Valance is prepared to say it in court has got the whole of Whitehall jumping through hoops to settle this case quietly. Apparently, the powers that be are under terrific pressure to appoint a senior British policeman to head an official inquiry."

Harry Strange had listened intently to what was said. He lay both palms on the table, his voice measured.

"What exactly are the prosecution offering?"

Monte pushed his pad back into his case.

"Valance to plead to the accidental discharge of his weapon, therefore the murder charge commuted to manslaughter, maximum term five years, and Jamie to plead to a charge of attempting to pervert the course of justice with the guarantee that he will serve no more than twelve months."

There was silence in the room.

Kane broke it. "If you want my professional opinion chaps, it is what the Americans call a 'slam dunk', a 'no-brainer'. Of course, both Valance and Jamie will be discharged with disgrace as a matter of course."

Jamie rubbed his face with his palms.

"Twelve months?"

"Better than life," said his father flatly.

Jamie couldn't think straight. "And what will I do without the Marines? Without the service? What am I going to do when I get out?"

Kane snapped his briefcase shut.

"If you turn down this offer, I will fight your case with everything I have Jamie. With the evidence from Valance, and your previous antecedence, I believe we would have a chance at a not guilty verdict; that said, a jury is always a gamble, and nothing is certain.

"I believe this agreement is for the best."

Jamie looked at his dad.

Harry nodded, and the deal was struck. Jamie would go to jail for a year.

*

The military trial of Richard Valance and Jamie Strange was listed for a guilty plea from both parties as agreed. Montague Kane sat in the judge's chambers, alongside his colleague Reginald Gold, who acted for Valance. The meeting no more than a rubber stamp, to confirm the agreed sentencing policy after pleas were submitted.

There had, however, been a sticking point, not considered when the deal was struck with prosecuting council.

If a soldier, sailor or airman is convicted of a criminal offence, and sentenced to fewer than two years, he or she would be incarcerated at MCTC Colchester. This, said the judge, was unacceptable, as the facility was too "comfortable" for his liking, and he would insist, no matter what political fallout, that both Valance and Strange be sent to a civilian prison of suitable category for the offences concerned. Therefore, the minimum term Jamie Strange could receive, would be two years, meaning, with full remission for good behaviour, he would be out in sixteen months, rather than the agreed twelve.

Monte Kane had dealt with many judges of this ilk.

It was his firm knowledge that, should the defence council baulk at his terms, a trial would ensue that would give His Honour, or in this case, His Lord, a great deal of publicity.

Some judges simply enjoyed the limelight, and Lord Justice Faversham was one of them.

Monte, never a man to lie down and accept defeat, trudged down to the cells below the courtroom to see Jamie and give him the news.

Jamie threw back his head in despair, "So, sixteen months then Mr Kane? I don't know . . ."

Monte sat.

"Jamie. From the moment the deal was offered, I began to examine the possibilities of an appeal for Richard Valance. Any appeal against his conviction, would automatically appeal yours, understand?"

Jamie looked confused. Monte ploughed on.

"I have yet to discuss the matter with Reginal Gold,

our co-council, but I feel that there would be a strong case. Now, I hear you say, 'Why not attempt this argument today?'

"Well, to test my theory in a trial, especially with a judge like we have here, would be a massive risk. Anything, and I mean anything, could happen if we go down that route. But, if we wait until Valance enters his plea and is sentenced, the appeal procedure is heard solely by the legal professions, and would be judged purely on technical argument. Do you understand that Jamie?"

"I think so."

"Look, an appeal basically takes the emotion out of the process. Trust me on this and you may just serve even less than your year . . . And don't forget, you've already served some time in Colchester, and that will count toward this pathetic sixteen months the old buffoon upstairs is insisting upon."

Jamie reluctantly agreed to the extra term.

As the pleas were entered, Monte commanded the courtroom as ever, pleading his client's previous good conduct and heroism under fire. It was purely for show, and of course, for the benefit of the amassed press crammed into the court. The verdict was never in doubt, and neither was the outcome.

Jamie Strange was sentenced to two years in jail, Richard Valance would serve five. Both were dishonourably discharged from the Royal Marines.

Montague Kane left the court immediately the verdicts

were issued. He walked alongside his colleague Reginald Gold.

"Well that was a load of tosh eh Reg?"

"I thought it went well Monte. Those boys could have been staring at a life sentence."

Monte stopped in the hall and gripped Reg by the arm.

"Listen, the fools up in Whitehall were so concerned to keep a lid on whatever is going on in Ireland, that they were too quick to hatch this carve-up. How can a man be guilty of manslaughter, when his only admission is to accidentally discharge his weapon? If we appeal Valance's conviction, I think we'd be onto a winner."

"You are a sly old dog Monte," smiled Reg.

Monte walked some more. "And, all money in the coffers Reg, money in the coffers."

*

Later that morning, Jamie was asked to change from his military uniform into civilian clothes before being transported north. Monte had once again, pulled some strings and Jamie would serve his time out in Walton Jail, Liverpool, enabling Harry regular visits that would not break the bank.

As the two now ex-marines were ushered to their awaiting transport, Bird stopped and waited for Jamie. It was the first time they had spoken since the day McGuire was shot. Both men stood opposite each other, handcuffed and disgraced.

"You doing all right there blue?" asked Valance.

"Under the circumstances Bird, yeah I suppose."

The Aussie nodded. "I'm sorry it turned out like this eh?"

"Me too, my dad is gutted."

"I'll bet . . . so I suppose you all hate my guts then?"

Jamie shook his head. "You saved my life Bird, I can't forget that. You made a mistake, that's all."

The prison guard gave Jamie a nudge to move the lads along. As Richard Valance was stepping into the back of his transport, he raised his hands, displaying the cuffs that bound him.

"You were right all the time about the Aussies Strange Brew . . . a set of convicts we are."

The doors were closed before Jamie could answer. He stepped into his own van, walked down a narrow corridor and sat in the end cell, a room not big enough to turn around in. He cricked his neck to see Bird's van move off.

"See you on the other side, Birdman," he muttered.

Detective Jim Hacker

The news that Jamie Strange had been incarcerated came as both a shock and a blow. I'd met with Harry just a month before Christmas 1983, and he was as down as I'd seen him since the loss of his wife, Rose. We'd sat in silence in the Hole in the Wall on Fylde Road, for over an hour, before Harry stood, bid me the season's greetings and left me nursing a half pint of best mild.

Sometimes, there is nothing to say.

*

The next morning, 26th November 1983, I arrived at my office to find the department buzzing with activity. A renowned cannabis dealer, one Mohammed Mahmood had been found dead on waste ground at the rear of Blackburn Rovers football ground.

Mahmood was a middle-ranking dealer. He had been arrested and charged with possession with intent to supply cannabis on two occasions and had spent three years in jail as a result. However, this had not cooled his ardour toward making his living importing the drug from his homeland, and distributing it all over the county. He had been on our top-ten list of targets for over two years, but had proved a very slippery character. He was renowned for his ability to move his drugs quickly and had a good solid client base. He was also known to be extremely violent if crossed.

The murder incident room at Eastern Division, had informed our team immediately and requested that I visit the scene and brief the incident commander, one Detective Chief Superintendent Alan Crocker, with all we knew about the victim.

I pulled Mahmood's considerable file from our records and made the seven-mile trip to Ewood Park in the company of our recently appointed collator Candice Ballantine.

Since the 3D Ice debacle, and the demise of our previous collator, Colin Whittle, Candice had proved to be a sterling worker and found the task of gathering the various strands of information on our targets fascinating.

She had a naturally analytical mind, and I had suggested that she might consider leaving her civilian role, and joining the force as a WPC.

The scene we were greeted with at Blackburn that day ensured Candice remained firmly office-bound from thereon in.

Mahmood had been killed on the spot where his body lay, but prior to the final act of murder, his attackers had systematically beaten him. This, however, had taken place elsewhere as the only blood at the scene was from a solitary shot to the back of Mahmood's head. The round had exited through his left eye socket and the pattern of blood, mixed with parts of the victim's eyeball had splashed out in front of his corpse and decorated the concrete in front of him.

He had been bound, both hands and feet, with what appeared to be nylon rope or washing line; there were also lesions around his throat, consistent with having a ligature placed around his neck at some earlier juncture. Then, it appeared he had been made to kneel on the ground, before the final act took place.

Mahmood appeared to have been driven to his final

destination in a Sierra Cosworth car, as it sat not ten yards from where his corpse lay, yet no attempt had been made to destroy the vehicle and any possible forensic evidence inside. A PNC check of the vehicle revealed that it was registered to Mahmood himself.

This killing was an execution in all but name, and a shocking a murder, yet as the morning wore on, it was to become as grisly a day as I'd ever known in my service.

As I and a very pale-looking Candice were about to leave the murder scene, we were informed that a further three bodies had been discovered in a terraced house in Whalley Range, not three miles from our position.

The house later transpired to be Mahmood's home address, and I then understood how his car had arrived at Ewood Park. The killers had taken both he and his vehicle from his home.

The bodies found inside Mahmood's home were identified as his girlfriend, Terresa Brownlow, 20 yrs, Mahmood's brother Iftekhar 25 yrs, and Terresa's cousin, James 19 yrs. All were bound with the same rope as Mahmood, yet the killers, probably not wanting to make so much noise in the confines of a terraced house, and in the grisliest of twists, had cut their throats, rather than use a gun.

The police surgeon was of the opinion that the three bodies found in the house had been killed some time before Mahmood and their attackers had used a large-bladed knife similar to a machete, to perpetrate each person's injuries. The doctor went to pains to suggest that such brutality had been used to inflict the victim's wounds, that two of the corpses were close to being beheaded.

I firmly believed they had been killed one by one, in front of Mohammed, before he was taken to his final destination and executed.

To me, this had all the hallmarks of a gangland killing designed to do one thing and one thing only:

To send a message to the competition.

Call me obsessive, but in my mind, the beating, the ferocious manner in which the victims were murdered, the seemingly casual attitude toward forensic evidence all pointed to Frankie Verdi, Eddie Williams and Tony Thompson as our perpetrators.

Detective Chief Superintendent Crocker wasn't so sure. Well, not until a near-perfect thumbprint belonging to Eddie Williams was found on a glass coffee table in Mahmood's living room.

The team were ecstatic a day later, when Lancashire HQ fingerprint department confirmed the presence of a second clear print inside the Sierra Cosworth car parked conveniently next to Mahmood's body.

Convenient? Handy? Easy?

Yes, very handy. My gut churned with acid bile as I heard that the two prints were so clear, that the number of matches found identifying Williams as being present at both crime scenes were almost double the legally required sixteen.

A more than perfect match?

Imagine my horror when it also transpired that both lifts had been of Williams' right thumb. There is no such thing as that level of coincidence. But, with the chief constable on his back and the press howling for a result, Det Ch Supt Crocker grabbed at his only real lead with both hands and arrested Williams.

I cast my mind back to June 1978 and the murder of Prison Officer Morris from Kirklevington. Williams had dropped his own name in the frame that time too. On that occasion using Fat Les Thomas, a known informant, as the delivery method. As a result of that debacle, The Three Dogs had lived off the infamy for the last five years.

I tried to warn Crocker, but it fell on deaf ears.

When you hold a suspect, and the only evidence you have is forensic in nature, it is the last subject you want to mention during the interview process. It is the only card you have. Play it too soon, and the interview will fail. The interrogator needs to establish the whereabouts of the suspect at the time of the incident, but most of all, to get him to deny that he, or she, has ever visited the scene in question, in this case, Mahmood's house in Whalley Range and the inside of his car.

As I suspected Williams gave a "no comment" interview, ensuring this was a lengthy process, involving three senior detective interviewers.

After twenty-four hours, Crocker was forced to apply for an extension of Williams' custody to continue the process. The chief hoped that the relentless questioning of the suspect would bear fruit. The press smelled blood.

At the end of the second day, Williams' solicitor stood alongside his client on the steps of Lawson Street Police Station. The team had failed to get their man. Eddie had been released without charge.

The grisly murders had captured the imagination of the nation's newspapermen, and they gathered like carrion crows to hear what the solicitor at law and, more importantly, his client had to say.

I watched from my office, live on *Granada Reports*.

The brief began:

"My client would like to read a prepared statement to you all, but first, I wish to make comment about the dreadful treatment he has received at the hands of Lancashire Constabulary, and, in particular, Detective Chief Superintendent Crocker.

"Despite his pleas of innocence, and repeated denials of any involvement in the brutal slayings of Mr Mahmood, his brother Iftekhar, and Terresa and James Brownlow, Edward Williams has been treated like a common criminal, rather than the successful businessman, and law-abiding member of the community he so obviously is. I would like to take this opportunity to demand a full and frank apology from the chief constable for his inherently poor treatment, and give notice that we shall be seeking redress through the courts."

The press babble instantly covered the brief's next line,

but they fell silent to a man the moment Eddie picked up his sheet of paper and began to speak.

It was the first time I'd laid eyes on him for almost five years. I'd seen odd pictures, but not like this. Eddie was dressed in a suit that would have cost more than my monthly wage. He stood, immaculately turned out, with the confident swagger of a man who had just won a bitter battle. Yet his eyes glowed with pure hatred.

"Ladies and gentlemen of the press," he began. "I had known Mohammed Mahmood for over three years. In that time, he had not only become a valued customer, but I would go as far to say, a respected friend.

"The sum total of the police evidence against me in this case was two fingerprints. One found at Mohammed's home, the other in his car. Had the senior detective in this case explored the history of Mr Mahmood's vehicle, something I am told would be commonplace in such a major investigation, he would have discovered that his treasured Sierra Cosworth was sold to him from my own car dealership. Indeed, Mr Mahmood was such a valued customer at Williams Performance Cars, that I delivered the vehicle personally to his home, just three weeks ago.

"A simple check of the vehicle's paperwork, including the receipt for the car could have prevented my embarrassing incarceration over the last two days. Thank you."

Out of shot, the hoard of press instantly erupted into a cacophony of questions. One rose above all the rest.

"James Dunn, *Daily Mirror*," shouted the voice. "Is it

true Mr Williams, that you are a member of a vicious and violent gang known as The Three Dogs?"

There was silence again. Eddie's eyes flashed at the man. The veins in his neck bulged.

"I think you're talking about a newspaper article that appeared back in 1976, when we were kids Mr Dunn, when me and two schoolfriends were still juveniles. We did get in trouble back then, but that was a long time ago and we paid for our crime. We are all respected businessmen these days. Everyone is allowed one mistake, Mr Dunn." Eddie pointed at the unseen questioner. "Even you."

I turned off the television and prepared myself for some sleepless nights.

Chapter Seventeen

Christmas Day 1983

Frankie Verdi strode proudly into his lavish dining room carrying a roasted turkey easily twice the size needed to feed his guests.

Laurie had spent most of Christmas Eve preparing the meal, the intricate place settings, the towering tree, and ensuring each of their guests had the perfect gift underneath it.

The work kept her busy, kept her out of the club for an evening, and best still, kept her away from Frankie.

"Wow Frank," blurted Tony. "That's the biggest turkey I ever saw."

Laurie managed a smile. "It only just squeezed in the oven, Tony. Frank nearly went out and bought a new model just to cook it."

Frankie started to carve. "Nothing's too good for my friends, eh girl? Nothing. No expense spared these days. Remember when we all lived on Moor Nook? Scraping a few quid together? Well not now eh boys?"

Eddie was quietly examining Cheryl Greenwood's boy William, who sat astride a plastic motorbike, courtesy of Father Christmas Frankie.

Cheryl, who Tony surprisingly announced was his girl, and was considering moving in with him in his new house in Fulwood, had initially seemed uncomfortable to be in Eddie's presence, sticking close to Tony, grabbing his hand whenever she felt the need.

Tony played the perfect protector, and managed to keep his massive frame between her and Eddie throughout the meal's preliminaries.

Eddie didn't give a fuck.

Williams looked at the kid again, his white-blonde hair curling down the back of his neck, just as Eddie's would, should he ever let it grow longer that his regulation number-one crew.

He piled roast potatoes on his plate alongside a mountain of turkey, then looked across the table at Cheryl, who he had to admit, had blossomed from the tarty teenager he remembered, into a beautiful young mother.

Cheryl met his gaze. He nodded toward William who was content, making vroom-vroom noises on the carpet.

"How old is the kid?"

Cheryl had been expecting the question. She and Tony

had talked about what they would say, and although Tony had been reluctant to lie to his lifelong friend, he'd also fallen for Cheryl and doted on William.

"He's two Eddie," she said calmly. William was nearer two and a half, but her answer wasn't an untruth, it just put a possible few months between the night Eddie forced himself on her and William's arrival.

Eddie stuffed a huge piece of meat into his mouth. He wasn't stupid. The resemblance was uncanny, but he really didn't give a shit about the kid, above all, one born from a little slapper from Avenham. If Tony was stupid enough to take on someone else's brat, that was up to him.

"Good-looking boy," he managed through a half-full mouth.

"Thanks," said Cheryl, instantly turning to Laurie, desperate to move the conversation in another direction. "How's the club doing Laurie? Tony tells me you run things over there."

Laurie wanted to say that she hated setting foot in Toast since she'd witnessed Frankie fucking a schoolgirl inside the club's toilets. That, and the fact he still insisted on inviting the little slut to the club, and disappeared with her at the end of most nights.

She wanted to say she really didn't give a fuck about Toast anymore, and that she knew Frankie had rented an apartment in town, where he had his little girl hidden away.

She wanted to say that she dreamt of being back in the arms of Jamie Strange, and she now squirreled away

£500 a week from the club's takings, right under the nose of her darling Frankie. And finally, she wanted to say that when she'd acquired enough cash, she hoped that Jamie Strange would forgive her, would take her back, and that they could run far away from The Three Dogs and their sick, violent ways.

Of course, she emptied her mouth of food, set down her knife and fork, and offered. "I help out when I can Cheryl. Frankie and the boys own the place, it's their business." She turned to Frankie and gave him a contemptuous look. "You're there most nights aren't you Frank? Hand on the tiller."

Frankie hardly noticed Laurie's derision. He draped an arm around her shoulders and drew her to him.

Laurie visibly stiffened.

"This girl is a rock Cheryl. I'll tell you this, Toast would not be the success it is today, if it wasn't for our Laurie here. If you look after our Tony, half as good as this little darlin' looks after me, you'll do okay."

Tony puffed out his chest. "She looks after me good Frank, she's a good girl is our Chez."

Frank gave Cheryl a lecherous look.

"Oh, I remember our Cheryl from the Red Lion days, don't I Chez?"

Cheryl knew what Frank was hinting at. She had been a bit promiscuous in her youth. But she'd learned fast, grown up faster. Where she'd lived, you swam. Or sank, without trace.

"That was a long time ago Frank. Things have changed now . . . now I've got William and Tony."

Frankie poured more gravy over his meal and managed a thin smile, yet his eyes, like two jet coals, bore into Cheryl. Frankie was sending his own very particular message. "Just be good to our Tony, that's all. He's very important to us."

Cheryl swallowed hard. "Course Frank, course I will."

*

The two women moved into the kitchen with the pile of dishes, whilst Frankie, Eddie and Tony found comfortable seats in Frank's new conservatory. They all smoked Cuban cigars, just like Frankie's hero, Al Pacino had in his favourite movie, Scarface.

Eddie admired the new build Tony's firm had erected.

"Your boys did a good job on this Tony. Reckon you could sort one for me at my gaff?" Tony looked puzzled. "But you live in a penthouse flat Ed. You're on the tenth floor."

Eddie ruffled Tony's hair the way he had when they were kids. "I'm teasin' you pal, just teasin'."

Tony didn't laugh. Tony didn't even smile. "Well, don't tease me Eddie. I don't like it."

Frankie sensed the atmosphere between his two friends. There was no doubt, Tony had come on over the years. He had begun to read books, to study, to improve his brain. He wasn't a fool anymore. Tony would never be Einstein, but he wasn't the village idiot either.

He was, however, one of the most vicious and dangerous men Frankie Verdi had ever known. Together with Eddie Williams, Frankie knew he had two men who would do anything he asked, no matter how gruesome or dangerous the task.

Tony and Eddie had cut the throats of Mahmood's three house guests as they begged for their lives. Tony had sawn at his victims with such gusto that Frank'd had to stop him from cutting their fucking heads off.

Mahmood himself had watched in silence as each body dropped to his living room floor, twitching and gurgling their last. He had been one tough fucker that was for sure, and even when he was kneeling on that patch of ground and Frankie held the pistol to his head, he never told where his stash was.

It was no matter. The fact was, now, rather than buying from the Pakistani at inflated prices, The Three Dogs bought directly from Holland. They had no need for Mahmood anymore. Indeed, they wanted his business, and with him gone, they could now move large quantities of cannabis across the county and beyond.

Of course, the stroke of genius had been Frankie's.

He smiled to himself as he recalled Eddie pulling off his latex gloves and pressing his right thumb on the Pakistani's coffee table, before sliding a receipt and the log book for the Cosworth car in the man's drawer. The totally bogus transaction had been completed by Eddie at his garage, yet the cops would be none the wiser.

Frankie had told him to use a different finger when he left his mark in the Sierra, yet when Eddie repeated his action using the same thumb, in truth, it only went to show further contempt for the law, and Frankie liked that.

They were the talk of the town again. There wasn't a criminal north of Watford Gap that didn't believe that they had executed Mahmood and his crew.

They had sent out a message . . . *don't fuck with The Three Dogs.*

*

Since Eddie completed the deal with the Dutchman, Joe Madden had proved his trustworthiness, and been promoted within the firm. Frankie had even given him a title, "Distribution Manager".

It was Joe, who took the delivery of large quantities of cannabis, amphetamine and cocaine from the boat in Kent, stored the drugs in various hiding places around the town and then distributed them to the smaller dealers, at a higher price. Joe had also been given the brief of recruiting more street dealers who would attend large events, concerts, festivals and nightclubs, not only in Lancashire, but Greater Manchester and Merseyside. Frankie had no fear of the big city gangs, confident that The Three Dogs had made their point strongly enough over in Blackburn.

So now Joe was the middleman, the buffer between The Three Dogs and the small-time boys, who might get lifted. If a street dealer gave anyone up, it would be Joe, but they all knew who he fronted for, so would do so at their own risk.

It was a dangerous job being a grass. Especially if you grassed on Frankie Verdi.

*

Laurie and Cheryl had loaded the dishwasher and were laying out the dining table for cheese and biscuits.

"I remember the first time I saw you," said Laurie. "Frankie was pawing at your boobs. You were sat near the pool table in the back of the Red Lion."

Cheryl looked embarrassed. "Yeah, well, we all do stupid things when we're young don't we? I just thought the lads were a good laugh, is all. You know, a few beers and a giggle."

She eyed Laurie. "I remember you too . . . that night. Frankie dropped me like a hot coal the second he saw you."

Laurie found two glasses and filled them with Blue Nun. She clinked hers against Cheryl's. "You're right . . . we all do stupid things when we're kids."

Cheryl examined Laurie, taking in her mood. "I seen the way you two are. I take it things are a bit rough between you and Frank at the minute then?"

"You could say that Chez, yeah."

"It'll work out eh? Everyone goes through rough patches."

Laurie took a large gulp of wine. She didn't have a shoulder to lean on. Frankie was all controlling. She had no friends, and anyone who worked for Frank couldn't be trusted to keep their mouth shut. Cheryl was turning out to be her only outlet.

"He's got a young tart holed up in a flat near the docks . . . he's there most nights. I caught him shagging her in the toilets at the club a few weeks back."

"Oh my God Laurie, I'm sorry love. You must be gutted, who is she?"

"She's just some little girl, I mean that too. She's Les Thomas' niece."

"Not Maisy Thomas? Lives on Moor Nook, next door to Les, the ice cream man?"

"Yeah, that's her."

"Fuck me Laurie, she's still at school, she's only fifteen you know?"

Laurie drained her glass a little too quickly and gave a cynical laugh down her nose. "So, call the cops, why don't you? Come on Chez, even her mum daren't say a word . . . and Maisy is loving it. New clothes, new shoes, nice little flat . . . that and all the coke she can stick up her nose. She's young, and stupid enough to think that Frank is going to kick me into the weeds and install her here."

Cheryl raised her eyebrows.

Laurie shook her head.

"Oh no, he ain't that daft Chez. He knows where his bread is buttered. You were right at the table, I run Toast,

I make the guys a lot of cash . . . and I mean a lot. Frank wants his cake and eat it. Me here . . . her there."

"So, what yer goin' to do Laurie?"

"I dunno . . . I made a big mistake with Frankie. I thought it would be all glamour, being a gangster's girl. Respect from everyone, money no object . . . Then maybe, I could calm him down a bit, get him straight and get married, you know, have a kid or two . . . But it ain't like that. It ain't anything like that. It's do as you're told, keep your mouth shut, and give him what he wants in the bedroom . . . or else."

"You mean he hits you?"

"He has done, but that stopped when I threatened to cut his cock off in his sleep."

Cheryl spat out her wine and guffawed. "Fuckin' hell Laurie, I can see how that did the trick."

Laurie poured more wine. "I should've stuck with my Jamie. A good solid lad."

"Jamie?"

"Yeah, Jamie Strange. He went in the marines, we were engaged, but stupid me, I wanted excitement, didn't I? Well look what I've got."

Laurie took another gulp, the wine kicking in, loosening her mouth.

"I think about him all the time Chez, Jamie I mean, I can't help it. We were like two love-struck kids. Just, I never appreciated it, or him, back then. I was stupid, and a bit of a tart with it."

Laurie ran her fingers through her hair.

"I suppose it could be just a good dose of regret, but I did love him, and he'd have walked through walls for me . . . probably still would."

Cheryl held out her glass for a refill of her own. "I went to school with him, Jamie Strange, yeah, big lad, nice, quiet."

Cheryl smiled a cheeky smile. "Handsome bugger too if I remember right."

Laurie nodded as she recalled her striking man. "Yeah that's him . . . probably got himself a nice girl now, settling down . . ."

Cheryl shook her head. "Oh, no Laurie. Ain't you heard? It was in the paper an' all. He's banged up. In nick."

"What . . . he's in jail . . . my Jamie . . . where?" Before Cheryl answered, Laurie turned toward the living room, a quizzical look on her face.

"You hear that?"

Cheryl shook her head. "Nope."

"Sounded like a car door slam."

Cheryl shook again.

A spilt second later the gunfire began.

Glass shattered and wood splintered as the powerful rounds from the unseen weapons slammed into the house. Laurie grabbed at Cheryl and pulled her to the floor as bullets thumped into the mahogany dining table above them.

Laurie could hear Frankie, Eddie and Tony shouting,

but couldn't make out their words over the cacophony of noise. Glass flew in all directions from the shattered windows, plaster dust fell from the ceiling.

Within seconds, it was over and there was the sound of squealing tyres.

Frankie barrelled into the room holding a sawn-off shotgun.

"You two okay?" he shouted.

Laurie nodded. "We're good."

Then somewhere in the house, Tony began to shout, to cry out. It was a woeful, awful sound. Laurie and Cheryl followed the noise to the living room.

Tony was sitting on the floor, cradling William in his massive arms. The toddler's toy motorbike torn to shreds by gunfire at his side. Tony's shirt was drenched in William's blood.

"Frankie," he wailed. "Frankie, do something . . . Aw look, look at poor Billy . . . Frankie, you always know what to do eh . . . Frank? Please Frankie . . ."

Cheryl began to scream.

Laurie turned and strode toward Frankie Verdi, who stood riveted to the spot, stunned by the sight of a murdered child in the middle of his own living room.

She clenched her teeth in rage and balled her fists, pummelling his chest as she screamed in his face. He stood and took the blows, hands at his sides, swaying slightly.

"This is you Frank! This here . . . this dead kid is your

doing. Do you understand me? This is because of you . . . and Eddie . . . and Tony and your pathetic reputations."

She swung an arm at the opulence that surrounded them.

"You would all be fucking millionaires before you're thirty . . . without the crime. Do you realise that Frank? Do you? Oh no . . . not the big-I-am, Frankie Verdi. No, you need the respect of all the scum that live in this town, don't you? You have to deal the drugs, to dish out the beatings. What about the good people Frank? What about gaining their respect? No, you just ain't interested in that, are you? Let the good guys fear you and the scum of the earth look up to you, that's what you want isn't it? Well look Frank. Take a good look at William lying there. Lying there because of something you did, something you planned, something to get some more fucking respect, some more fear."

Laurie fell into a chair, exhausted and traumatised. She let her head fall into her hands and spoke to the floor. Questioning herself as much as Verdi.

"What did you do Frank? What did you do this time?"

She raised her head and met his black eyes.

"You killed those people in Blackburn, didn't you? Shot that man and cut the throats of three more. This is connected, isn't it?"

Laurie's face became one ugly sneer.

"You disgust me Frank," she spat. Then turned to Tony,

still sitting on the floor cradling William with one arm and Cheryl with his other, as she sobbed uncontrollably. "And you Tony . . . yes you and Eddie are just as bad as Frank. You do his bidding. You killed that little boy in your arms, just as if you'd pulled the trigger yourself."

Eddie had heard enough. He grabbed Laurie roughly by the arm and began to drag her out of the chair and from the room. "Come on, you're fucking hysterical, I'll get you a drink." He turned to Frankie. "You calling the cops, or you want me to do it?"

Frank seemed to snap out of his trance. He walked to the phone.

"I'll do it," then, suddenly finding his most vicious tone, pointed at Laurie. "And you . . . you keep your fucking mouth shut."

Frank lifted the receiver, but before he dialled, he turned, his mouth turned in a vicious sneer.

"Tony! Tony . . . For fuck's sake . . . put the kid down and get Cheryl a fuckin' brandy to shut her up. She's giving me a fucking headache."

*

Christmas Day is usually the quietest day of the year for all public services. The police are no exception.

PC 2211 Evans was the lone patrol on duty for the twenty-five square miles of rural and urban stretch between Fulwood and Garstang sections. The southern-most part of that area containing the Verdi household.

Before the call came that would affect Dave Evans for the rest of his career, he'd been driving along Whittingham lane, when he'd noticed smoke up ahead.

Moments later, he discovered a transit van smouldering at the side of the road, completely burnt out. The number plates were unrecognisable and as the vehicle was still way too hot to start poking around under the bonnet, he called the incident in, refused the assistance of the fire brigade and sat pondering his next move.

When the report of a shooting incident at the Verdi home in Broughton, not a mile away from the burning van came over his radio. Evans was experienced enough to know the van was an important piece of evidence, rather than a bunch of joyriders covering their tracks.

He contacted force control room and asked for a search of recently stolen Ford Transit vans, gave an approximate year of manufacture, and, as there was just enough paint left on one section of the vehicle, the colour blue. Then, being fully aware of the Verdi reputation, asked for all available patrols to assist him.

Dave Evans was a family man. Wife, three kids, two boys of school age, and a girl, Emily, a toddler. Dave was what some would call a "man's man". Big, burly, naturally strong, played rugby for Preston Grasshoppers, liked a pint. But when Evans walked into Frankie Verdi's front room, all that strength, all that brawn, was of no use to him.

Verdi opened the door to him, his trademark black eyes dark and foreboding.

"This way," he said, turning on his heels and walking Evans into the room.

The cop took in the awful scene. Almost all of the windows were shattered. Shards of broken glass littered the floor, mixed with splinters of wood from the frames. Dave Evans' boots crunched across the carpet and he walked toward the heartbreaking sight that lay in the centre of the room.

A plastic tricycle, moulded to look like a police motorcycle, was on its side, torn open by the bullets fired indiscriminately through the windows of the house. Next to the bike, equally ripped open was the body of two-year-old William Greenwood.

Dave Evans swallowed hard. William would be close to Emily's age. He knelt by the obviously lifeless body, yet did his duty and checked the child's vital signs. Standing, he noticed the right knee of his uniform trousers was soaked in blood.

Evans stepped away from the body, doing his best to retrace his original footprints and found himself in close proximity to Frankie Verdi.

Evans felt rage burning in his gut. Hatred. He towered over Verdi, he wanted to smash his face to pulp, to hurt him. The man lived by the sword, yet it was an innocent who had died this day.

The cop took a deep breath and did his best to calm himself.

"Who did this?" he said quietly. "Who in God's name did this?"

Verdi walked around the body toward the kitchen. "That's your job isn't it copper?"

Detective Jim Hacker

The murder of the toddler, William Greenwood sent shockwaves around Lancashire and beyond. If Frankie Verdi had hoped for infamy after the gangland slaughter of Mohammed Mahmood, then whatever notoriety he, Eddie Williams and Tony Thompson had accrued was washed away, along with the toddler's spilt blood.

The investigation had such obvious links to the Blackburn slayings, that the chief decided to give the Greenwood murder case to the same group of officers following the Mahmood slaying, allowing easier cross-referencing and sharing of information.

The transit van, found by PC Evans, burnt out close to Verdi's home, had been stolen from Croxteth in Liverpool. House-to-house inquiries revealed that three men, seen in the proximity of the van, boarded another vehicle that had been described as a light grey Ford hatchback, and had made off at speed.

A stolen grey Escort was later found in the same condition as the Transit, just off Upper Parliament Street in Liverpool 8, the scene of such vicious rioting in 1981, and home to several well-known drug gangs. If the team investigating The Three Dogs were finding witnesses hard to come by, then the officers tasked with the door-to-door work in that area of Liverpool were on a hiding to nothing.

The truth was, the Mahmood investigation was going nowhere, and despite Verdi virtually shouting his guilt from the rooftops, the detectives had no firm evidence to back it up. As I have iterated before, people talk, and people listen, but when it comes to giving evidence against an individual who will cut your throat and laugh as he does it, well, witnesses get to be few and far between.

Verdi, Williams and Thompson, had all come up with the same story about Christmas Day.

They had just enjoyed their turkey, when several unseen and unidentified attackers opened fire on the house with big bore semi-automatic weapons. Their only possible explanation was one of mistaken identity, and although they would assist the officers in any way possible, they had no idea why anyone would wish them harm, or any clue as to their identity.

Cheryl Greenwood and Laurie Holland, unsurprisingly, backed this story to the hilt. No one knew anything.

That said, the death of a child loosens the tongues of even the most hardened criminals, and I had the feeling that someone, somewhere may just drop the dime on either Verdi, or the Liverpool gang who had sought revenge on him.

For now, however, both investigations trod ever deepening water.

If the public were reluctant to talk to the cops, the

same could not be said for the press. It appeared, unnamed but well-informed insiders were willing to part with all kinds of information on The Three Dogs and their business dealings, both legitimate and criminal. Even, it would seem, their private lives.

When Eddie Williams stood on the steps of Lawson Street nick and made a veiled threat toward the *Daily Mirror's* crime correspondent, James Dunn, he probably never gave it a second thought. However, Williams had shown his lack of savvy when dealing with the media. All he achieved, was to irritate a very old hack, who had never been shy when it came to exposing villains from all walks of life. Dunn had written "exposés" on the vilest creatures ever to walk the earth and had never given two hoots what they thought.

The Thee Dogs were about to get both barrels, from a very different gun.

Chapter Eighteen

27th December 1983

Laurie stood in the kitchen drinking coffee and waiting.

Frankie was incandescent with rage and was busy smashing up what was left of their home after the attack. He'd spent a good ten minutes screaming down the phone at his lawyer, and like a petulant child, when he didn't get the result he wanted, had gone about throwing his toys out of the pram.

Finally, there was quiet. Laurie risked a peek around the door frame and found Frank, bathed in sweat sitting in the only undamaged chair they owned. He was re-reading the *Sunday Mirror*. Laurie, had always thought that Frank craved infamy and she felt a secret inner contentment that he now appeared to have achieved his goal.

"They say, there is no such thing as bad publicity," she offered with no mere hint of sarcasm.

Frankie couldn't take his eyes off the front page of the paper. It showed a large picture of him helping Maisy Thomas out of his Jaguar, she was dressed in her school uniform. The headline read:

"*Dog on heat*," with a tag line, "*Gangster in schoolgirl love triangle*."

He threw the paper to the floor.

"This was you, weren't it?"

Laurie gave a meek smile. "No honey, it wasn't me. The whole fuckin' town knows about you and your little slut. If I'd wanted to hurt you Frank, you wouldn't be able to read that rag, believe me."

Frankie grimaced. "Well when I find out who it is, I'll . . ."

Laurie took a step closer and pointed. "You'll what Frank? Cut their throat? Have you not seen enough blood to last you a lifetime?" She threw back her head a laughed. "If I were you, I'd be more worried about the last line in the article. What does it say? '*A spokesman from Lancashire Social Services, says the Children and Young Persons Bureau is investigating the allegation?*' . . . I reckon that means charges Frank. Charges that will make you a sex offender . . . a nonce . . . think on that."

Laurie turned for the door.

"I'm going to see Cheryl. See how the poor woman is. If you're not here when I get back, I'll presume you've been nicked."

Laurie slammed the door behind her, found the keys for her MGB in her handbag, and fired up the car. Were things finally unravelling? For the first time, Frankie seemed rattled. Whoever had hit the house on Christmas Day was a big-time villain, and Frank had got Eddie, Tony and Joe Madden on the case full-time. Laurie considered that The Three Dogs may have bitten the wrong guy this time, and that maybe, her longing for pastures new, was not so unrealistic after all.

As she pulled the car from the driveway and headed to Cheryl Greenwood's flat, she pondered on what Cheryl had told her, just seconds before the shooting started that afternoon.

Jamie Strange was in jail. The mere thought of him filled her stomach with butterflies.

How could she have been so mean . . . so stupid? And look at her now. Fancy car, big house, designer clothes. Yet no friends, and no love in her life. Why Jamie was in jail, she had no idea. But she intended to find out, and she intended to go and see him.

Detective Jim Hacker

The funeral of William Greenwood was not only an extremely sad affair, but one that created a mass of media interest.

Fortunately, on that day, 16th January 1984, I was not required to attend. I did, however, see the press reports and images that were splashed across the daily papers.

The murder, and therefore, Frankie Verdie and his gang, were now national news. Indeed, Mr Dunn of the *Mirror* had taken it upon himself to lambast Frank, Eddie, and Tony at every opportunity. He would light a fire under one of the gang, and as fast as Verdi and co. extinguished it, another ferocious blaze would appear the next day.

Frankie's affair with schoolgirl Maisy Thomas, Tony's building firm's tax affairs, and most recently, the allegation that Eddie had been seen in a notorious club in Liverpool, regularly visited by the city's homosexual community, had all graced the *Mirror's* gossip pages.

All these petty matters grabbed the headlines, but another reporter, James Garner of *The Guardian* was concentrating far more on the gang's illicit dealings. Garner had supposedly found a mole in the Dogs' camp who, albeit anonymously, was willing to spill some beans. The broadsheet had published a full-page spread alleging drug dealing, punishment beatings and money laundering.

It all made interesting reading, yet allegations are one thing, proving them is another.

*

William's service itself was an awfully small affair. Cheryl had asked that neither Frankie, Eddie or Tony attend, therefore denying the press further fodder at the expense of her dead son's memory.

Contingency plans for armed police officers to be placed in and around the burial site had been put in place. Lancashire Constabulary had no intention of having another shooting incident on its patch, especially at an event that was covered on national television. But with The Three Dogs elsewhere, the chief constable considered this unnecessary and other than the media, who were kept at a sensible distance, Cheryl had her privacy.

The boy was laid to rest in the presence of his mother, his grandmother and Laurie Holland. Why no further friends or relations attended on that bleak and rainswept morning, I will leave you to decide.

*

They say that today's news, is tomorrow's chip paper, and they are correct.

Unbelievably, as January froze the bones and February blew down gates and fences, the boys of the press grew tired of Frank and friends. Worse still, the tandem murder investigations were no nearer a result. By the end of March, both inquiry teams were reduced by half.

As I've said before, life goes on.

Thankfully, this is true, and as winter was giving way to spring, on April Fool's Day 1984, I was blessed with a son.

Paternity rights for fathers were still a long way off, and I was only able to sneak in two days with our new arrival before returning to duty. This meant a trade-off, the joy of Daniel James coming home, and the daunting prospect of having my mother-in-law as a house guest until my wife was on the mend.

Yes indeed, life goes on.

Chapter Nineteen

7th April 1984. The Stanley Arms, Anfield, Liverpool

Although born to Jamaican parents, Arron Tower was a Scouser, born and bred. He'd first stood on the Kop to watch his beloved Liverpool FC as a twelve-year-old, in 1968. Arron was a rarity back then, a black man standing amongst the thousands of white faces. Then, throughout the 1970s, as black players were introduced to the various league teams, he would stand alongside men who threw bananas on the pitch and made monkey chants . . . and worse.

Quite often, they would turn to Arron during these incidents and say, "We don't mean you mate . . ." as if that made it all okay.

Arron had grown up with racism, indeed, he'd stood alongside it.

Today, at just over six feet five and weighing in at sixteen stone four, he cut a formidable twenty-eight-year-old figure. It would be a brave, or incredibly stupid man, who made monkey chants anywhere near Arron Tower now.

Arron had grown up with violence. His parents had sailed from Jamaica in the late 1940s to fill the employment crisis that England suffered in the post-war era. His father had worked on the docks, his mother as an ancillary nurse in Walton hospital. They were law-abiding, hardworking souls, who took the bigotry thrown at them with all the serene grace of the devout Christians they were.

Arron did not.

He did, however, find some solace, as part of a group of Liverpool fans who didn't care what colour you were, so long as you could fight. Arron stood out like the proverbial sore thumb as a lanky black man with dreadlocks, surrounded by pasty skinheads as the Liverpool hooligans took on all comers, home and away in organised mass street brawls. The 1970s were not a pretty time in English football history.

Arron quickly got his reputation as a hardman and gained the respect of his peers. But his real breakthrough came when he began to deal cannabis in and around his home area of Toxteth. Arron started small, just buying an ounce of resin a week, chopping it up into small deals and selling it to other kids his age.

It wasn't until he was twenty-four that he met the Dutchman Luuk De Jong. Tower had been on a short trip to Amsterdam, when he had been introduced to the obviously wealthy and equally obviously homosexual, De Jong.

Arron didn't give a shit what the Dutchman liked to do in his bedroom, or who with. All he cared about was that the man could supply just about any drug, in large quantities, at great prices.

Within a year, Arron Tower was driving a Mercedes, carried a Colt 45 everywhere he went and was the most feared man in Liverpool 8.

However, the trouble with people like De Jong, is they have no respect for their customers. If you have the cash, he will supply you. Hence the issue with The Three Dogs' crew over in Lancashire. They had decided to cut Arron out of their business and deal direct with De Jong. This, of course, could not happen. This was about face. People would talk. People would say Arron and his crew had gone soft. Hence, Christmas Day.

*

Today was matchday. Liverpool were playing Spurs, and The Stanley was full to bursting. Arron took a gulp of his beer, sandwiched between his fellow supporters and considered the cock-up over in Preston.

He was bothered about the death of the kid. That said, he wasn't crying into his beer about it, after all, kids got killed all the time, all over the world, but he could have done without it. Had his boys killed one of the Preston crew, particularly that queer bastard Eddie Williams, the heat wouldn't have been so great.

As it was, the bizzis had been on top for over two

months, kicking in doors and being generally a pain in the arse. It was only just beginning to die down, so Arron could start to make money again.

De Jong was the real problem. Every time he'd visited the city, he had insisted on visiting Tina's Bar on the Albert Dock. The place was full of queers and lezzers. Arron would sit with his back firmly to the wall. Seeing those men snogging made him feel sick to his stomach. But De Jong was the main man; without him, there would be no Mercedes and no Jamaican holidays, so Arron sucked it up.

He knew the second Eddie Williams and De Jong set eyes on each other, it meant trouble. They had gone off to some disgusting sex party together. Eddie had always been a sly one and Arron just knew he would try to deal him out. And he'd been right.

That said, after the little visit to Verdi's house, it appeared that the so-called Three Dogs had got the message. If they hadn't they were more stupid than he thought.

Arron checked his watch.

Ten minutes to kick-off.

He finished his beer, pushed his way out of the door and into the crowded street.

*

Eddie Williams stood outside the chip shop opposite the Stanley pub. He wore a Parka coat, hood up, red-and-white Liverpool scarf pulled up over his mouth. Tony Thompson, who had never seen Arron Tower was leaning against the

240

Stanley's front window. He noticed the big powerful black man push his way out onto the pavement, glanced over the road to Eddie, who gave the merest nod, then set off behind Arron Tower.

The pavements were thick with fans, full of excitement as their team prepared to take on the mighty Tottenham Hotspur. Tony found the going difficult, but as Tower was so tall, and his dreadlocks so easy to spot, he stayed on track. Tower was a mere ten feet from Tony, as he stopped to light a cigarette. He pushed the fag into his mouth, pulled a zippo from his pocket, flicked the top open and cupped the combination with both hands as he sparked up.

It was a perfect opportunity. The thick crowd, Towers elbows raised.

Tony slipped in behind the giant of a man, pulled his machete, and with all his brute strength, plunged it into the left side of Tower's chest cavity.

Arron didn't move, or even cry out, he just dropped his lighter. Tony pulled out the knife and forced it in a second time, a fraction lower, closer to the heart.

Arron Tower's knees buckled and he fell to the pavement. The crowd hardly noticing, filed past him, or stepped over. Tony backed away and walked against the tide of bodies for a minute before crossing the road.

Within a minute, Tony had dropped the knife into a waste bin and stood alongside Eddie as they heard the first shouts from members of the public to call an ambulance.

It was a pointless exercise. Arron Tower was already dead.

Chapter Twenty

4th July 1984. Fulwood, Preston

Cheryl Greenwood teetered on a set of small steps as she clipped brightly coloured curtains to a rail in her new home.

Tony walked into the small bedroom, recently painted in pale shades. He grabbed Cheryl around the waist and lifted her to the floor in one swift movement.

"Hey Chez, now come on, what have I told you about climbing ladders?"

Cheryl draped her arms around Tony's neck and looked into his handsome face.

"I need to get stuff done Tone."

She let go of her man, took a step back and smoothed down her T-shirt with both hands.

"I'm starting to show, see? Soon I won't be able to help so much."

"You don't need to Chez, I told yer. I got blokes who can do all that. In fact, I got one coming over in an hour or two, to put up that fancy light, the one for the ceiling, you know, that one that twists round with cartoons on."

"You mean, the mobile."

"Yeah, that."

"Well, just help me with these for a minute then. Laurie will be here soon, we're going shopping to Manchester, to that big place, you know, The Arndale."

"You're going to pick out the pram then?"

"I reckon, come on, give a hand."

Tony struggled with the small curtain hooks, his thick fingers not made for the delicate task, but he went along with Cheryl. After all, she was carrying his child, and this was to be the nursery.

No sooner were the curtains in place, a horn blared at the bottom of the drive. Cheryl looked out into the bright sunshine of the summer's day, to see Laurie with the top down on her new car.

Cheryl waved through the window, kissed Tony on the mouth and skipped down the stairs.

She pulled on a lightweight jacket, found her bag, that contained more cash than most families would see in a month, and made for the car.

Cheryl dropped into the passenger seat of the VW Golf Gti Cabriolet and rubbed the leather seats with her hand. "Nice car Laurie . . . very nice."

Laurie was power dressed to the max, in a white linen

two-piece with massive shoulder pads. Underneath she wore a blood-red silk blouse with a long pointed collar folded over the top of her jacket.

"And you're looking fab girl," added Cheryl. "You look like you just walked off the set of Dynasty."

Laurie fired up the Golf and the two pulled away. "Frankie bought me the car as a present. He's trying to get back into my good books, now he's had to fire off that little tart Maisy."

Cheryl smiled. "It'd take more than a bloody motor to get me to forgive the cheating bugger, I'll tell you."

Laurie didn't answer, just changed the subject.

"You're looking great too Chez. You and Tony all okay?"

Cheryl knew exactly what her friend was hinting at. There had been some dark and terrible days since Christmas. More tears than you could believe a person could shed. But Tony had been a rock, and now she was expecting his son.

"I still think about William every day Laurie, if that's what you mean. He's the first thing that comes in my mind every time I wake up. Some days, when I open my eyes, I forget . . . you know? My head still thinks he's here. I expect him to be buzzing about the place, getting into mischief the way he did, then I realise that he's gone and ain't ever coming back, and the pain is so bad, I feel like I can't even get out of bed . . . like I'll never get up again, coz there's no point . . . does that make sense?"

"Perfect sense . . . but I'm so pleased to see *you* happy again Chez."

The pair lapsed into silence. Cheryl thought that there was more to Laurie's last remark than she was letting on.

*

Manchester was heaving with shoppers and visitors taking advantage of the beautiful sunshine. The two women had shopped till they dropped and sat in an outdoor café, watching the world walk by, enjoying a glass of wine.

Cheryl eyed her friend. "So . . . come on, really, how are things between you and Frank these days?"

Laurie pursed her lips and tapped the table with her nails. Considered her real answer, then offered, "He's trying Chez. In his own way, he's doing what he thinks is right. What he thinks will make me happy."

"But you ain't?"

Laurie shook her head. What was the point in lying to Cheryl. After all, she had no one else to confide in.

"It was bad enough before Maisy," she said. "I mean, he never showed me any affection back then . . . not unless he wanted sex. Then, well, it was just that. He'd paw at me for a minute or two, then . . . wham-bam. Fuckin' hell Chez, it was like being a kid again, you know, when you didn't know any better."

Cheryl gave a wry smile. "Oh, I know honey."

"Anyway, once I found out about Maisy, well things got even worse. We were like strangers. Ships in the night.

"Then . . . well then there was Christmas. I don't know how you coped Chez. I mean, he's got such an evil streak

245

in him. I . . . I just can't live with the violence anymore. I seen it all my days. You know my story. I told you . . . with me mum an' all."

Cheryl sipped her wine and took a deep breath.

"Yeah, you told me all about it love, but let me tell you somethin', I was brought up in a proper shithole too. My mum was not much different from yours. She weren't on the smack or anythin' but she was on the game for years. I had more fuckin' uncles than you could shake a stick at. And, just like you, some of 'em tried it on. Some, not many, got what they wanted too. If my old mum needed the money, there was no arguing with her, and I was told to do what the blokes wanted. The odd wank here, the odd BJ there. It was fuckin' horrendous. I couldn't wait to get away, I was desperate. Then, after a one-off shag, I go and get myself caught, and William comes along. I figured that was me lot. Single mum at nineteen, stuck in another shithole on benefits. I never thought for one minute I would ever meet a bloke as good as Tony. He's kind . . ."

Laurie couldn't stop herself. "He's a gangster Chez. He's a . . . a murderer."

Cheryl waved a hand. "Oh! And this is who talking here? How come you suddenly got all pious? Sitting there in your posh suit, driving your new car? Come on Laurie, wise up. What kind of bloke do you think we would both have ended up with eh? With our track records? At best, a decent lad with a job in a factory, renting a flat on the Grange or Callon? Or maybe we'd end up with a petty thief or burglar, or maybe just a fuckin' loser who gets himself locked up every Friday night scrapping with the coppers.

"Girls like us Laurie, we don't get the good guys. We might turn a head or two, but we get the bad guys, or maybe, if we are lucky, the not so bad. So I reckon I've fallen on my feet with Tony. I know what he is."

Cheryl lowered her voice.

"And I know he topped that bloke over in Liverpool too, the one who did for my William. He told me as much. And you know what Laurie? I'm fuckin' grateful for it. I wish I could have been there and seen the bastard bleed out. I'm happy Laurie, for the first time in my life, I'm happy, and I love him."

Laurie managed a thin smile. "I know you are Chez, and I'm happy for you . . . but it ain't for me . . . this . . . this constant looking over your shoulder. I mean, our house is like a fortress these days, cameras everywhere, panic buttons. It's more like a prison than a home."

Cheryl turned down the corners of her mouth and shrugged.

"Is that the real problem?"

Laurie looked puzzled, Cheryl clarified her position. "The lad in prison. Your first proper fella, your first love . . . what's his name?"

"Jamie."

"Yeah, that's him, Jamie. Is he the reason you can't get it back together with Frankie? I mean, I know what a mean bastard Frank is but you knew that when you took up with him. I reckon that's what turned you on about him in the first place. So why not give it a go, spice things up in the bedroom for him, you know, make him see what he's been missing? Why not forget about Maisy, and Jamie, I mean, after all, she's been kicked into touch, and your old flame is in the nick. I mean, what was I just sayin' about losers? Come on, the lad can't be no angel; apparently, he's in nick for a shooting."

Laurie shook her head. "It was me that was the loser Chez. I had a good bloke there. A proper decent man. And if I know Jamie, there'll have been a good reason behind what happened; somethin' to do with the Marines. I can't stop thinking about him Chez, about how things could have been. I know it was me that messed up. I just want a chance at being happy, like you. I want someone who loves me, treats me nice. And I don't mean new cars and clothes either. That don't prove nothing. I mean affection, real affection."

To Laurie's surprise, Cheryl darkened. "Well I think you need to realise how lucky you are. And I'll tell you this much. Don't go sniffing around this lad Jamie either. If Frankie gets wind of it, he'll top you both."

Laurie, eyed her friend. She was tainted, touched by the madness. She had lost a child due to the violence and thuggery, yet here she was, loyal to the cause. Blind to the wickedness.

"Maybe he will Chez, but I didn't escape one whore, to become one myself."

Chapter Twenty-One

"So how long you got left now, Jamie lad?"

Jamie's cell mate was the talkative type. A small wiry burglar by the name of Cook. In the whole time Jamie had been banged up with the guy, he had never found out his first name.

"I've another six months I reckon. Unless this appeal that Birdman has going on gets anywhere. I mean, if they quash his conviction, they have to look at mine too don't they?"

"Suppose they do Jamie, but you know what these fuckers are like. They can drag out the whole thing for so long, it won't be any good to you."

Jamie stretched out on his bunk. "You might be right Cookie, but you never know your luck in a raffle."

Cook rolled off his own bed, unceremoniously pulled down his trousers and sat on the steel toilet in the corner of the cell. Privacy didn't come anywhere or anytime in Walton. Over the past ten months, Jamie had become immune to the indignity of it all. He had thought that life in military barracks would have somehow prepared him for prison.

It had not.

"Well you know what I think," said Cook, wiping and flushing. "I've said it before, and I'll say it again. You shouldn't be in here. You and your mate Bird, should have got a fuckin' medal. That's just what's needed with them paddies. They come over here putting bloody bombs all over the place, killing women and kids, and then expect our lads to play by the rules. I tell yer, I'd've done the same as your mate. Slotted the fucker there and then."

Jamie had heard it all before, and not just from Cook. Several other inmates, especially those that had served in Belfast before their fall from grace had intimated their disgust at Jamie and Bird's treatment.

Even some of the POs had conceded that they felt some sympathy for Jamie. It was of little help. He was still locked in a cell, twenty hours a day watching another guy relieve himself.

There was a knock on the cell door and the hatch opened a split second later. It was Gilbertson, a wise old PO close to retirement. Jamie quite liked the guy, he had a good way about him, treated people with respect and got it back in spades.

"Now then Jamie lad," he chirped. "You have a visitor."

Jamie looked puzzled. In the ten months he had been in jail, only his father had visited him, and Harry had already used all his VOs for the month.

"I wasn't expecting a visit Mr Gilbertson."

The aging guard took off his cap, and ran gnarled fingers through his silver hair. "Well you have one son, and I think you might enjoy this one too. She's as bonny a sight as I've seen in here in many a year."

Jamie sprang from his bunk. "You mean a woman?"

Gilbertson laughed. "Aye lad, I mean a woman."

"From Montague Kane's office then . . . about the appeal?"

Gilbertson shrugged. "That, you'll have to find out for yourself lad."

Jamie was escorted along the myriad of corridors and through the dozens of locked gates until he reached the visiting area. Gilbertson searched him as per the prison regulations, and would search him again after his visit. Jamie scanned the room for his mystery visitor.

Then he saw her.

Laurie Holland was sitting at table ten. Her beautiful blonde hair flowed over her tanned shoulders. She wore a short white summer dress with thin straps to hold it in place. She was stunning and radiant. Everything Jamie remembered and more. There wasn't a man in the room that didn't risk a second look.

When she saw Jamie stride toward her, she stood, revealing those legs of hers. She smiled, a welcoming but apologetic smile. Her dazzling blue eyes glistened with the merest hint of tears. Laurie bit her bottom lip as he closed on her, and opened her arms to hold him.

He took her to him, pulling her into his taut muscular body.

Within seconds, a guard was over. Understanding, but firm. They must release each other and sit.

Jamie wanted to hold Laurie for the rest of his life. He would have given the world just to feel her body next to his for one more second, but he knew he could not, or the visit would be terminated.

They sat.

Laurie gripped his hands across the table. Silent tears rolled down her cheeks. He was just as handsome as she'd remembered. The good looks were still there, yet he had matured. He looked even stronger, more rugged than before. She felt her heart would burst.

"How are you Jamie?"

Jamie could barely speak. "I'm okay . . . how . . . I mean why . . . erm . . . when did . . .?"

Laurie wiped her cheeks. "I heard that you were in jail at Christmas, but didn't know where. It . . . it took me a while to find you . . . and pluck up the courage to come, of course. I mean, I wasn't sure you would want to see

me again after so long, and well, after, you know . . . Oh
Jamie, I'm so sorry."

Jamie shook his head. "No need to apologise. It ain't
your fault I'm here is it?"

"That's not what I meant."

Jamie wore a puzzled frowned.

"I don't mean that. I mean, I'm sorry for . . . for
everything Jamie. For how we . . . I . . . behaved toward
you. I never really got the chance to . . . to . . . I mean,
I was so caught up in wanting a different life from what
I'd had as a kid, I didn't see what was in front of me all
the time."

Jamie waved away the apology. He was far too pleased
to see Laurie sitting in front of him, having taken the
trouble to find him.

"We were probably too young anyway Laurie. To be
honest . . . I just thought that you didn't love me anymore,
you wanted Frankie Verdi instead of me, end of."

Laurie visibly stiffened at the mention of Frank's
name.

"You're right Jamie, we were just kids back then, too
young to know better. But let's not talk about Frankie eh?
We ain't got much time."

Jamie noticed Laurie's discomfort instantly. He gripped
her hand across the table. "There's something wrong isn't
there? Between you and Frankie I mean. I can see it in
your eyes. I seen the papers and . . ."

Laurie managed smile and took in the man she had

once agreed to wed. She didn't want to ruin the short visit by discussing Frankie Verdi.

"Like I said Jamie, let's not talk about him eh? I mean, look at you, you're certainly not wanting for anything in here Jamie, the size of you."

Jamie's muscles bulged, his prison shirt struggling to contain his massive shoulders and arms.

"We're locked up twenty hours a day. The other four, I train and eat."

"It must be horrible though."

"I've stayed in better places, yeah."

"I believe you have another six months."

"That depends on Birdman's appeal."

"Birdman?"

"Richard Valance, the Aussie guy I was partnered with, the guy who shot McGuire."

"This McGuire was a terrorist, right?"

"Right."

"So why not shoot him? He'd tried to kill you, hadn't he?"

"Yes, but he'd thrown down his gun."

"You mean he'd surrendered?"

"Yes."

Laurie shrugged as if this information didn't change anything.

"So, what will the appeal be about?"

"It's a little complicated, but the lawyers are saying that as Bird only admitted to an accidental discharge of his weapon, he can't be guilty of manslaughter. In the end, it's more political than legal. We just have to wait."

Laurie gazed into his eyes.

"And you are stuck in here for nothing."

"I knew what he'd done, but . . ."

"But what?"

"Bird had saved my life Laurie . . . I owed him . . . so I lied for him."

"Always the honourable man eh Jamie?"

"Seems I made the wrong choice this time though."

Laurie leaned forward. Jamie could smell her, almost taste her.

"It looks like I made the wrong choice too," she said, her tears falling freely again. "Oh Jamie, could you ever forgive me. I've been such a fool."

Jamie felt his stomach turn. Was he really hearing this, after all this time?

Laurie put her head in her hands for a second before locking eyes with Jamie. She knew it was probably a hopeless cause. No one could forgive a person for being so heartless, so cruel.

"Frankie and me . . . it's over Jamie. He hits me, he treats me like dirt. I hate him." Laurie gripped Jamie's hand again. "Look, I know what I did to you was horrible and hurtful, but I was young and stupid. I don't expect anything from you darling, I know it's probably all too late but I just wanted you to know that . . ."

Jamie felt all the old emotions come flooding back. He

done his best to stop them over the years, but there had never been another woman in his life that could hold a candle to Laurie.

"It's never too late Laurie . . . never."

Jamie wanted the table that separated them to disappear. He wanted to pick it up and hurl it across the room so he could hold her. As Laurie's tears tore at his heart, he wanted to hurl Frankie Verdi across the room too.

"Look, I've read the papers, seen what Frank and the gang are up to. The rumour in here is that they topped Arron Tower, the guy from Toxteth. He was a face, a big player in this part of the world. The word is, it was over drugs, that Tower ordered the attack on Frankie's place, and they ended up killing that kid by mistake."

Laurie nodded fiercely, there were more tears.

"I was there Jamie. It was horrible. That poor child."

Jamie sat back in his seat and blew out his cheeks.

"So, you've left Frankie now then?"

For the first time, he saw the slightest indecision in her. She squirmed in her seat, fear in her eyes.

"It's not so simple Jamie, not so easy. If he knew I was here today, talking to you, I swear he'd kill me. Kill me with his bare hands. You don't know what he's capable of Jamie. He doesn't want me, but nobody else can have me . . . I made a terrible mistake Jamie. I should have stayed with you, married you."

She pulled another smile from somewhere deep inside her. "We'd probably have kids by now eh? But I ruined it all, through my stupidity, my greed. I know you could never take me back after everything I've done to you, and I deserve everything I've got, but I can't . . ."

More tears fell. "I just can't go on Jamie . . . I . . ."

Laurie broke down into hacking sobs. Jamie stroked her hair, the way he had back when they were dating. The way he had when she'd broken her heart over what her mother had done to her.

"Don't worry about Frankie Verdi," he said flatly. "The minute I'm out of here, we'll be together and he'll never hurt you again."

Chapter Twenty-Two

Toast Nightclub, Preston

The Three Dogs sat in the VIP area of the club. They were completely alone. One huge doorman stood at the entrance barring anyone else from entry. This was a private celebration. It was just before two in the morning.

On the table in front of the men were three silver ice buckets, each containing the finest champagne Frankie could find. Nestled next to each bottle was a crystal glass, a small mirror, a razor blade and a small packet of white powder.

"Champagne and cocaine," toasted Frank. "The breakfast of champions."

The three chinked their glasses and smiled. The coke had negated the alcohol in the champagne, leaving the men in a permanent state of euphoria.

Tony, who for so long had avoided any drug other than a little cannabis, had found this new powder irresistible. The overwhelming desire to chop out another line after each glass of fizz was too much for him.

He was flying.

"I think we should make a toast for Eddie," he said, wiping his nose and sniffing loudly. "I mean. It was Eddie who did the deal with the bloke from abroad wasn't it?"

Frankie's eyes flashed with a hint of jealousy, but the moment passed and he raised his glass alongside Tony's.

"To Eddie," he shouted above the last of the DJ's offerings for the night.

Tony mimicked his mentor and swallowed the contents of his glass in one gulp.

"Thanks, lads," said Eddie. Genuinely pleased to have his efforts recognised. "Joe is travelling south tomorrow, to collect the next shipment. A big one, all of fifty grand."

Tony whistled. "Fucking hell Eddie. Can we shift all that?"

Eddie chopped out a line of his own. "Course we can, and with the festival season here, we could actually move more. By this time next year, we could double that amount, each shipment.

"Joe's done a great job with the dealers. He's also a clever guy and spends hours with the music papers finding the right concerts and festivals for his runners to work.

"He keeps all the bulk buyers happy too. Syd Bullen in Skelmersdale, Big Jimmy Glass in Blackpool, Charlie Croft in Blackburn and Sly Smith in Lancaster, they're all happy as pigs in shit. They love the quality and the price, and that it always shows up on time."

Frankie nodded. "It's a smooth operation Eddie, I'll give you that, and now that we've got the newspapers off our backs, we can breathe a bit easier."

Eddie grimaced. "You're not still shagging that Maisy are you Frank?"

Verdi took a swig from his glass, placed it on the table and rubbed his hands together like an excited child. "Got her waiting for me in the Tickled Trout Motel, room 103, with a new set of stockings on . . . That girl can do things with her mouth you wouldn't believe."

Tony laughed. "Fuckin' hell Frank, you have to hope your Laurie don't find out. She'll have your balls for breakfast."

Eddie, was suddenly sullen. "Well I think it's a risk you don't need to take Frank. There's enough pussy about without having an underage. Especially as you are feeding her the charlie like it's going out of fashion. She could fuck you up big style if she goes to the coppers. And take us all with you."

Frankie pulled on his jacket, his eyes like coals in the half-light.

"They've already tried that, and I sorted it. They couldn't prove nothing and her mum wouldn't give a statement so what's the fucking problem?" Frankie's line kicked in and his mouth ran away with itself. "You stick to hanging around in gay bars Eddie, and let us real men do what we do best eh?"

Eddie stood up instantly, fists balled, unable to control his anger. "You know I was just there for business Frankie," he hissed. "I'm as much a man as anyone here."

Tony did another line, wet his finger, wiped up the remnants of the drug and rubbed it on his gums. Too stoned to know better, he blurted. "Frankie's pulling your leg Eddie. I know that William was your kid, so you can't be queer eh?"

Frankie's eyes widened. He fixed them on Eddie. "This true?"

Eddie calmed some. He didn't want this conversation, but it was better than the one about gay bars in Liverpool.

He shrugged his massive shoulders. "Could have been. Me and Cheryl did have a bit of a thing back then. The kid did look like me, I suppose."

Frankie laughed. It was a raucous bawdy sound. He slapped Tony on the back and ruffled his hair. "Fuck me Tone . . . looks like we've all shagged her then."

Faster than his size should allow, Tony grabbed Frankie by the wrist. His sheer power holding him in place. Frankie was unable to release himself.

Tony raised his eyes to meet Frankie's. "Don't ever talk about my Cheryl like that again Frank, okay?"

The club's music was turned off and the lights were raised. The uncomfortable and dangerous stand-off lasted no more than a few seconds, yet it changed a lifetime's order.

Tony loosened his grip and Frankie snatched his arm away. He snarled and made for the door.

"If you need me, you know where I am."

Eddie sat back down and poured more champagne. "Well that went fucking well."

*

James Dunn sat in the car park of The Tickled Trout Motel in his old Cortina.

He could have afforded to buy a Rolls Royce had he so desired, but the old Ford did him just fine. No one noticed it.

Sitting alongside him was Jeff Brown. He'd known Jeff since school, when they'd hung around the playground together at Hackney Secondary. Jeff was the best photographer James had ever seen. He'd covered wars, coups, famines, riots, hangings, murders, and more. But tonight, James Dunn needed Jeff's uncanny ability to get clear shots in almost total darkness, both with and without using a flash.

Dunn was fifty-five years old. He'd seen the likes of Verdi and his cronies come and go. He'd covered the Kray Twins, the Moors Murders and the rest. He'd seen more blood spilt than some war correspondents. James knew, however, the one thing that tied so many villains, pop stars, politicians and other famous faces together. It was the thing that brought so many down too.

Sex.

Men having sex with boys, girls with girls, orgies, sado-masochism, bondage and blow-jobs, James had seen it all and Jeff had photographed it for him.

These Three Dogs were fucking amateurs compared to The Krays and the like. The day that Eddie Williams pointed his finger at James Dunn was his undoing. But at least he'd had the sense to keep his head down recently. James would have to wait, and be patient, before exacting his revenge on Williams. Frankie Verdi, however, couldn't keep his dick in his trousers.

Like taking candy from a baby.

Dunn knew Maisy Thomas was in 103. A quick twenty quid to the night porter had seen to that.

Room 103 was on the ground floor of the Tickled Trout Motel. A decent-quality establishment, boasting four stars and a gourmet restaurant. It sat close to the junction of the M6 and M55 and therefore was popular with travelling salesmen.

Jeff Brown had found his way around the back of the block Maisy's room was in, and despite almost closing her curtains, by using a clever little device fitted to the lens on his camera, had been able to fire off some shots of Maisy dressing in Frankie's preferred undergarments.

All this was well and good, but James Dunn knew he couldn't use those pictures without the arrest. Dunn knew his only way of gaining access to the room was by finding a cop that would play ball.

He wanted the money shots. He wanted Verdi, balls

deep in this fifteen-year-old schoolgirl. Frankie Verdi, gangster of this parish, who had groomed this poor vulnerable child for his own sexual pleasure.

Dunn was already writing the headlines.

At exactly 0300 hrs, Frankie Verdi parked his Jaguar not three spaces from the *Daily Mirror's* finest and strolled into the foyer.

Dunn followed a moment later, found the payphone, and dialled Det Ch Supt Alan Crocker's personal number.

Crocker was not a bad policeman. Indeed, he'd served twenty-six years without a blemish on his record, receiving two commendations for good policework. He was a man averse to breaking even the smallest of rules. As careful and consistent a performer as you could wish for.

Nevertheless, Alan Crocker had never been under so much pressure to solve a crime, or in this case, five grisly murders. And Frankie and crew had embarrassed him, and his inquiry team.

Crocker was in no doubt that Verdi was behind the four Blackburn killings, and maybe the stabbing over in Merseyside. Yet there was nowhere near enough evidence to arrest him, let alone charge him, or any of The Three Dogs for that matter.

Even so, despite the pressure, it was with some reluctance that he agreed to work with a reporter.

Dunn assured Crocker, that he could deliver Verdi on a plate, so long as he could be present at the arrest and take photographs.

The deal was struck.

At 0315 Alan Crocker walked into the reception of the Tickled Trout, flanked by two burly uniforms.

Dunn and Brown, kept their distance in the car park awaiting the nod.

Crocker slid his warrant card across the desk to the night porter. "Do you have a duty manager on call son?" he asked curtly.

The porter was still coming to terms with the bribe he had just taken from some reporter and instantly figured he was in the shit.

His eyes darted between the obviously senior man, and the two massive uniformed officers. Whoever the cops wanted, they were expecting trouble.

"Erm . . . yes sir. Mr . . . Mr Wallace, but he'll be asleep."

"Then wake him," barked Crocker. "Tell him that there is a Detective Chief Superintendent Crocker standing in his lobby and that a serious crime is currently being committed in room one oh three of his motel."

The night porter went a funny shade of white. "One oh three you say?"

"I did. Also inform Mr Wallace, that unless we can gain access to the said room PDQ, then he, and this establishment could be considered to be aiding and abetting this said crime."

The porter was almost green. The twenty-pound note given to him by Dunn earlier, burning a hole in his pocket for a very different reason than an hour ago.

He lifted the receiver and dialled.

Crocker could just about make out a very sleepy voice at the other end of the line. As the porter relayed Crocker's information, the voice awoke and became instantly agitated.

"Tell him we want the master key, and we want it now," said Crocker, turning up the heat. "Or these two lads here will just make a mess of his door."

Mr Wallace was now shouting so loudly down the phone, that Crocker could hear him just fine.

"Give him the fucking key you idiot!"

The porter locked a set of watery eyes on the detective. "Mr Wallace . . . erm . . . well he said . . ."

Crocker held out a large hand. "To give me the fucking key."

The party had got started in room 103. Frankie had brought more champagne and more cocaine to help it go with a bang. Maisy had brought a black satin basque, silk stockings and five-inch stilettos.

Both were so deep in their own throes of passion, they never noticed the hotel room door swing open.

Crocker kept his part of the bargain and let Jeff Brown into the room first. He had two cameras around his neck, one set for high speed multiple exposures, the other for single shot flash.

Frankie had insisted on leaving the lights on as he pounded Maisy on the bed.

Jeff Brown didn't need the flash. He had a field day.

Frankie was so stoned, that he kept on thrusting even as the three cops entered the room. It was actually Maisy who noticed their presence first.

She let out a scream and pushed Verdi from her. Frankie rolled off the bed and hit the floor with a bump. Maisy tried to find the sheets and cover her modesty.

The two uniforms were around the bed in an instant. Verdi tried to kick out at them as he lay on his back on the floor, but he was too far gone and the two cops too experienced and strong. He was unceremoniously rolled on his front and handcuffed.

Both Verdi and Maisy began to hurl insults at Crocker and the two uniforms. It was water off a duck's back. One of the huge uniformed cops took a quick look at Verdi's now flaccid member as he stood naked and whining in the corner.

He gave his partner a nudge. "Don't know why she bothered with that eh Fred?"

Fred sniggered.

Verdi's eyes burned into the first cop. "I know where you fucking live," he spat.

The cop grabbed Frankie by the throat and slammed him up against the wall. "And I know where you live too you piece of shit. I also know what happens to nonces inside. That little pecker of yours won't be of any use to you in there son."

The cop released Frankie, who fell to the floor gasping for breath.

Crocker stepped over. He was waving an evidence bag under Verdi's nose. It had three single gram bags of white powder in it.

"Frank Verdi, I'm arresting you for unlawful sexual intercourse with a minor and possession of a class-A drug, with the intent to supply. You are not obliged to say anything unless you wish to do so, but what you say may be given in evidence. Do you understand?"

"No comment," said Frankie.

Crocker turned to the uniforms. "Right lads, get a WPC down to deal with Maisy here. She'll be going straight to the police surgeon for examination. Then wake up the SOCO lot. I want this room sealed off until they have done a full sweep." He turned to Jeff Brown.

"You get what you wanted?"

"Oh yeah," he said, and turned to Frankie. "His arse will be more famous that his face by tomorrow night."

Detective Jim Hacker

The arrest of Frankie Verdi, in itself, did nothing to move the murder investigations forward. Although, purely on a personal note, it did put a spring in my step as I walked into my office. There was little doubt, Crocker hoped, that as Verdi would be charged with not one, but two serious offences, he may be held in custody until his trial.

With Frankie off the streets, maybe, just maybe, a witness could find the courage to come forward.

In 1984, the offence of unlawful sexual intercourse had a statutory defence. That being, that the male party had no way of knowing that the girl in question was under the age of consent. This proviso was put in place for the benefit of young men, who, for example, had met a girl in a nightclub, presumed she was over eighteen and found themselves in trouble the next morning when the parents found out their dear fifteen-year-old daughter had been sexually active. This proviso also came with its own condition. The male in question must be under the age of twenty-four.

Presumably, the lawmakers considered an older man should know better.

Frankie Verdi was twenty-three, but as he had already been photographed with Maisy in her school uniform, he would find this defence difficult to employ.

On the other hand, Crocker would undoubtedly find Maisy to be a difficult witness, and it was obvious she was a willing participant in the matter. Therefore, the second charge was a far more serious matter and the one Crocker would hope to make stick. Again, in the early eighties, even possession of cocaine was a very serious matter.

Selling at around £80 a gram and with the average weekly wage in the north of England being just £30 more, you could see how expensive a commodity it was. It was also viewed by the courts as a dangerous substance, ranking alongside heroin. If the prosecution could prove Frankie had supplied the drug to Maisy Thomas, a minor, then he would undoubtedly receive a lengthy custodial sentence.

There were many ifs, buts and maybes for Crocker to overcome, but this was the closest anyone had been to bringing any of The Three Dogs to justice.

As a matter of course, directly after his arrest, Frankie Verdi's home, car and the nightclub, Toast were thoroughly searched. No further drugs were found, but it was noted that a large quantity of cash, exceeding thirty thousand pounds, was held in the safe at the club. Crocker would undoubtedly inform the Inland Revenue about the find.

Sometimes, there is more than one way to skin a cat.

Chapter Twenty-Three

Eddie Williams sat in The Soup Kitchen, a greasy spoon café just off New Hall Lane. Sitting opposite him was Cyril Norman, ex-detective and now solicitor's runner for Dundonald and Partners, The Three Dogs' chosen legal representatives. He was demolishing a full English with extra toast. Eddie stuck to coffee, his cocaine hangover ruining his appetite.

Norman had run the full scenario of Frankie's arrest by Eddie, and what needed to be done in order to ensure Frankie's release from custody.

Cyril may have been an ex-cop, but there was no such thing as fair in Cyril's book, just who paid the highest price. And Frankie was a very rich boy indeed. No one liked dealing with Cyril, cops or villains. A bent cop is a bent cop, but today Eddie had no choice. Needs must.

*

Eddie left the café feeling like he needed a shower and drove to Moor Nook council estate, the place of his birth, the place where he, Tony and Frank had grown up. He pulled up behind Fat Les' ice cream van. Frank had given Les one of the old models as a golden handshake when they had sold the 3D Ice business.

Les had quickly restored himself as the local cannabis supplier using the van. Of course, he now bought his drugs from Joe Madden, and therefore, essentially, The Three Dogs.

However, it wasn't Les that Eddie wanted to see, it was his sister, Margaret Thomas, mother of Maisy, who lived next door.

Eddie strode up the path to the front door. The garden was overgrown, almost concealing a rusting old washer that had been dumped there sometime in the last ten years. Weeds poked through the cracks in the concrete, a dustbin overflowed under the front window.

Nice.

Eddie knocked and got nothing.

He knocked again, harder. Finally, the door was opened.

Margaret Thomas was in her late thirties but looked nearer fifty. You could see that at one time she had been a looker, just like Maisy, but time had not been good to Margaret.

She took one derisory look at Eddie and turned back into the house, shuffling along the linoleum-clad hallway in grubby slippers and dressing gown.

Eddie reluctantly followed and they stopped in her small kitchen. A whole week of plates, pots and pans were stacked, festering in the sink. Margaret flicked fag ash into the mountain of crockery.

"What the fuck do you want?" she croaked. The forty Bensons a day giving a guttural edge to her voice.

There was a funny smell coming from somewhere that Eddie couldn't or didn't want to identify. He had no desire to spend a moment longer in Margaret's filthy stinking house than was necessary.

"Now, that's not polite, is it Marg?"

"I don't give a fuck for polite Eddie. I know what's happened. The pigs rang me in the middle of the fucking night to tell me. Our Maisy's banged up alongside that dirty bastard Frankie Verdi. He's been fucking her again. I told him the last time, when he came round wanting me to keep my mouth shut. I told him, 'All right Frank,' I says, 'I'll do it this time, but you leave my girl be from now on.' And has he? Has he fuck."

"How much did Frank give you the last time Marg?"

Margaret either didn't hear Eddie, or chose to ignore the question.

"Now they want me to go down and sit in on the interview, 'cept, not yet as she's so fucking high, they can't talk to her till she's straight. He's been giving her drugs Eddie, drugs, so she'll do things for him. Fucking kinky stuff I'll bet, dirty bastard he is."

"How much?" pressed Eddie, his infamously short temper not helped by his banging headache.

Margaret threw her fag in the sink and lit another.

"Hundred," she said flatly.

Eddie looked about him. "You didn't spend it on bleach did you Marg?"

"If you've come to take the piss Eddie, you can fuck right off now. I don't need it, okay?"

Eddie managed to control himself. "How would you like to get out of here Marg?"

"What you mean?"

"I mean, how would you like to leave this shithole behind, live in a nice new flat down the docks, even take a holiday in the sunshine, Benidorm maybe?"

Margaret's ears pricked up. *She fucking heard that*, thought Eddie.

"Benidorm? That's abroad ain't it?"

"Spain, last time I looked Marg. Why not take a couple of weeks away, pick a nice hotel out the brochure, all five-star luxury, get a tan, there'd be plenty of cash to spend too. And when you get back, your nice new, clean flat, will be ready for you, rent free."

Margaret looked at Eddie, eyes full of suspicion.

"You are talking a lot of money there Eddie . . . hundreds."

"Not hundreds Marg . . . thousands. New everything; furniture, carpets, clothes . . . even get your hair done all nice for a change. What you say Marg, come on, you're still a good-looking woman."

Margaret touched her hair absently, a flicker of a smile crossed her lips, before it disappeared and she fell back to reality.

"What you want me to do for all this money Eddie? Top someone?"

Eddie managed a smile of his own. "Don't be silly Marg, we ain't like that. Don't believe all the gossip about us three. We're just businessmen these days. Look, Frank has been a silly boy, and he knows it. He just can't keep his hands off your Maisy, and from what I've seen, the feeling's mutual. And she'll be sixteen in a few months, won't she? Come on Marg, I bet you had some fun before you were of age eh?"

"Might've done. But not with a grown man . . . with a boy me own age."

"Marg, like it or not, your Maisy loves Frank, she wants to be with him, wants what Frank can give her too. A better life, better than this. Why don't you have a slice of the cake too eh?"

Margaret dropped her second stub into the pile of dirty plates and pursed her lips.

"What you want me to do?" she said.

*

Maisy Thomas sat alongside her mother in the interview room. Mother and daughter had been allowed a short visit prior to the start of proceedings, affording the appropriate adult the same rights as a legal representative.

A surly looking detective sat opposite, together with a uniformed WPC. A tape recorder whirred on the table.

The detective began the introductions, and after

everyone had spoken for the benefit of the tape, he asked his first question.

"Maisy, how old are you?"

"Fifteen."

"And when are you sixteen?"

"Six weeks."

"On the tenth September, right?"

"Right."

"Are you aware, that it is illegal to have sex before your sixteenth birthday?"

"Yes."

"She's been brought up right," butted in Margaret.

"Quite," said the detective, acknowledging Margaret's input. "But Maisy, you have been having sexual intercourse with a man called Frankie Verdi have you not?"

"Only the once," said Maisy, all sweetness and light.

"Once?"

"Yes, just last night. See, I told Frank it was me birthday, so he booked that posh hotel and brought champagne to make it special. We love each other see. I mean, Frank said we would have to wait till I was sixteen before we could do it, you know, sex like, but I wanted it sooner, so I lied to him. I told him my birthday was yesterday . . . sorry."

"You lied to him?"

"Yes, I told him I was of age."

"She did," added Margaret.

The detective ignored the obvious collusion.

"So, Maisy. Did you lie to Frankie Verdi because you were under the influence of cocaine?"

"I've never taken drugs."

"Is it not true, that Frankie Verdi gave you cocaine last night, before and during sexual intercourse?"

"No sir."

"Then how do you explain the three packets of cocaine found by police officers on the bedside table? Cocaine residue found on the surface of the same table, and residue on a five-pound note, found in your handbag, young lady?"

Maisy took a deep breath and began her rehearsed speech.

"My little brother found those three packets of powder outside our house yesterday, dropped on the pavement."

"Your little brother?"

"Yes, our Terry, he's four. He came in with them. I took them off him and put them in me bag. I was going to hand them into the police station, 'cos I figured they looked a bit dodgy, but I forgot in all the excitement of meeting Frankie."

The detective was losing patience. "Maisy, don't lie to the police. It will only be worse for you in the end. We know that Frankie Verdi gave you the cocaine and we know that you took some last night."

Maisy shook her head.

"I went in me bag for a condom and pulled out the bags of stuff at the same time by accident. One of them had come open and there was powder in me bag and some spilt on the table. Frankie told me to flush the lot down the toilet, but before I could, you lot burst into the room."

"So, your little brother will tell us the same story then?" said the detective wearily.

Margaret leaned in. "You are not going to interview my four-year-old, sunshine, dream on, and anyways, he's a bit on the slow side and wouldn't remember . . . but I do, I remember clear as day. It's exactly as Maisy said. She found them packets out in the street. I was there. I saw it with me own eyes."

*

Det Ch Supt Alan Crocker sat looking at the transcript of Maisy Thomas' interview with his head in his hands. Alongside it, was a sworn statement from Margaret Thomas relating to her youngest child Terrence, and how he'd miraculously found three bags of white powder in the street worth £240.

Then there was Frankie Verdie's transcript, a pointless exercise, every question answered with "no comment".

A forensics report stated that they had found two partial prints on the bags, neither useable in court, but both belonged to Verdi.

Sitting next to it all, was a copy of the *Daily Mirror*, and on pages three and four, James Dunn had the whole sordid tale laid out in pictures and sensationalised text. Maisy's face had been pixelated, a new technique used by the press to hide the identity of juveniles or other persons the editor may deem too sensitive to publish. But Frankie was there in all his naked glory with only a cartoon carrot, carefully placed in shot, to hide his modesty and keep the *Mirror* from being hounded by Mary Whitehouse.

Sitting opposite Crocker was Assistant Chief Constable Peter Davies.

"This is a mess Alan," said the senior man tapping the *Mirror* with a clean, clipped nail. "A bloody mess all round. What were you thinking?"

Crocker looked up, eyes bleary from lack of sleep. "I was thinking, sir, that we might just nail this bastard."

"Except we haven't nailed him, have we Alan? We haven't even got enough to charge them with possession, and I've got the chief bellowing down the phone, wanting to know exactly how James Dunn of the *Mirror* happened to be present at the scene of the arrest."

"He must have followed us sir," said Crocker weakly.

The ACC exploded. "Fucking followed you! So, you, a senior detective, and two uniforms didn't notice a little fat cockney and his sidekick carrying God knows how many cameras standing behind you as you entered the hotel room. For goodness sake . . . no, for your sake Alan, you need to do better than that. I would suggest that Verdi's solicitors are rubbing their hands with glee as we speak, and Discipline and Complaints are already filling out your form fourteens to start your investigation. Get a grip Alan, and sort this mess out. Release them both ASAP and I want a full, and I mean *full*, report on my desk by this afternoon."

*

Laurie Holland scanned the *Mirror* newspaper in disgust. She had long since given up hope of ever having a normal loving relationship with Frankie.

Even so, the newspaper article mentioned Laurie by name and even had a picture of her alongside the vile shots of Frankie straddling Maisy Thomas.

Eddie had been on the phone. He had it all in hand, not to worry, he'd said.

Laurie wasn't worried. She didn't care anymore.

Even so, she pondered how much longer she would have to tolerate being embarrassed and scared in equal measure.

Not long now she hoped. If Jamie's appeal went well, he could be out within weeks. So, things had to happen quickly.

Laurie needed a new escape plan. An escape into the arms of Jamie Strange.

She had to ensure that she and Jamie could make a new life, a new start, away from Frankie Verdi, and away from The Three Dogs.

So far away, they could never be traced.

Australia maybe?

Frankie was a very rich man, getting richer by the day. Laurie had been just as instrumental in him accumulating that wealth as Eddie fucking Williams or Tony Thompson had ever been. Without her, Frankie would still be knocking out pizzas and selling eighths of resin on Moor Nook.

No.

No matter what happened now, she was not going to walk away empty-handed, and she didn't mean that paltry five hundred a week she was putting away either. Jamie had told her he still loved her and everything was going to be just fine.

And Laurie believed him.

There would be no more exposés, no more murder, no more drugs. A real life, a real home, marriage, children.

She peeked out of her bedroom curtains.

They were still there, the press, all wanting a comment.

Laurie dropped the paper and checked herself in the full-length mirror. She wore a figure-hugging designer number she'd picked up with Frankie's money in Manchester last month, red as claret, with matching killer heels. Her hair and make-up were perfect.

She trod the staircase to the front door, and opened it with a theatrical swish.

Instantly, the crowd gathered at the front gate began to shout questions, cameras clicked, flash guns flared. Laurie slowly trod the path to the main gates, swinging her hips, a big smile fixed on her face.

As she reached the amassed hacks, she stopped, held up a manicured finger and touched it to her ruby lips.

She waited.

Within seconds, every man stood silent in a mixture of apprehension and appreciation. One or two visibly held their mouths open.

"Thank you boys," said Laurie huskily. "I'm so glad to see

you all here, as I appear to be left alone in the house again."

One caddish photographer shouted. "Make us a cuppa then love."

Laurie smiled. "Don't worry lads, I'll bring out some tea and biscuits shortly, but first . . . who's here from the *Mirror*?"

A short, portly middle-aged man stepped forward, leaning over the gate. "That will be me love, James Dunn."

"Ah, yes James," said Laurie, cocking her head to one side quizzically. "The crime reporter, right? So, you are the one who keeps putting my picture in the paper then?"

"That's me," said Dunn, eyeing Laurie up and down and feeling a great follow-up coming on.

Laurie pulled back her fist and slammed it into Dunn's nose with everything she had. All her frustration, all her anger behind the blow. Dunn's nose exploded, blood spurted in all directions. The reporter fell backwards, landing with a nasty slap on the pavement. The surrounding press looked on in shock, until the photographers, usually the first to react, began to snap the prostrate crime correspondent.

Laurie turned on her heels, then, looking over her shoulder, she said, "That's what I call a slap in the face Mr Dunn. Now you know how I felt, reading your rag this morning."

Once Laurie made it back to the house she made two calls; the first was to Walton Jail. The second was to her bank, to ensure they had an overseas office. She and Jamie would be needing an offshore account.

Her goals for the morning achieved, she wandered to the kitchen and began to make a tray of tea and biscuits.

Chapter Twenty-Four

As Laurie kept the press happy, Frankie Verdi sat drinking tea in Tony's front room. Eddie munched on a sandwich, having rediscovered his appetite; Joe Madden abstained.

Tony checked Cheryl was out of earshot in the kitchen, closed the lounge door for good measure, and joined the meeting.

Frankie held up both palms.

"First off, I want to say sorry to you all for bringing us some heat."

"Your dick will get us all hanged up," muttered Eddie.

Frankie's back ached from lying in his cell. He was in no mood to be treated like a child. "I said I was sorry, didn't I?"

"Yeah, Frank is sorry Eddie," placated Tony. "Let's not have another fall-out eh?"

Frankie arched his back and groaned. "Tony's right, we

need to stick together and just ride this little matter out. After all it's my arse all over the papers, nobody else's."

Joe Madden managed to stifle a smile. "Have to say boss, that Maisy looked well fit in them pictures, you'd be hard pressed to say no to a piece of that."

Eddie still wasn't impressed. "There ain't no bird worth going down for, and definitely not one that could interfere with our business. You need to keep your hands off Maisy, Frank . . . and no more fucking free charlie either. Keep it in your pants for a few weeks for fuck's sake. Laurie's stamping around the club like a wounded rhino. Women scorned are fucking dangerous animals Frank. You have to remember, with what she knows, she could bring us all down."

Frankie waved a dismissive hand. "You let me worry about Laurie. She knows where her best interests are," he prodded the table with his finger. "And that's right here. She wouldn't dare grass on me, or any of us. If she risked opening her mouth, she knows we'd find her, and what the consequences would be."

Eddie sat back and folded his arms. "I'm just saying, keep an eye on her, that's all."

Frankie had heard enough. "Look, you take care of your little Dutch pal, and I'll take care of Laurie. All she does is get pissed all night, and sleep it off all day. If she ain't at the club, she's at home or fucking shopping."

Then Joe Madden dropped the bombshell. "She was in Walton nick the other week Frank."

Verdi's eyes burned into Joe Madden, his voice barely a whisper.

"What you say there, Joe?"

Joe squirmed in his seat, instantly regretting opening his mouth. "Well, not a hundred per cent like Frank, I mean . . ."

Verdi flew into an instant jealous rage, knocking over his tea. "Not one hundred per cent? Then what exactly do you mean then Joe? Fifty? Seventy? Was my Laurie in Walton nick . . . or fucking not?"

Joe hunched his shoulders. "Well . . . fuck me Frank . . . calm down will yer . . . Look, you know Billy Clayton? He's doing a two-stretch in Walton for dumping all those dodgy chequebooks."

Verdi's face was contorted with temper. "What the fuck has that twat Billy Clayton got to do with my Laurie?"

"Nothing Frank, he ain't got nothing to do with her exactly," Joe chose his words carefully. ". . . 'cept his missus, Sandra went to see him the other week, and she said, she swore she saw your Laurie there, visiting some mush."

Verdi stood over Joe, fists clenched. "Some . . . mush? Who exactly Joe? Who was she visiting?"

Joe was getting worried. "I . . . I don't know Frank, I never asked like."

Frankie bawled at the top of his voice. "Then make it your fucking life's work to find out, you fucking prick!"

The lounge door opened. Cheryl walked in carrying a

bowl and a sponge, determined not to have a tea stain on her new carpets.

"I think I know who she went to see," she said.

*

Harry Strange had ridden the train from Liverpool Lime Street into Preston Central. As he walked up the pedestrian ramp onto Fishergate, the sun was just dipping down behind the Railway pub.

Harry licked his lips.

It had been a long day, but well worth the trip. Jamie had received good news; his release date would coincide with Richard Valance's new date, after his successful appeal against his manslaughter conviction.

Harry would have his son home before the end of the month.

Harry tripped into The Railway and ordered a Guinness. Friday nights were a lively affair in the main bar. Irish music played and a raucous crowd, who had settled in the area from across the water, threw pints down their necks like there was a drought. Preston boasted a large Catholic population, hence the name, a derivative of "Priest Town", and The Railway's clientele were notoriously sympathetic toward the PIRA.

Harry had fought the Irish, but held no grudge against them. However, had they known who his son was, he may not have been so welcome.

He settled in a corner with his back to the wall and a good view of the main door.

Old habits die hard.

Harry sipped his pint and, for the first time in a long time, felt good. He sat and planned the redecoration of Jamie's room; a small surprise to welcome him home. His good feelings, however, were to be short-lived.

Before he was halfway down his drink, in walked Laurie Holland. It could have been sheer coincidence of course, but Harry didn't believe in such things. The girl hadn't left quite enough time, from watching him leave the station, to entering the pub.

Laurie wore a long-sleeved black dress, large dark glasses, and turned every head in the bar as she scanned the crowd. Finally, she spotted Harry and walked over.

"Hello Harry," she said quietly. "Long time no see."

Harry nodded. "Laurie," was all he offered.

There was a flicker of a smile from the woman. "You look well."

Again, Harry didn't have a reply to the small talk. He waited for the real reason to arise. The reason that Laurie Holland was standing in front of him.

She tried again. "How's Jamie?"

"You saw him a couple of weeks back didn't you? He told me. What did *you* think?"

Laurie seemed surprised that Jamie had mentioned the visit. "Oh, well, yes, he looked good. He's made a big lad eh?"

Harry shook his head. "Look Laurie, it was good of you to look the lad up after all this time, but you have to realise, that when a man is locked up like that, after all that has happened, he starts to read things into a visit that, well, that don't really exist. Do you know what I mean?"

"No . . . no Harry I don't."

Harry put down his pint. "Well I do. And I also know there is something else going on here. So, let me put this to you. You rang the prison for another VO. As Jamie can only have one visit every seven days, they tell you Jamie is booked. Obviously, that visitor would be me. You figure that as I don't own a car, I'll take the train. You check the timetable against my visit time. You wait at the station for me to walk out, and see me drop in the pub for a beer. After five minutes, you follow me inside and pretend that it's pure coincidence. Am I right?"

Laurie looked sheepish. "I suppose."

"I know I am Laurie, this stuff was my world for years. Now, what I don't know, is why you would do such a thing when you know where I live?"

Laurie removed her dark glasses to reveal two black eyes. "Because, I think Frankie may have me followed, and if he finds your house, you could be in danger."

Harry took hold of Laurie's chin and inspected her injuries. "Frankie did this?"

She nodded. Tears fell.

"Because you went to see Jamie?"

"Yes. And he knows Jamie's getting out soon. I don't know how he found out. I think someone in the prison is feeding him information. He's obsessed with Jamie; always has been. I'm scared for him, and you Harry. For both of you."

Harry sniffed and rolled his tongue over his teeth. Laurie had seen Jamie do exactly the same thing when he was angry.

"It's not the first time Frank has tried to find my house, is it?"

Laurie shook her head.

Harry sniffed again. "There's no wonder Frankie Verdi is obsessed with Jamie love, because deep down, so are you. I'd hazard you lie awake at night and wonder what life could have been like had you not chosen the path you are on. I'm right aren't I? But, look, it's of no consequence now . . ."

Laurie shook her head. "But it is Harry. It is of consequence, because Jamie and me are going to try again."

Harry was open-mouthed. Jamie hadn't mentioned this snippet of information, probably as he didn't want to hear Harry's opinion on the matter.

Harry was incredulous.

"Try again? So, you've left Frankie?"

"I'm scared to leave, Harry. But I'm . . ."

Harry cocked his head, another Jamie trait, when he wasn't all too sure he was being told the truth.

"Scared to leave the money too eh Laurie? You forget girl. I spent a long time in your company. I'll be honest with you, because I'm an honest man. When you broke my son's heart, I was glad. I was glad because he could never have lived up to your expectations. He could never have provided what you craved. I mean look at you now. Your sunglasses cost more than a marine's weekly wage. You were his one true love Laurie. But you were unfaithful and ungrateful, you were nothing but trouble . . . and you still are."

Harry drained his pint. "And now, well, it seems you have managed to drag us all down with you. You visit my son after all this time to raise his hopes. To raise his hopes and to gain his favour. I bet you told him you still loved him, didn't you? But really all you need Jamie for, is to do your dirty work, and you'll be off again. Off with the next bad guy with pots of money.

"You batted those lashes of yours, and he jumped, just as you knew he would. You know what he'll do to Verdi, the first time he sees those bruises. He's not even out of prison yet, and you are aiming to send him straight back there."

Laurie was close to tears. She knew she deserved all Harry had to give, but she had to make him understand. "It isn't like that Harry, I know what you're thinking, but I made a mistake . . ."

Harry pointed. "No, Jamie made a mistake, ever getting with you in the first place. Now just do me one favour Laurie . . . leave him be eh?"

Laurie watched the old soldier stride out of the door. She wanted to say he was wrong, wanted to tell him that she really did love his son, but he wouldn't believe her.

Who could blame him after all she'd done? Harry wanted to protect his only kin, and that was understandable. Laurie wanted to protect him too, and Harry. That's the reason she'd taken the beating. Somehow, Frankie had found out about the Walton visit and once again was desperate for Harry's address.

All she could hope for, is that with time, Harry would come around, forgive her and accept that she really did love Jamie.

*

That same evening, Laurie examined her bruises as she sat at her dressing table mirror. Frankie stood behind, watching her attempts to cover them with make-up.

He knelt behind her and wrapped his arms around her waist.

"Where did you go today?" he asked. A hint of accusation somewhere in his tone.

"The bank," she said, truthfully, as she'd deposited a large sum of cash in her newly opened offshore account, before visiting Harry.

Frankie looked at her damaged face.

"You know I hate to hurt you, don't you?"

Laurie didn't answer. She wanted to move his arms, but it would only make further trouble.

"It's just that you make me so angry sometimes."

Frankie moved his hands inside Laurie's dressing gown. They were cold against her warm skin.

"I mean, I just can't have you seeing that soldier boy. And now, well, when he comes out, I'll have to make sure you never see him again."

Frankie cupped her breast and squeezed it just a little too hard.

Laurie knew what was coming.

"Don't Frank. I have to get ready. I have to open the club."

Verdi nibbled her earlobe. He whispered. "Come on babe, we can work this out. You don't need that soldier boy. And me and Maisy are over, finished. I told her as much. We're the team, the team that built all this."

Laurie squirmed. "Is that why you stink of her Frank? Is that why I smell her all over you?"

Verdi held onto her, in no mood to set her free, his other hand now reaching between her thighs.

"Please Frank, don't."

Verdi's tone changed. Instantly all attempts at romance discarded, the quiet whisper suddenly surplus to his requirements. Here, was the true, sinister, insistent Frankie, the unrelenting controlling Frankie, the man of violence. He pushed his hand further upward, probing with his fingers.

"You live in my house, you eat my fucking food and drink my fucking booze. You drive the car I paid for and wear the clothes that I work for . . ."

Laurie dropped her make-up brush and grabbed his hand, but Frank was too strong.

". . . And if I want to fuck you . . ." Verdi released her breast and grabbed her long locks, dragging her from her seat to the floor.

He fell on her, grabbing at his fly to release his manhood. ". . . I fucking well will."

Laurie didn't struggle, just as she'd learned not to struggle as a young girl on those awful nights when her mother had brought grown men to her.

Now, twelve years on, as Frankie humped and grunted on top of her, racing toward his orgasm, she lay there once again. Like a rag doll thrown from a pram.

*

Laurie shook with fear, with resentment, with disgust. Her hands trembled as she pulled herself to her seat.

She went back to applying her make-up as if nothing had happened. Forcing herself not to cry, to show weakness to the man she hated.

Verdi sat on the bed sweating.

She eyed him in the mirror. Her voice was flat calm.

"You need to let me go Frank," she breathed. "You need to let me go, or kill me . . . or I swear, I'll kill you."

*

The office of Toast was hot and humid.

No windows to open, no air conditioning. Not built for the summer months. Frankie sat in front of the CCTV monitors, flicking through the cameras in no particular order. He was bored.

Bored with Maisy, bored with Laurie, bored with, well, just about everything.

He needed a holiday, some sun on his back, some fresh pussy to play with, away from the prying eyes of the press.

There was no doubt he had the money. His restaurants almost ran themselves, his managers so terrified of him, they wouldn't dare take their foot off the gas. Laurie looked after Toast, and Joe Madden had turned out to be a diamond when it came to the darker side of the business.

So why not go? Thailand maybe. He'd heard all the stories of the whores there. They'd do anything for a couple of dollars. Pretty young things who did as they were told. Just his type.

He flicked on the camera for the main bar.

Laurie leaned on one corner, still wearing her dark glasses. She took a long drink from her glass and looked unsteady on her feet. Not a good advert for his business.

He zoomed in on her image. She was a fine-looking woman, no doubt. But she wanted what Frankie couldn't or didn't want to give. Marriage, kids, normality. A recipe for a lifetime of tedium.

It was as he examined Laurie, that he noticed that she'd left her bag on the table alongside the monitors.

Frankie looked at it for a moment, then stood, feeling an irresistible urge to open it.

Inside, he found all the things he would have expected

to find. Her purse, keys, lipstick, tissues, two spare tampons; a couple of old receipts.

Then he noticed that the bag had a centre compartment. It was zipped closed.

Frankie took a glance at the screen. Laurie was ordering another; not going anywhere soon.

He furtively opened the centre compartment to find a bank book and other papers from NatWest Bank. His company, and to his knowledge, Laurie, banked with TSB.

He instantly felt his stomach churn. Something wasn't right. He slowly opened the book with shaking hands. The account holder's name was printed on the first page, together with the account number and sort code. "*Laurie Marie Holland 24433567 20-30-19*".

He turned the page.

The book showed regular weekly deposits of £500. Every Friday since before Christmas, Laurie had been paying in the same amount in cash. The current balance was £15,000.

Frankie noticed the book was shaking as much as his hands. His stomach now in knots. Bile filled his throat.

She wouldn't, would she? Would she dare steal from me? Steal from Frankie Verdi? If so, why? Well there was only one reason for that. She was planning to run away, to run away with that fucking fag soldier boy, the one who would be out of jail in a matter of weeks. Well, she wouldn't get far on fifteen grand, would she?

Frankie examined the other papers stuffed into the

pocket alongside the bank book. One was a letter, headed *"The Bank of Jersey"*.

Laurie had an offshore account. It showed an opening balance of £20,000, paid in just this morning.

Now you could go a lot further with thirty-five.

Frankie thought his head would explode.

He strode around the office, spittle forming at the corners of his mouth, unable to control his rage. He lashed out at the furniture, sending chairs tumbling, turning over desks, files flew through the air, paper covered the floor.

Sweating, he stopped dead in his tracks, a light flickering in his head.

Frankie rooted underneath the piles of paper, and found a desk phone he had thrown across the room, checked for a tone, and dialled the main bar.

Head barman, David Reece, answered almost immediately.

"Davey boy . . . Frankie here. I see that my dear Laurie is having a few tonight."

"Erm, well yes boss, looks like it."

"Don't worry son, it ain't a problem, she's just had some bad news is all. Just make sure when you serve her refills, that they are doubles from now on eh? On me."

Frankie could tell that Reece wasn't sure about his orders, but he wasn't going to argue with Frankie. He valued his job. And his kneecaps.

"No problem boss," he answered.

Frankie, then dialled the VIP area. Tony Thompson picked up the phone. He sounded high as a kite.

"Who's calling the Golden Shot?" he shouted.

"Tony . . . Frankie here . . . get your arse to the office now, and bring Eddie and Joe with you."

Tony was quiet for a second as he took in Frankie's tone. "Oh, okay Frank, I'll get them now."

The three men stepped into the mess that was the back office. Eddie scanned the room and dared comment.

"Been having a smashing time Frank?"

Frankie's eyes shone like polished black marbles. Sweat formed on his top lip.

"Don't be fuckin' funny Eddie. This is no laughing matter. Find a chair and sit the fuck down . . . all of you."

Moments later the three men sat in silence awaiting Frankie's obviously serious message.

"We have a fucking dirty thief amongst us boys," he began. "A dirty thieving whore, stealing our hard-earned cash, so she can run off with her fag soldier boyfriend."

Frankie scanned the faces of his three comrades in arms. All looked blank.

Verdi held up Laurie's bank book and the letter from the Jersey bank.

"Thirty-five fucking grand boys. Thirty-five grand, in just eight months."

A light came on in Joe Madden's head. "You're talking about your Laurie ain't yer Frank?"

Verdie curled his lip. "You bet your fucking arse, I'm talking about my dear Laurie."

Frankie stood and prowled about.

"After all I've fucking done for the bitch . . . she's stealing from me, so she can run away with the soldier boy."

Madden nodded. "You mean the one who gave me the kicking on opening night, yeah?"

"One and the same Joseph," pointed Frank.

Tony scratched his head. "What we going to do, Frank?"

Verdi rooted in Laurie's handbag, found her car keys and threw them at Joe Madden. "Go get her motor from the house Joe, and bring it here to the club. Eddie, Tony . . . stay here."

*

Joe delivered the car to the front of the club, locked it, slipped by the door staff and over to Tony Thompson who was waiting in the foyer. Tony held out a massive hand. Joe handed him the keys for the Golf, and wandered into the VIP area.

Strangely, he found himself alone. That said, he didn't want, or need to know any more than he already suspected. He ordered himself a beer, and watched the main bar.

Laurie was still there. She looked dishevelled, unlike her normal professional self. As she downed another Jack and Coke, Tony appeared, took her firmly by the arm and went to lead her away.

Laurie appeared reluctant, and there were words exchanged that Joe couldn't make out. But from Tony's body language, he seemed conciliatory rather than aggressive. Even so, it didn't look good.

Joe took a long drink from his pint. Left more than half on the table and made to leave. He said a little prayer to himself. Thankful he'd remembered to put on gloves before he'd touched Laurie Holland's car.

Tony held onto Laurie as she negotiated the steps of the club.

She was so drunk, the fact her car was waiting outside didn't register in her muddled brain. Tony opened the passenger door and made a big show to the doormen.

"Come on Laurie," he said in a stage whisper. "Let's get you home eh?"

The two doormen sniggered, half at Laurie's condition, and half at the fact that Tony had been given the thankless task of taking the boss' drunken girlfriend home.

Tony gave the two men a hapless look and shrugged his shoulders.

One gave him the thumbs up.

As Tony pulled away, Laurie slumped forward in her seat, close to unconsciousness. She mumbled something about a taxi.

Tony ignored her. He had a job to do.

Before he had reached Preston's ring road, Laurie was asleep. He checked the rear-view mirror. Eddie was behind in an unregistered and untraceable car he'd bought cash, from the auctions.

All going to plan so far.

Rather than take the A6 toward Broughton and Frankie's

house, Tony made for the M6 turning south one junction, then taking the M61.

Again, one junction.

Another left, then another half a mile of A road before hanging a right and starting the steep climb toward Rivington Pike and Winter Hill, the tallest peak of the West Pennine Moors.

Whether it was the twisting country lanes, the climb, or just the fact that something had recorded in Laurie's subconscious, Tony didn't know, but she woke suddenly and peered out of the windscreen.

"Where are we Tony?" she slurred.

"On our way to your house Laurie."

She turned down the corners of her mouth and did her best to focus on the road ahead.

"This isn't the way home."

"Yeah," bluffed Tony, hoping he could keep the false-hood going for a little while longer. "It is, I'm just taking a short cut."

Laurie was coming around, her head clearing by the second.

She turned and eyed the man she'd known since a teen. "What's going on Tone? What are you up to?"

Tony slammed on the brakes. The German car slewed left, then right. Laurie held onto her seat to steady herself.

Sensing real danger, the moment the car came to a halt, she made a grab for the door.

She was way too slow.

Tony reached out with his left hand and grabbed her

hair, snapping her head violently backwards. He twisted his body in his seat and slammed his massive right fist into Laurie's face. Once, twice, three times.

There was blood, lots of blood. It was splattered up his forearm, on his shirt, his cheeks.

He examined Laurie's mangled features. She rasped short breaths through her mouth, her nose badly broken.

Tony shook his head. "Oh, look now, why'd you go and make me do that?"

He pushed the car into gear and resumed the climb toward Laurie Holland's final destination.

*

Eddie William's unrequited love for Frankie Verdi had always ensured his quiet hatred of Laurie Holland. He knew, of course, that even if Laurie hadn't been around, his relationship with Frank would still have remained that as one of friends. Yet he couldn't hide his pleasure at seeing the woman in the position she was.

Tony had parked the Golf in a sweeping layby that was a popular spot for sightseers as it overlooked the whole of the moor. It was also equally popular with climbers as it boasted a sheer two hundred feet drop directly onto jagged rocks.

Eddie wandered over to the edge of what was essentially a cliff and looked down. "Shame about the motor. It took me ages to find one in such good order."

Tony was busy pulling Laurie from the passenger seat

and sitting her in the driver's side. Eddie wandered over and examined her ruined features.

"Fucking hell Tone, you gave her a good slap there pal."

"She woke up Ed, was about to start kicking off like."

Eddie shrugged, "Whatever . . . right start her up."

Tony leaned into the car and turned the key. The Golf fired first time.

Eddie pointed, "Handbrake off."

Again, Tony obliged.

"Now," said Eddie. "You're going to have to ram it into first without pushing the clutch, so give the stick a good shove."

On Tony's second attempt the car lurched forward sending it toward the edge of the precipice. Eddie ran over and slammed the driver's door shut.

The car trundled along, over the rough ground, but as its front drive wheels went over the edge of the cliff, it stopped, stuck on the ledge, engine revving, the bonnet dangling precariously in mid-air.

"For fuck's sake," spat Eddie. "Fucking front-wheel drives. Come on Tone. We'll have to shove her over."

Both men leaned into the rear of the car. There was a grating sound as the exhaust scraped over the rocky edge, then, moments later, the weight of the engine see-sawed the car over.

The air was suddenly silent.

The cabriolet landed nose first with an almighty crash then teetered for a moment before falling on its roof.

Eddie checked his watch. "Come on Tone, still time for a beer."

*

Laurie knew she was dying.

Not because of the pain, but because there wasn't any. She couldn't feel anything, couldn't move. She was upside down. Something, she presumed the engine, had been pushed into the footwell and trapped her legs, but there was no sensation down there. There was no sensation anywhere below her neck.

The sun began to rise. It was going to be a beautiful day, it felt warm on her face, at least God had left her with something.

She began to cry. What had her mother used to say? "You've made your bed girl, so you better lie in it."

Well here she was, paying the price. Because that is what her mother really meant wasn't it? Pay the price for your actions, your deeds, good or bad.

Laurie hadn't been to church since Rose's funeral, so she figured praying was a little pointless. She'd been a bad girl, plain and simple. She'd put money and possessions above love, and this was the ultimate fee to pay.

She closed her eyes and tried to imagine Jamie's face, his smile, his eyes.

Then Laurie Holland took her final breath.

Detective Jim Hacker

It is a natural thing for a policeman to be inquisitive; not to accept what you are expected to believe to be true.

Instinctively, a cop should question everything. He must look beyond the obvious. Good coppers are just like that. I happen to believe you are born with it.

Sgt Gerry Smart was one such officer. For nineteen years, Gerry had worked traffic. Eleven of those on Lancashire's motorway network.

Now, just as it takes a certain type of policeman to become a detective, the same must be said for motorway coppers.

Gerry Smart would tell you that the motorways are the safest roads in the country. But he would also tell you that when it goes wrong on there, it usually means fatalities.

Sgt Smart was one of Lancashire's most experienced road traffic accident investigators.

I sat alongside him in Headquarters canteen. He'd been investigating Laurie Holland's fatal accident, and I'd asked to meet with him, as my team had been looking at her death from a completely different angle.

Too many people who came into contact with Frankie Verdi had ended up dead.

I too was blessed with that natural inquisitiveness, that suspicion, distrust, scepticism even, especially when it had anything to do with The Three Dogs.

Gerry was none too happy with Laurie's "accident" either.

Firstly, just as any good detective would, he looked at what we were meant to believe to be true.

Allegedly, Frankie Verdi had organised for Laurie Holland to be driven home in her car, by Tony Thompson as she had been drinking heavily after receiving some "bad news". Thompson had been followed in another vehicle, driven by Eddie Williams who had brought Thompson back to the club a short time later.

Once Laurie Holland was safely at her home address, we were asked to believe that for reasons unknown, she then re-entered her car, with four times the legal limit of alcohol in her bloodstream, and drove it to a secluded beauty spot on the West Pennine Moors.

It is then supposed, that she lost control of her vehicle, which plunged over a precipice. As a result, Laurie suffered catastrophic and, subsequently, fatal injuries.

Armed with this information, Gerry then examined the scene of the crash and Laurie's VW Golf Cabriolet.

He found that the car was well maintained and had no mechanical issues at the time of the accident.

There were no brake or steering faults.

There were no skid marks at the scene, either on the road or the layby where the car had exited.

The car had fallen within feet of the cliff face.

The car was in first gear when it crashed.

There was damage to the underside of the VW,

consistent with the vehicle being stuck on the ledge at the top of the cliff prior to it falling.

Gerry had only two possible conclusions.

Laurie Holland had slowly and deliberately driven off the cliff and, with the car stuck, rocking on the edge, somehow managed to pivot her VW over so she could end it all. That, or foul play was at work.

That afternoon, I sent two of my detectives to recover the CCTV footage for the night in question from both Toast nightclub, and Frankie Verdi's home address.

Both tapes had been wiped.

By the time I was leaving my office for the day, Lancashire's Fingerprint Department had confirmed that the palm-prints of Tony Thompson and Eddie Williams were present on the rear of the VW and were consistent with the owners having pushed the vehicle with both hands.

Foul play indeed.

But Eddie had sold the car to Frankie, and Tony had driven the car that night, so both had reasons to have their prints all over the car, no matter how suspicious the placings.

Once again, despite the mountain of circumstantial evidence, we were stymied.

Out of sheer frustration, I made a call that I knew I really should not.

Chapter Twenty-Five

Harry Strange shook as he read, and re-read the evening newspaper. A picture of Laurie Holland's mangled car, lying on its roof at the bottom of a ravine, sat alongside a shot of the girl herself, looking beautiful, the picture of health.

Harry had bought the paper after receiving a call from Jim Hacker. He shook his head and threw it to the floor.

Laurie may have been many things, but she didn't deserve to die.

It had been years since Harry had felt so angry.

Angry with himself as much as anything else.

He had berated Laurie Holland, not given her a second chance. He, a Christian man, should have done the right thing. Everyone makes mistakes, and she had admitted hers to him and to Jamie. She had taken a beating to keep him safe from the clutches of Frankie Verdi. Now, she had lost her life, and Jamie, his chance of love.

Adrenaline coursed through him, his fury threatening to bubble up to the surface at any moment. His mind worked overtime.

*

After seeing Laurie Holland in The Railway pub, Harry had walked all the way home. He'd needed to clear his mind, take in what Laurie had told him.

He'd strolled past Toast, the club still locked and bolted, awaiting its first revellers. Awaiting Frankie Verdi.

Harry had known Frankie's parents well. He and Rose had visited the couple's small eatery every Friday night for years. Frankie had been a gangly teenager then, waiting tables and washing up for pocket money. The friendship between Harry and the Verdi family had ensured the Verdi's presence at Rose's funeral and wake. And that, in turn, had introduced Laurie to Frankie.

The rest, as they say, is history.

Verdi had become obsessed with Jamie, even before he'd found out Laurie had visited him in jail. Harry had no idea why, but he knew what men like Frankie, Eddie and Tony were capable of. He'd heard all the gossip about the so-called Three Dogs gang; read the press reports of drug dealing, money laundering and murder.

It hadn't been enough that Frankie had taken Laurie

from his son. For some reason, known only to Verdi himself, he wanted to go to war with Jamie.

Harry mused that, once Jamie found out about Laurie's death, Verdi may have achieved his goal.

Harry truly believed The Three Dogs had killed Laurie Holland.

His good friend Jim Hacker had phoned him and said as much.

Yet he'd also intimated that, once again, the police didn't have enough evidence to arrest Verdi, Williams or Thompson, let alone obtain a conviction.

Jim Hacker was a good family man, and a good friend. So now, for Laurie, for Jamie, and for Jim, it was time to restore the balance. To restore order.

*

Durham jail nestled inside the city walls. Walking distance from the station. Harry Strange sat in a pub not a hundred yards from the prison gate.

Checking his watch, Harry downed his pint, found his visiting order in his jacket, and set off to see Richard Valance.

Durham is an ancient jail, yet Harry considered it smelled and sounded the same as Walton. He figured that probably every jail in the country held the same aromas and atmosphere. He also hoped, that he didn't end up on the other side of the gates any time soon.

Valance strode to Harry's table and looked like he'd

been eating the same diet as Jamie and lifting the same weights in the gym. The man was built like a wall. Yet whereas Jamie had kept his boyish good looks, Valance had suffered damage to his facial features during his obvious love of hand-to-hand combat. Indeed, Harry noticed recent pink scar tissue over Richard's left eye as he sat.

He nodded toward it. "Forget to duck Bird?" he said, holding out a hand.

The Aussie took it and shook firmly. "I walked into a door Harry."

"How's the door?"

"In the medical wing, I believe."

Harry smiled. "You look good . . . bit pale, same as Jamie, but still good."

Bird dropped the niceties. "Fuck me Harry, I'm so glad you came mate. I thought you'd never speak to me again after everything. You know, after what I did."

"You made an error of judgement in combat Richard, no more. Your mistake was not slotting the boy before he reached the corner of the alley."

Valance managed a half smile, but it soon disappeared and he shook his head ruefully.

"I lost the plot Harry. I'd never been shot at before. I was so fucking wired mate, the red mist was on me, I just wanted to kill the little bastard. I admit it. Thing was, the unforgivable thing, I dropped Jamie in it big style. I should've just taken the rap and had done with it."

Harry held up a hand. "We are where we are Bird. You will be out in a couple of days, and so will my boy. Both of you are alive, fit and well. You've both lost the careers you loved and you've both spent time in jail. As far as I'm concerned, the slate is clean. You've paid your dues. If I were the Irishman's father, I'd not be so kind, but I'm not. I'm Jamie's, and that's that."

"Well I can't say how much I appreciate that coming from you Harry. I just hope Jamie feels the same."

"I reckon he does. He owed you a great debt I believe. Maybe you should just consider that debt repaid."

Bird leaned back in his seat. "That's as maybe, but you ain't come all the way to Durham to tell me you love me Harry. I ain't that daft . . . So come on, why are you here?"

Harry considered his next words carefully.

"Laurie Holland," he said.

Valance shrugged. "Jamie's ex-bird? The blonde, the one from the club?"

"One and the same."

"What about her?"

"She's dead . . . murdered by Frankie Verdi and friends."

"Fuck me Harry, yeah . . . Verdi, he's the one who tried to get me and Jamie followed that night when we was home on leave."

Harry nodded. "Well the coppers know it was them that killed her. They tried to make it look like an accident, but it wasn't. I have a good friend in the force, he tells me it was them, but there's not enough proof."

"Jeez, does Jamie know? He'll be gutted."

Harry shook his head.

"Not yet. I have that job to do tomorrow. See, to make matters worse, Laurie went to see him a week or two back. They'd made up, were going to give it a go again. Seems Frankie found out and gave Laurie a beating. Then she came to me, tried to warn me that Frank was out gunning for Jamie and me. That night, something else must have happened and Frank had her killed."

Bird looked about him and lowered his voice. "You know you ain't going to be able to stop Jamie from topping this Verdi bloke eh?"

Harry locked eyes with Richard Valance.

"We need to take all three Bird."

The big Aussie stretched out a huge hand. "I wouldn't miss it for the world Harry."

Chapter Twenty-Six

Frankie sat on a stool in his kitchen drinking black coffee. Sitting opposite, was his long-time ally and legal representative Trevor Dundonald.

James rarely gave Frank bad news, but on this particular morning, he had no choice.

"What do you mean I can't get my fucking cash back?" spat Verdi.

"Exactly that, Frank. That money forms part of Laurie's estate, and in her last will and testament, made just days before her death, she left any money in her accounts to Jamie Strange."

Frankie almost exploded, just at the sound of Jamie's name.

"Come on Trevor, what do I fuckin' pay you for eh? I mean, she was obviously stealing from me. Not to mention, mentally unstable. Even the coroner said that she topped herself 'cos she had depression."

Dundonald had first sat opposite Frankie in a police cell back in 1976. Back then, he'd been a scruffy urchin, his school blazer covered in the blood of another schoolboy. He hadn't been able to help Verdi that day either. However, since then, there had been nothing but a string of victories. Frankie's exploits had ensured Trevor and his partners had become rather wealthy over the years. The bottom line was he knew Frankie about as well as Frank knew himself.

Frank, just like many wealthy men, didn't like being told "no".

Dundonald corrected his client.

"The coroner's verdict was accidental death, Frank. If you'd bothered to attend, you would have known that. His presumption, was that Laurie had let the car roll forward by accident. And although, he did comment that she may have been depressed prior to the accident, that doesn't mean she was mentally unstable at the time she made her will. Indeed, I would suggest that her solicitor, who witnessed the document, would argue fervently against that."

"Well what about the fact that the money was nicked then? What about that?"

Trevor took a sip of coffee and raised his eyebrows. "Do you really want to release your books to the police Frank? I mean, they are already crawling all over the fact that you had thirty grand in the safe when they searched Toast the last time. I'm sorry, but there is just no way of recovering your money."

Frankie slammed down his cup, causing Trevor to jump.

"Well I expect you to fucking find a way Trevor. That's why you are on such a fucking big retainer isn't it?"

The solicitor quietly put down his own cup. "The only way to get your money Frank, is to get it back from Jamie Strange once he collects it."

A wry smile came over Frankie's face. He pointed a finger. "Now that's what I pay you for Trev my old son. That is what I pay you for."

Chapter Twenty-Seven

It had been three weeks. Three weeks since Tony Thompson and Eddie Williams had left Laurie to die slowly in her car.

Jamie Strange had attended the coroner's hearing, listened to all the testimonies, and armed with evidence of his own, had come to his own conclusion.

Laurie had been murdered, and today, he would attend her funeral. Today, he would look her murderers in the eye.

*

Jamie had been in a dark place ever since Harry had broken the news of Laurie's death to him. He had taken in the information in silence before indicating to the guards that he wished to return to his cell. Harry knew his son's heart was broken all over again. He also knew what was to come on his release.

Harry and Bird were already dressed in their best suits. Jamie sat on the sofa and polished his shoes.

His father looked down at his son. "You'll rub the leather off them if you carry on," he said, doing his best to lighten the mood.

Jamie gave a thin smile and pulled the now immaculate brogues onto his feet. He then found his jacket, slipped his arms into it and turned to Bird.

"No matter what those Dogs do today, we keep our heads Bird, okay? I don't want Laurie's service ruined."

Harry strode to the door.

"We have our plan lads, and we stick to it. Come on, let's pay our respects."

*

It didn't seem right to Jamie that the sun shone. It didn't seem right that the birds sang. Even though it was the height of summer, it still didn't seem appropriate.

Jamie walked the gravel path of the graveyard toward the assembled mourners, listening to the stones crunch under his feet. For a moment, he was back at his mother's burial, and remembered how he'd trod the same path, only to find Laurie flirting with Frankie Verdi.

Richard Valance strode to his left, his father to his right, their jackets flapping open in the gentle breeze. The words of the priest carrying on it.

Jamie could see Frankie.

Dressed in his black suit, white shirt, black tie, his

317

trademark, funeral or not. Thompson stood to his left, Williams and Joe Madden to his right. All had their heads bowed, playing the part of the bereaved.

Jamie wanted to tear them apart with his bare hands, but this was not the time or the place for violence.

They reached the graveside just in time for the last prayers. As the priest threw a handful of soil down into the grave, Frankie looked up.

There was a hint of shock, before his eyes burned into Jamie's. Jamie didn't show any fear, because he didn't feel any. He held Frank's gaze, the two men, like a pair of boxers eyeing each other up before the first bell, the priest's final words lost in a haze of viciousness, an atmosphere of mutual hatred.

Jamie heard the mourners mutter the word "Amen", breaking the spell. He stepped forward and dropped a single red rose onto Laurie's coffin.

"Goodbye my love," he whispered.

Then, turning to his father, he said, "Did you get a good look at all three?"

Harry glared at Verdi, Williams and Thompson, and nodded. "Oh yes," he said. "I've seen enough scum for one day."

As Harry, Jamie and Bird turned to leave, there was the sound of a scuffle behind them. Eddie and Tony were holding onto Frank for grim death, his face contorted in rage.

Unable to prise himself from the grip of his two

fellow gang members, Frankie began to shout out in frustration.

"You're fuckin' dead soldier boy. You hear me? Dead. I'll fucking kill you myself, and your old man, you hear? Are you listening you fucker?"

Jamie, Harry and Bird strolled along the gravel toward their car. Harry smiled and turned to his son. "Perfect," he said. "Just perfect."

Chapter Twenty-Eight

Frankie was inconsolable.

He sat alone in the VIP area of Toast, drinking straight scotch and snorting cocaine. Not even Tony and Eddie wanted to be close to him.

The club had been especially opened for Laurie's wake, and dozens of so-called mourners and well-wishers took advantage of the free food and booze, milling around the main bar, believing Frankie's exile and temper to be born out of grief rather than anger.

Of course, none of the mourners knew Laurie too well. Frank had seen to that. Laurie hadn't been allowed friends. There was the odd old school chum, a couple of folk from Laurie's first job at the hairdressers on Ribbleton Lane, but no one of consequence. No one from outside the circle.

Finally, Frank staggered from his private den, bumping

into guests too scared to say anything about their spilled drinks or stained clothes.

Finding Eddie and Joe Madden leaning against the DJ booth, he clinked his glass with both men.

"Good fucking riddance to the thieving bitch, I say."

Eddie furrowed his brow. "Come on Frank, I know you're pissed off, but keep it down a bit eh? Just play the game for an hour or two and it will all be over."

Frankie bared his teeth, the drugs and whiskey talking. "Don't tell me what to do, you fuckin' queer."

Eddie went instantly pale. "What you call me Frank?"

Verdi was so drunk he almost fell over. He grabbed onto a nearby speaker for support. "You think I ain't known all these years Eddie? You think I'm fucking blind?"

Eddie was close to smashing Frankie in the face. Joe shuffled from foot to foot, unsure what to do, which side to fall on.

"Come on lads," he managed. "No need for this eh? It's the drink talking here innit?"

Eddie squared up. "Take that back Frank, or me and you are gonna have a tear-up here and now, an' I'll show you who's fucking queer. God help me, I'll smash you up good."

Frankie laughed in Eddie's face. "Come on Ed, it's a joke eh? Just pulling your leg that's all, just a laugh."

Eddie looked around for potential witnesses to Frank's outburst. Happy no one else had been party to it, he hissed. "Very funny Frank. But don't ever call me that name again, or you won't be laughing next time yeah?"

Frank pulled a bag of coke from his pocket and stuck his car key into the powder. "Aw fuck it Eddie, I'm sorry pal, come on, let's do a key each eh? Take the edge off."

Eddie leaned in, sniffed the powder from the end of the key and wiped his nose. Frank offered the same to Joe, who followed suit.

Frank took the last snort and put the drug away.

"Listen lads, I want that soldier boy sorted . . . and soon."

"Shouldn't be a problem," said Joe.

Frankie sneered. "You didn't do too well the last time, eh Joe?"

Madden looked a little hurt. "Well it was two on one Frank, come on."

Eddie found his own bag of charlie and began to chop out a line on the DJ booth.

"I say we find where his dad lives, and torch the place."

Eddie took the line and awaited the hit. He blew out his cheeks as his heart rate went through the roof. "Somebody must know where the gaff is, and we might strike lucky and get all three of them fuckers in one go."

Frankie was about to comment when Cheryl Greenwood wandered over, her pregnancy now obvious.

"All right lads . . . how you bearing up Frankie? Must be hard for you today mate, eh?"

Frankie looked down his nose. Annoyed at the interruption. "I'm doing okay Chez . . . we was just saying how, if it weren't for that soldier boy, we reckon that Laurie would still be here. We think it was him that turned her head, got her all confused."

Cheryl nodded. "You might be right there, Frank. That said, he was always a nice quiet lad when I knew him like."

Frankie darkened. "You knew him?"

Cheryl took a step away. "Yeah Frank, but only like you lot did. He was at our school eh?"

Frank pulled out his coke bag again and started to chop. "I don't remember the fucker myself."

"Yeah," said Cheryl. "Probably because he was so quiet. Nice lad, lived on the Greenlands estate."

Frankie took his line and wiped the residue with his finger. The hit was instantaneous, the drug counteracting the alcohol in his system, clearing his head. He bristled with venom, his voice no more than a murmur, yet all knew it could break into a tumultuous tirade at any moment and become an outpouring of bitter frustration.

"Are you telling me you know where the fucker lives?"

Cheryl looked about her. Where was Tony when she needed him? Why did she have to open her stupid mouth? How many times had Tony told her? Don't get involved in The Three Dogs stuff. Leave Frankie and Eddie be.

"I . . . I'm not too sure exactly Frank . . . I mean it was a long time ago like. Erm . . ."

Frank looked for witnesses, saw none and grabbed Cheryl by the arm, causing her to cry out.

"Listen to me you little slut. Just because you're Tony's bird now, don't think you can keep things from me. You ain't nothing . . . understand? You're just the same as your slag mother. I don't know what Tony's thinking taking up with you. You must be good for something though eh?"

Frankie winked at Eddie and Joe, and tugged harder on Cheryl's arm.

His eyes flashed, full of evil, bursting with wickedness. "You used to be fun Chez, you were good for that all right. Remember when I used to fuck you behind the Lion? Up against the wall? You loved it eh? Do anything for a dab of whizz you would. Eddie is testament to that ain't he? That's how you ended up with his kid."

Cheryl's eyes widened in a mixture of shock, fear and anger. How did Frankie know? She and Tony had kept it so quiet.

Frankie didn't even notice Cheryl's quandary.

"Now," he spat. "Do you know where this fucking soldier boy lives, or not?"

Cheryl's own temper was coming to the boil, her fury overcoming her anxiety. She grabbed Frankie's hand and prized herself away from his grip. She looked across to Eddie, he had a smug grin on his face. She felt suddenly dirty.

Straightening herself, she did her best to regain her composure.

"I know what I was back then Frank, but I'm not the same girl now. I was young and stupid. Stupid enough to get involved with you."

Cheryl turned on her heels and put distance between her and Verdi.

"Laurie was right about you. You are a mean bastard Frankie Verdi . . . and there was no need to treat me like that." She pointed from a safe distance. "No need at all. No wonder Laurie wanted away from you. Just wait till I tell my Tony what you just did. You won't be fucking laughing then."

Frank turned to Joe Madden. "Don't worry, she won't say a fuckin' word. Go find out what she knows about this soldier boy." He slapped him on the back and laughed again. "You're good with whores."

Chapter Twenty-Nine

Joe Madden sat in his car, watching the front door of 11 Greenlands Terrace.

The older bloke, that had been at Laurie's funeral, had been in and out a couple of times. Once to buy his morning paper, and once to buy a bag of groceries.

However, there was no sign of Jamie Strange or his flat-nosed Aussie mate.

Joe was bored shitless. He was not cut out for observation duties. That said, he wasn't cut out for killing either.

He didn't mind dishing out a bit of pain to the odd wayward dealer or late payer, but murder? No way. Joe knew his limits. His job was to watch the house, and as soon as the soldier boy was confirmed inside, to ring Frankie at the club.

End of.

*

Jamie Strange climbed the stairs to the landing and walked into his father's bedroom at the front of the house. He opened the curtains and stood at the window looking out on the street below.

Harry shouted from the lounge downstairs. "He seen you yet?"

"Oh yeah," said Jamie. "He's seen me all right, he's scuttling off to the phone box right now."

"Has Bird seen him?"

Richard Valance was sitting two cars back from Joe Madden's.

Jamie turned on his walkie-talkie. It was only a cheap model from the electronics shop in town, but good for a couple of hundred yards.

"You there, Birdman."

"Roger, he's dropping the dime as we speak Strange Brew."

"Nice one. Don't get too comfy there pal. I reckon we'll have company shortly."

"I'm on it Strange Brew, you and Harry get your kit sorted. I reckon we're in for a lively night."

Jamie dropped back down the stairs and into the kitchen. Harry had already pre-empted Bird's request, and was laying out their meagre arsenal on the table. Claw hammers, crowbars, axes, anything he could find in his garden shed. Even though they would all wear gloves, Harry had taped the handles of each of the tools in order to hamper any fingerprint evidence should they get torn or lost.

Alongside the almost medieval array, were the gloves, two sets of black coveralls and two black balaclavas.

Bird was already kitted up, and had a pickaxe handle and a meat cleaver for company in his car.

"I wish we had a couple of Brownings to go along with that lot, Dad," said Jamie, pulling on his coveralls. "I reckon Frankie will be tooled up."

Harry picked up a claw hammer and tested it for weight. "We have to make the best of what we have son. Let's kit up and get settled eh?"

*

The company didn't arrive until darkness fell, and it came in the shape of a red Audi Quattro, driven by Tony Thompson.

Jamie's radio crackled into life.

"Big Tony's on plot Strange Brew."

"Roger that. Any sign of Eddie or Frank?"

"No mate, just him."

Of course, Jamie, Harry and Bird had no way of knowing how many would come. They had planned and prepared for a possible full-on onslaught, yet one thing was for certain: one way or another, this would all be settled tonight.

Valance watched as Thompson walked around to the rear of his car and opened the boot.

He pulled out a large petrol can and a bunch of rags; set them on the floor and took a long look at number 11 Greenlands Terrace.

Bird was on the radio in an instant. "Fuck me Strange Brew, he's only planning to torch the house."

Jamie was about to instruct Bird to take Tony in the street, before Harry grabbed the comms unit and stopped him.

"Let him come," he said. "Tell Bird to get in close as he starts the fire. And the moment my front door opens, give the boy a quick shove in the back."

Jamie looked at his dad. Calm, collected and in charge. He'd always known Harry had seen a lot of combat. He'd always known he'd had to kill many of his opponents, both overtly and covertly, but he'd never dreamed he would be working alongside his father this way.

"You're the boss, Dad," he said, and relayed the message.

Harry smiled. He hadn't felt so alive in years. "Now, go get a couple of blankets off the bed and get them soaking in the sink . . . quick sharp."

Bird, slumped down in his seat. He watched as Tony dowsed the rags in the petrol. Parked just two car lengths away, he could even smell the fuel. He'd no idea what Harry had in mind, but whatever it was, it was going to be hairy.

The street was quiet, half an hour to pub closing. The drinkers still drinking, the abstainers ready for bed.

Finally, Tony appeared happy with his work and strode off toward the house. Can in one hand, rags in the other.

Bird quietly opened his car door and crouched by the car.

Thompson was indeed a big guy in every way. Powerful, young and muscular. Bird selected his pickaxe handle as his preferred weapon and, using the garden hedges as cover, set off after him.

Harry strode down his hallway and stood to the left of the door, back to the wall, within reach of the handle.

He figured that Thompson would pour the accelerant through the letter box, then push a burning rag or two through to ignite the carpet beneath. He just hoped that the sets of coveralls he'd dug out from his time in Aden were still fireproof after all this time.

He forced himself to relax, but gripped the claw hammer in his right hand, ready to pounce.

Jamie stood at the end of the hallway holding the sodden blankets, awaiting his father's instructions.

The summer night was quiet, still, with no breeze to hide the slightest sound. Harry heard the latch on his gate open. He nodded at Jamie who depressed the pretzel on his Walkie Talkie twice to indicate to Bird, they were ready.

Tony Thompson set the petrol can down on Harry's front step and took another good look, up and down the street.

All quiet.

He pushed the letter box open with a gloved thumb

and wedged it with one of the petrol soaked rags. Then he lifted the can and began to pour fuel inside the home of Harry Strange.

Tony thought that the glug-glug noise the can made was loud enough to wake the dead, yet no one stirred.

Thompson smiled to himself. Once the soldier was burnt to a crisp, then Frank would be happy again, and they could all get back to how things used to be.

He found his Zippo and lit it, touched the flame to a second rag and stuffed the burning cloth through the door.

The rag dropped to the carpet. Instantly, there was a *whoomph* as the petrol fumes ignited and the subsequent fire sucked air from the hallway to feed itself.

Harry grabbed at the handle and swung his front door open.

Thompson stood rooted on Harry's doorstep, plainly shocked at the sight of two men, standing in the hall, knee deep in flames.

Right on cue, Bird arrived behind Thompson and gave him an almighty shove in the back.

Tony couldn't steady himself and fell forward toward Harry and the fire. The old marine was quicker than anyone could have thought and grabbed Tony as he teetered, pulling him face down into the flames.

Thompson crashed to the floor and was instantly engulfed. His long curly locks instantly aflame. He began to scream as the fire ignited his shirt, he rolled on the petrol-drenched carpet in agony, the movement only soaking his clothing in more accelerant, feeding the flames, searing his skin, boiling his blood.

Harry stepped over, raised his hammer and brought it down on the back of Tony's head with all his might.

The boy was instantly quiet.

Jamie wrapped a blanket around the smouldering legs of his father's coveralls, then dropped a second onto the body of Tony Thompson extinguishing the fire.

"You okay Dad?" he asked, coughing through the smoke that now filled the hall.

Harry nodded. "Never better son. Now, you let me deal with this, take what kit you want from the kitchen, and get off through the back. You two know the script. Go and finish this. Make them fucker's pay lad."

Jamie held his father in his arms.

"I love you, Dad."

*

Eddie checked his watch.

"Tony should have been back by now."

Frankie eyed his own timepiece. "Maybe. Maybe he had to wait for the street to get quiet?"

Eddie shrugged his powerful shoulders and took a drink. Frankie had invited half a dozen women into the VIP area. They guzzled free Asti Spumante wine, laughed inanely and did nothing but annoy him.

One redhead insisted on sitting close to Eddie and

periodically rubbed his thigh. It was only a matter of time before she offered him more than a thigh-rub, so Eddie leaned in close, his lips touching the girl's ear. "Fuck off, slut," he whispered.

Red stood up, all indignant and offended, but it didn't last. Minutes later she was giving Frankie the same treatment.

Frankie got the charlie out and theatrically rolled up a fifty-pound note to snort it with. Red squealed with delight and her hand moved north to Frank's crotch.

The whole show made Eddie sick. Maybe it had been better when Laurie was around? At least it kept a lid on the number of tarts Frankie groped in an evening. He'd also noticed that, with no one to guide the staff, the club was already slipping away from the high standards that Laurie had insisted upon. He'd seen at least three guys wandering about in jeans, and one openly smoking a joint.

He needed to drag Frankie away from the redhead, and talk to him about appointing a new manager.

But first, he'd do a line or two himself.

*

Jamie and Bird had driven to Toast in a stolen Ford Granada. It was ten years old, rusting and smelled vaguely of sweaty feet. But it was big and quick, so would do just fine.

It was Harry who had selected the car, as his neighbour Kevin Jones had the identical model. It had been a simple task to copy Kev's number plates, and stick them on the stolen motor.

Should the cops randomly check the number, the old Ford would show it was Harry's kosher neighbour driving around town. The ploy wouldn't stand up to intimate inspection, but it was good enough for the boys' needs.

They pulled up just thirty yards from the front door of the club. People queued patiently awaiting entry, and it took Jamie back to the night he and Bird had visited the place. The opening night, when Laurie had looked so beautiful. When she and Frankie had argued, when Frankie had tried to have them followed.

Since that night, Verdi had made Laurie's life a misery, treated her like dirt, beaten her, and just as she had come back to Jamie, just as they had started to make plans, had taken her life. Well, it was time for vengeance, and it wasn't going to be pretty.

Bird pulled on his balaclava. Between his knees he gripped his pickaxe handle and meat cleaver. Jamie already had his mask in place and held a hammer in each fist.

The boys knew, that if this was to work, they would need maximum aggression, and give no quarter. They also knew, however, that innocent people were inside the club. People there simply enjoying a night out, people doing a job. And that made the task harder.

First, they had to take out the door staff. They needed a swift entry and exit and it was the lads on the door and the guys working the floor inside, that could slow them down, so they had to be dealt with first.

These guys would be handy lads, but they didn't deserve the hammer and meat-cleaver treatment, it had to be elbows, knees and feet, that did the required amount of damage.

The pair slipped from the car.

"You ready Bird?" asked Jamie.

"I ain't going to let you down a second time Strange Brew," answered Bird, and sprinted toward the door.

A split second before they reached the main entrance, some of the queueing public saw them and there was instantaneous panic.

The sight of two six-foot-three, sixteen stone, muscle-bound men, dressed in black coveralls, wearing balaclava masks and wielding hammers and meat-cleavers, spread instant terror.

The orderly line became a melee of confused, scared men and women who began to run about like headless chickens.

One of the guys on the door stepped forward to try and calm them, then turned to see the reason for the alarm in the crowd.

At that moment, he was met by Richard Valance in full flight. Bird lifted his elbow and smashed it into the man's jaw. The guy staggered and as Bird passed him, he swung the pickaxe handle in a downward arc, catching the guy in the right knee.

The bouncer fell to the floor, writhing in pain.

Jamie was powering up the steps to the foyer. The second doorman took one look at him and turned on his heels.

They were inside.

Running at full pelt, they barged into customers, sending people flying, glass breaking, people screaming.

Left turn.

More people, more shouts. Another bouncer, a big tall brute of a man.

Jamie headbutted him flush on the bridge of his nose and he went down.

Sensing something serious was happening, the DJ pulled the plug. This caused even greater panic and Jamie and Bird had to fight their way through a crowd determined to exit the club. It was like swimming upstream, but they were prepared for it.

Like a pair of rugby players locking up for a scrum, they powered forward heads down, thrusting, unstoppable.

Within thirty seconds of leaving the old tired Granada, they stood at the entrance to the VIP area of Toast, the town's "number one music and entertainment venue".

Tonight, there was to be a very different form of theatre.

The lone doorman standing guard at the VIP room was a pale, blonde guy with a ponytail.

Bird raised his cleaver and the guy sprinted off toward the exit, his blonde locks bouncing behind him.

"Let's go do this," shouted Jamie over the cacophony.

The pair burst into the tight space that was the VIP room.

Chesterfield sofas and plush armchairs only acted as obstacles, barring their way, preventing access to their targets.

Jamie kicked them aside, opening a path to their ultimate goal.

Frankie Verdi was sitting in a corner, head back, eyes closed. A skinny woman with red hair, kneeling in front of him, her head bobbing up and down at his crotch.

Eddie saw them first. He bawled at Frankie to get his shit together, but Verdi seemed too out of it to care.

Several other women who were scattered about the room started to scream and push toward the door.

Eddie picked up a stool and threw it at Bird.

The big Aussie simply batted it away and strode over toward the sharp-dressed gangster.

Eddie picked up a second stool, this time holding onto it, using it as a shield to protect himself from Bird's cleaver.

It was never going to be enough. Valance brought up his right foot, and simply kicked the stool from Eddie's hands.

Williams' eyes flashed with fear, but he knew he had no choice but to try and fight his way past the monster of a man in front of him. Dropping his head, he went for Bird with everything he had.

Valance swung the cleaver and caught Eddie, slicing open his shoulder. Williams tried desperately to get in close to his attacker and throw some punches into his torso, maybe grab the cleaver. Valance shrugged off the blows and raised the axe again, this time burying the weapon deep into Williams' back.

Eddie cried out as Bird shoved him back against the wall, to give him room to attack. Williams staggered, blood soaking through his suit jacket from the first blows. Bird took his time, calm, calculated. He knew exactly what he wanted to do and with his fourth strike, opened a massive wound in Eddie's neck.

Williams fell backwards and slid down the wall to the floor, holding his throat, blood pouring through his fingers, and painting a grotesque mural behind him.

He looked about, confused, almost childlike.

Finally, he seemed to notice the masked man who was brandishing the cleaver high above his head, ready to strike the final blow.

Eddie held up a bloody hand. "No Mister . . . no . . . please don't," he pleaded.

Valance brought down the axe and lodged it in Eddie's skull.

Williams teetered for a second, then fell forwards onto his face, the cleaver buried in his head.

"I'll leave that with you," said Bird. "Let's call it a present from Laurie, shall we?"

Frankie cowered in the corner. Jamie towered over him, menacingly brandishing two claw hammers.

"Look, lads, c . . . come on," stammered Verdi. "I've

got cash, p . . . plenty of cash, in the safe, I'll open it for you. Must be twenty-five grand. What d'you say eh?"

Jamie didn't speak. He pulled two long strips of cotton sheet from his coveralls. Bird grabbed Verdi and threw him to the floor.

"What? What the fuck you doing?" he wailed.

In seconds he was bound, hands and feet.

Jamie and Bird took an arm each and powered Frank through the half-empty club. Customers were still doing their best to escape without any help or direction, all the door staff left standing had long since saved themselves. The punters were so intent on making their own getaway, they didn't even notice Frank being dragged out of his own door, kicking, screaming and pleading for his life.

Bird opened the boot of the Granada and Verdi was pushed inside.

As Jamie slammed the lid, their entry and exit had taken just one minute and eleven seconds.

Both men removed their masks and slipped into the car.

Jamie drove steadily away.

Bird began to wriggle from his bloodstained coveralls. They joined his equally claret-covered gloves and the two balaclavas in a black bin liner on the back seat. He pulled a pack of baby wipes from the glovebox, wiped his hands and face and turned to Jamie.

"Will I do?" he said.

Jamie nodded and pulled the Granada to the side of the road. "Pretty as a fucking picture Birdman."

Valance took Jamie's hand. "Was good knowing you Strange Brew."

And with that, he was gone, strolling back toward the club, just to see what the fuss was all about, why all the cops were there.

Then of course, he would eat, Indian maybe, a cold beer or two, then find his hotel, get a good kip. After all, Manchester to Sydney is a long flight.

Jamie, however, drove on. Nice and steady. Frankie banging about in the boot, making threats. He turned left into New Hall Lane, keeping to thirty. Several cop cars with their lights flashing and sirens wailing flew by him in the opposite direction. Too late.

Jamie turned up the radio to drown out Frankie's tirade of abuse.

Then it was the M6 southbound. One junction. Left onto the M61, one junction. Left again and onto the A road. Half a mile, turn right and start to climb.

The air was fresher near the summit of Rivington Pike. The muggy, feverish ether of the town in high summer replaced by a cooler, cleaner, calmer atmosphere.

Jamie peered over the edge of the precipice where Laurie had lost her life. The night silent, except for the bangs and the muffled abuse emanating from the car behind him.

"I wish I could have been here for you," he whispered

to the night. "But this is the best I can do for you now."

Jamie turned and strode to the car.

He popped the boot, and for the first time, Frankie Verdi got a look at his attacker. He instantly flew into a manic rage, flailing about in the confined space of the boot, banging his head against the bodywork.

"Fucking soldier boy," he screamed. "It had to be you eh?"

Jamie had heard enough. He leaned into the boot, grabbed at the ties that held Frankie's legs and with one swift pull, released them.

Verdi immediately lashed out with his feet.

Jamie, despite his great size, was quick and light on his feet. He simply stepped away and let Frank thrash about some more.

Eventually, unable to gain enough purchase to release himself from to boot, Verdi stopped his squirming and lay still, breathing hard and sweating. One loose leg dangling over the lip of the boot.

Jamie wandered closer so he could see Frankie's face.

"One Dog," he said flatly. "That's what you are now, eh Frank? One Dog. With Tony and Eddie gone. Doesn't have the same ring eh?"

Verdi screwed up his face. "Tony? Tony too? You fuckin' killed Tony?"

"Actually, it was my old man who finished him off. I

341

mean, he would have burnt to death had Harry not caved his scull in with a hammer. Act of mercy it was."

Frankie's eyes flashed. Jamie wasn't impressed. "Your fault that Frank. It was you who sent him, wasn't it? It was you who guided him to his death. Sent him to burn down our house, with me and my dad inside. You wanted me dead, but you didn't have the bottle yourself, so you sent your halfwit mate to do it."

Jamie leaned into the car and grabbed Frank by the lapels. In one powerful move, he lifted him bodily from the boot and stood him on his feet.

Frankie looked about him.

Jamie smiled. "Ah! The light comes on. You know where you are Frank eh? This is the place ain't it? The place where you told Tony and Eddie to bring my Laurie."

Verdi snorted. "Your Laurie? She was never your Laurie. She couldn't wait to run to me the second you left town, to climb in my bed. She was mine, and no one . . ."

Jamie slapped Frankie so hard, it echoed off the cliff walls below. Verdi hit the floor, cracking his head.

Blowing hard, he rolled himself onto his face. Slowly, he managed to get into a kneeling position. He spat blood from his mouth and managed a sick smile.

"You think I killed your childhood sweetheart, don't you? Your first fuck? Well you got it all wrong soldier boy. The stupid bitch topped herself. She was drunk, as usual, and she killed herself. Ask the fucking coppers. Ask anyone."

Jamie pulled Verdi to his feet. He was desperate to untie him, to fight him, to smash his face to pulp, but that couldn't happen.

Not yet.

"Oh, but I did ask, Frankie. I asked a lot of people. You see, I know you sent Tony and Eddie up here to kill Laurie, and I know why you did it too. I know you found out that Laurie had been to see me in Walton, and I know you gave her a beating for it. What you don't know Frank, is she went to see my father too, she wanted to warn him about you, about what you might do. She told him, she wanted to leave your nasty little clutches, but she was too scared of what you might do to her."

Jamie pointed. "Now, let me tell you how things went from there. Something happened in the club that night, and I'm guessing, that as I have a solicitor's letter on my mantle at home, telling me I just inherited thirty-five grand, that you found out Laurie was squirreling money away."

Frank spat some more claret. "She was a thieving bitch, and that money is mine."

"Correct so far then Frank?"

Verdi snorted and turned his head away. Jamie grabbed his chin, forcing him to look into his face.

"So, you make sure Laurie is drunk and you have her taken up here. Tony and Eddie force her into the driver's seat, just where we are standing right now Frank. They set the car off in first gear and it trundles over to the ledge there. Trouble is, neither of your two chums are that bright, and the car gets stuck. So, the dimwits push the car over, leaving their prints all over the boot."

Frank shook his head free. "It's a nice fairy tale soldier boy, but if that's the case, why weren't they banged up for it?"

"Because both Eddie and Tony had access to the car before that night."

Frankie laughed. "So, the prints prove nothing, soldier boy. You got nothing. The cops got nothing. So . . . fuck you."

Jamie just managed to stop himself from inflicting more damage.

"Officially, I agree . . . but unofficially . . . well . . . the cops got tired Frank. They got tired of you and your gang, and finally, they let things slip. They let it slip about the wiped CCTV tapes from the club and your gaff. They let it slip that Laurie's blood was found on the passenger seat and glovebox. Consistent with her being "beaten in that situ". They let it slip about Tony and Eddie's prints being fresh, two palms each, either side of the boot, consistent with the vehicle being pushed by the two men, they said.

"And you know the worst thing Frank? She didn't die straight away. She hung there, upside down slowly fading away. That beautiful, intelligent woman that you murdered. They let that slip too, you piece of shit."

Frankie glared. "Oh, I get it. So now, the big brave soldier boy is going to top me with my hands tied."

Jamie shook his head.

"Oh no Frank, I'm going to untie you. Because I'm not like you, I'm going to give you a chance. A chance to fight me here, in this place. Fair and square. Whoever wins, drives the car away. The loser ends up like Laurie, at the bottom of this cliff."

Jamie stepped forward, pulled on Frankie's ties, and the cotton strip fell to the ground releasing his hands.

Frankie instantly moved to his left, placing Jamie's back to the ravine.

He felt his jacket pockets, and couldn't believe his luck. In all the excitement, Jamie had never thought to search him.

Verdi slipped his hands into his black jacket. When they reappeared, both fists boasted Frank's trademark, brass knuckle dusters.

Jamie was bigger and stronger than Frankie, but with his trusty weapons on his fists, Frank believed he could take the soldier boy. Take him, and throw him down the cliff to join that thieving slag he was so fond of.

"You're a fool, soldier boy. You should have thrown me over when you had the chance."

Frank threw a right. A real haymaker, a one-punch wonder, but Jamie was too quick for him. He read the punch a mile away and slipped it, countering with a straight left, leaning in, all sixteen stone of him behind it.

He caught Frank on the chin, not clean, a glancing blow, enough to send him staggering backwards, struggling to keep his balance on the uneven ground.

"You'll need more that a pair of dusters Frank," spat

Jamie and threw a massive clubbing right hook to Frankie's temple.

Again, Frank managed to avoid the full force of the punch. Bending at the waist. As he came up, he threw an uppercut of his own. Two stones lighter than his opponent, the blow from his fist alone would not have done the amount of damage he needed. But with the brass dusters, it was a whole new ball game. Frank caught Jamie on his cheek. The age-old fighting weapon tearing into his face, slicing his skin open down to the bone.

It was Jamie's turn to falter, his standing foot slipping on the gravel, he almost went down. Frankie steamed in for the kill, sensing his moment, but Jamie put space between them.

Step back. Step left.

He needed a second or two to clear his head. Once again Frankie missed with big swinging punches.

Verdi was starting to blow. The drugs, the booze the lifestyle, starting to show in seconds. "I'm gonna knock your head off soldier boy," he panted.

Jamie feigned a left, dropped his right shoulder and swung a huge shot into Verdi's gut. Frank doubled up and dropped to his knees.

"You don't look much to me Frank. All mouth . . . You scared of heights son? 'Cos you're going over."

Jamie stepped in, pulled back his right, determined to finish Verdi. Ready to smash his massive fist into his smug face.

Frank had other ideas. He grabbed a rock from the ground with his right hand and threw it with all his might toward Jamie, the stone smashing into his left eye.

Jamie felt suddenly sick. He staggered, out of control. Bright stars appeared in his peripheral vision as he sucked in lungful after lungful of the cold air, trying to clear his head.

Verdi pounced, driving his shoulder into Jamie's midriff, pushing him ever backward toward the cliff edge.

Jamie was off balance and disorientated. Frank was on top of him now, slamming punch after punch into his already damaged face. The dusters tearing his flesh. Jamie knew he was close to unconsciousness. He was also close to the cliff edge. So close, his head was in mid-air.

From somewhere, he found some strength and gripped Verdi by the throat. Finding the larynx with his thumb he dug in with everything he had.

Frankie instantly stopped punching and grabbed Jamie's hand. He couldn't breathe.

Jamie was back in control.

Frankie was forced to roll off his foe, his only way of releasing himself from the vice-like grip that cut off his air. As he rolled to his left, he arced one final punch into Jamie's face with his right hand, a devastating blow.

Frank was free again.

He pulled himself to his knees, exhausted, his throat on fire. Blood poured from his nose, it was all he could do to take a single breath.

Jamie lay on his back breathing hard, eyes open but motionless.

Frank scrambled over to Jamie's feet and began to lift them.

"Right you fucker," he screamed.

Verdi hadn't the strength to push Jamie over, but he sure as hell could pivot him. Just like Eddie and Tony had done with Laurie's car.

Frankie laughed manically, hysteria overtaking his senses. "Who's the winner now eh soldier boy? Who's the fuckin' winner?"

Verdi knew once he got Jamie's feet to shoulder height and leaned in, he could get him over.

"Come on, you fucker, over you go. Just like your thieving bitch."

Jamie drew back his right foot, and slammed it into Frank's face. Verdi staggered backward, one step, two, then faltered and finally fell.

Jamie had so much blood in his eyes he could barely see. He forced himself to his feet. Frank rolled over, desperate to regain his own footing but his feet couldn't find the leverage and he slipped again. Like a drunk on a greasy bar-room floor.

With a massive hand, Jamie grabbed Frank by the collar and began to drag him to the edge.

Frank twisted and turned. He flailed his arms in attempt to throw punches, but he was spent. He had nothing left.

They reached the edge.

Jamie took a deep breath, bent his knees and picked Frank up, forcing him to stand and face him one last time.

He locked eyes with Verdi.

"Rot in hell Frank," he said.

And pushed him over.

Detective Jim Hacker

Harry Strange was arrested by the first officers who arrived at the scene of the arson attack on his house.

On his arrival at the police station, he requested his lawyer, Montague Kane.

Kane argued that Harry, a decorated, retired soldier, had fallen victim to an arson attack by a known gangster.

And even though this cowardly attack on a law-abiding citizen was obviously a serious case of mistaken identity on the said criminal's behalf, what was Harry to do?

Harry openly admitted striking Tony Thompson with a hammer, as he strode into his house and set fire to it.

He had no intention to kill the lad. Just stop him in his tracks. It was an act of self-defence, pure and simple.

Harry was released without charge.

The murder of Eddie Williams by two masked raiders at Toast nightclub was instantly connected with the ongoing warfare between Liverpudlian and Lancashire drug gangs.

It was, however, a mystery why Frankie Verdi was not killed alongside his partner in crime in the VIP room at the club, and how he ended up smashed beyond recognition at the bottom of the same cliff where his girlfriend Laurie Holland had met her end only weeks earlier.

Ironic wouldn't you say?

*

Connections.

As a policeman, you are often party to connections. Some of these associations are gained via your duties, some from personal experiences.

Of course, had the investigating officers realised that Harry, Jamie, Laurie and Frankie had such binding connections, their inquiry might have taken a far different course.

But then, that would have entailed yours truly giving them that line of inquiry to follow.

Something I was not inclined to do.

*

I last saw Harry Strange in the winter of 1985. We met in the Old Black Bull tap room for a quiet pint. He'd decided to move house.

Bad memories he said.

I wished him the best, and sadly, never saw him again.

Chapter Thirty

Cheryl Greenwood sat on her sofa in her small council flat, watching breakfast TV. Her baby boy, Anthony, lay quiet in his cot.

She heard the postman at her door.

Cursing the arrival of more bills, she plodded to collect the pile of mostly brown envelopes from her mat.

One in particular took her eye. It had an American postmark. She examined it closely.

Atlanta, Georgia.

She shrugged and tore it open. Inside there was a typed note. It simply said, *"It's what she would have wanted."*

Cheryl turned the paper over to check for a name, but there was none. She looked in the envelope again and removed a second item.

It was a cheque for thirty-five thousand pounds.

ENDEAVOUR INK

Endeavour Ink is an imprint of Endeavour Press.

If you enjoyed *Breaking Bones* check out
Endeavour Press's eBooks here:
www.endeavourpress.com

For weekly updates on our free and discounted eBooks sign up
to our newsletter:
www.endeavourpress.com

Follow us on Twitter:
@EndeavourPress